NEVER FORGET

THE SAFEGUARDED HEART SERIES BOOK THREE

MELANIE A. SMITH

WICKED DREAMS PUBLISHING

Published by
WICKED DREAMS PUBLISHING
info@wickeddreamspublishing.com
Boise, ID USA

Edited by Jennifer Gardner

Cover design by Wicked Dreams Publishing

Formatting by Wicked Dreams Publishing

eBook (K) ISBN: 978-1-7323900-4-1
eBook ISBN: 978-1-7328154-8-3
Paperback ISBN: 978-1-7323900-5-8
Hardback ISBN: 978-1-952121-04-3

CONTENTS

PART 1

"And think not you can direct the course of love, for love, if it finds you worthy, directs your course."
—Khalil Gibran

ONE

"Hmmm, forever is a long time," Bryce hedges. "I think I'll give you some time to get sick of me before I propose for real."

I can't help but laugh. "Seriously? I admit that I want to be with you forever too and that's all you've got?" I shake my head and poke him in the stomach.

He gives me a lascivious grin and rolls on top of me so suddenly it takes my breath away. "That's not even *close* to all I've got," he promises in a whisper as he nuzzles my neck, his warm breath tickling my ear. He pulls back suddenly and climbs out of bed, giving me an eyeful of his six-foot-four, ridiculously well-muscled body. "But first, breakfast."

"Naked breakfast?" I ask hopefully as he walks away.

He laughs and shakes his head, retrieving his boxers from the floor. "Just based on the ravenously horny look on your face, I'm going with no," he teases. "You know, because I actually want to eat. Food." He runs a hand over his short, chestnut brown hair, his blue eyes sparkling mischievously.

I pretend to pout a little. "Have it your way," I reply nonchalantly, making a show of stretching widely and letting the sheet slip off of me. I watch his eyes rove over my full chest and soft curves and I try not to let it excite me. But my stomach rumbles loudly and, as usual, he's right. I definitely need food.

Still, I take my time slowly sliding out of bed and pulling an oversized shirt from my bottom dresser drawer — which I bend down slowly to retrieve. Once I'm covered I saunter casually past him. He shakes his head and laughs, following me down the stairs.

I make a stop at the bathroom. My long, wavy brown hair is an absolute mess, so I take a moment to untangle it with my fingers before meeting Bryce in the kitchen.

I note that he's already started a pot of coffee. While it percolates, I examine the pitiful contents of the fridge and cupboards.

"Your choices are cereal and cereal," I announce.

Bryce smirks at me as he pours himself a cup of coffee. "Cereal it is," he agrees. "But we're going grocery shopping today." He passes by on his way to the dining room and plants a kiss on the top of my head.

I watch him sit down and find myself welling up a little.

He notices and gives me a quizzical look. "Everything okay?"

"Perfect," I admit breathlessly. Utterly. Fucking. Perfect. It's everything I've hoped for since I opened my heart back up to love not many months ago. And with all we've gone through to get here, I can't help being anything but blissfully happy.

I join him at the table with the food and we munch quietly, shooting each other furtive smiles, the freshness and excitement of our new relationship coursing through me.

"What else is on the agenda today?" I ask as we finish.

Bryce leans back in his chair. "Well, if I'm going to be staying here, I'm going to need to get some stuff from my place," he replies.

The thought is still a little overwhelming, but I'm thankful it'll be Bryce here with me instead of the personal security guards I'd had twenty-four-seven due to recent events. Though I'll still need them at least part of the time until the danger has passed. Whenever that is.

"What do you need to do today?" he asks.

"I have some phone calls to make," I admit sheepishly. "I wasn't just ignoring you and Emily this week."

During the epic pity party in which I thought I'd be alone forever, Bryce's sister had paraded over unannounced the night before last, tired of being ignored and raring to convince me into chasing her brother down. Fortunately, confiding in her led him to me. And I'm sure she'll be happy to hear that. But I should really call my mother, father, and my best friend, Allie.

"Funny you should mention Em," Bryce replies, taking our dishes into the kitchen. "Because we're seeing her tomorrow for brunch." His feigned casualness rouses my suspicion.

"Brunch?" I ask sharply, following behind him.

He turns away from the sink, wrapping his strong arms around me and gently stroking my backside. "At my mom's house," he replies, again too casually, but I can see the worry in his eyes. "That okay?"

"You know I love your mom," I reply. "But if you don't want to introduce me as your girlfriend yet, I completely understand."

Bryce pulls a face somewhere between offended and confused.

"You looked worried," I explain.

Understanding dawns on his face at my explanation. Bryce huffs a laugh and shakes his head.

"Baby, I want to shout it from the goddamn rooftops," he replies, looking intensely into my eyes. "But from now on I want this to go at your pace. Not mine. That's all."

I can't help but smile. This man. He's always looked out for my feelings first. Even when that meant watching me date a selfish, lying charmer of a man. Hell, not just watching, but helping me find the bastard when he "went back to Italy" or, as it actually happened, San Francisco. Only to stop hearing from him after a month when he did actually go back to Italy after all, but not because he'd planned to. The whole chain of events ultimately led to my being stalked and attacked by whatever criminals were after him, trying to get to him through me. Luckily, I'd already realized by the time he reappeared that my feelings were better spent on the man who'd always been there for me. This man.

I slide a hand over his gorgeous, taut chest, looking up at him from under my eyelashes. "I'd love to go," I respond. "Though I can't promise I'll behave." I slide my hand down, running a finger along the waistband of his shorts.

He laughs and shoves me backward, pressing me against the fridge. His soft lips run over my collarbone, his hands roving under my shirt. As his fingers find the tips of my breasts, his mouth presses over mine. I revel in the taste of him, the sweetness of being tangled together, getting to touch him in ways I'd only dreamed of before. But he pulls away before it can go very far.

"I see I'm not the only one who likes to play dirty," he says huskily.

I bite my lip to suppress a smile and he sucks in a sharp breath, his pupils dilating and fixing on my mouth.

"I'm going to do all kinds of amazing fucking things with that mouth later. But right now," he says, kissing me on the top of the head, "you need to get ready to go."

"I don't know where you get all this self-control," I mutter.

Bryce barks a loud laugh and runs a finger down my jaw. "Lots of practice," he replies.

I blush to the roots of my hair, and it just makes him laugh again.

"Sera, baby, please don't be embarrassed. It all worked out. And good things come to those who wait." The look on his face is full of promise and desire, and it's all I can do to keep breathing. And standing. He releases me slowly, leaning back against the counter behind him.

Somehow, I tear myself from him and drag ass back upstairs to take a shower. A very cold shower.

∽

WHEN I MAKE MY WAY BACK DOWNSTAIRS, BRYCE IS standing in the living room, dressed, with his phone pressed to his ear and a frown tugging at the corners of his mouth. I sink into the oversized white sofa, watching the dim sunlight that has broken through the clouds sparkling on downtown Seattle outside of the large wall of windows that makes up one side of the living room. Bryce doesn't say a word, simply listens for a few more moments before slipping his phone into his back pocket and sinking into the couch next to me.

Slinging one arm on the couch behind me, he runs his other hand over my leg. "I have to go into the office today," he conveys grumpily. "But hopefully it won't take long."

I fold my hand over his, dipping my head so he doesn't see the disappointment on my face. "Everything okay?" I ask, tracing the veins in the back of his hand lightly.

He flips his hand over, squeezing mine. "It will be," he assures me. "It's nothing too out of the ordinary. Part and parcel of being in charge now. But it's not something I can really discuss. Corporate security issues and all." He winks at me.

I smile vaguely, curious but knowing I shouldn't press. It's how we met, after all, months ago when my own company was facing security issues, and he swooped in like the knight in shining armor that he is. But now that his father is gone, it's up to Bryce to actually run the corporate security company his grandfather created. It was a natural fit for him after leaving the Navy SEALs. Though I knew he was reluctant to accept the burden so soon, and with it already encroaching on his weekends I can understand why.

"Does that mean one of my bosom buddies will be back?" I ask warily.

Not that I necessarily mind any of my guards, but I'd much rather have some time alone, all things considered.

"Unfortunately, yes," he replies. "I'll call Tristan. I'm pretty sure he's available today."

I smile, perking up a little at the thought.

Bryce laughs. "I can see that you approve. I don't have anything to worry about, do I?"

I shove him lightly, not sure if he's really jealous or not. "Of *course* not," I reply. "We just get along well. He's a nice guy."

Bryce cocks an eyebrow at me. He's got eyeballs too, so I'm sure he knows how ridiculously attractive Tristan is with his blond hair, green eyes, and charming personality. And by charming personality, I also mean amazing body. Though not quite as amazing as Bryce's, admittedly.

"Well, as long as you don't get along *too* well," he replies, pulling his phone out of his pocket.

I give him a funny look and put my hand over his phone. "You know he's gay, right?" I ask.

Bryce's eyes widen. "Now I do," he responds. "I can't believe I didn't realize that."

I laugh and let go of his phone. "Hmm, I guess your know-it-all security guy superpowers have their limits," I tease him.

He sticks his tongue out at me and places the call. I arch my eyebrows and resist the urge to make a comment about his tongue. His wicked, amazing tongue. Shuddering lightly, I get up to retrieve my own phone.

It's not long before Tristan arrives, once again in his

fitted black suit with matched, skinny black tie over a crisp white shirt. With fall arriving, it's cooler, but I can't imagine how they wear those suits in the heat of summer.

"Are you going out?" Bryce asks as we say our goodbyes at the door.

"No. I can order groceries to be delivered. Anything particular you need?" I respond.

"Eggs," he responds. "Lots." He leans in and plants a chaste kiss on my lips.

I scrunch up my nose grumpily. "That's all?" I pout.

His eyes flick to Tristan, who is looking out the window wall with his back to us, politely giving us space. Bryce's mouth drops to my ear.

"I've only got so much self-control. Any more and I'll end up doing what I've been imagining doing to you for the last fifteen minutes. And I think it would be inappropriate if I took you against the windows right now," he murmurs. "Tristan might notice."

A low gasp escapes my lips as my insides clench.

Bryce smirks and uses the opportunity of my speechlessness to leave with a wink. "Bye, Sera."

The door clicks shut softly behind him. But it takes me a few more moments before I catch my breath enough to return to the living room.

I take a few minutes to chat with Tristan before

excusing myself and heading upstairs to my makeshift office, where I place an order for groceries to be delivered in an hour. If I'm not going out, I'm going to need the food for lunch. And I'm sure Tristan will appreciate it too.

Next, I hunker down and try to decide who to call first. I realize quickly that it's a no-brainer. I don't even really want to talk to my mother or father, and it's been nearly two weeks since I've spoken to Allie. And she's had enough of her own problems to deal with that I realize I've, once again, gone bad friend. So I call her immediately.

"Hey, stranger," she answers, sounding decidedly cheery.

I'm instantly grateful that she doesn't seem upset with me. "Hey, Allie," I greet her. "I'm so sorry it took me so long to respond to you."

"Let me guess. A lot has happened?" she replies with a smile in her voice. "Yeah, after our brunch two weeks ago, I figured that might be the case. Again."

"Yes," I agree softly. "A lot has happened."

"Give me all the juicy details," Allie insists.

I can't help but laugh. "It's not all sunshine and roses," I amend. "But okay."

Might as well lead with the least pleasant stuff. So I start by telling her how I was followed two nights in a row the week after we had brunch. I also explain suspecting Bryce was seeing his ex, Madison, then having it confirmed when I went to see him last Saturday night. But unable to face it, I ran out of his apartment building, not wanting to have to compete with Madison for his attentions. And unfortunately ended up being attacked. Which requires me to then explain *why* I was attacked, which in turn requires me to explain finding Alessandro at my door the next day, since it was ultimately his drama spilling over into my life.

I find having to talk about Alessandro Giordano bittersweet, to say the least. I'm hard-pressed to think of him as a selfish, lying bastard. Even though he is. He's also charming and he loves me, though in the end not enough to get over himself. And I loved him. But when he returned after weeks of not speaking to me to tell me he wanted me to leave with him, so he could protect me, so we could be together, it's no surprise to Allie when I explain I just couldn't. I couldn't leave my home, my friends, my work, and the man I'd realized I truly belonged with.

"Well," Allie says, finally breaking her silence. "At least you got some closure?" I hear her take a deep breath. "That's some heavy stuff, Sera. So what happened with Bryce? Is he still seeing his not-so-ex?"

"Ex," I reply firmly. "He ended it with her the

same day I saw Alessandro. As it turns out, it was mostly a mistake. He'd lost his father, made a bad decision in his grief, and it took some time for him to disentangle himself."

"Well, that's a relief," she replies. "Are you okay?"

"There's more," I admit.

"Of course there is," she groans, laughing.

"I hired personal security guards after Alessandro left. Just in case. It really led me to isolate myself this week. That's why I wasn't responding to calls or texts. That made some people impatient. Eventually Emily marched over here demanding to know what my problem was," I explain. "Once I told her what happened, naturally, she told Bryce."

"Bet he's happy to see the back of Alessandro," Allie replies wryly.

I hadn't even thought of that aspect. Bryce has always disliked Alessandro. Now that I've got some distance, I can't really blame him.

"Probably," I agree. "But he came to tell me he still loves me." I flush at the memory of his admission, and everything that came after.

"Oh, Sera," Allie breathes. "Did you tell him you love him too?"

I snort. I'd never dared to admit to Allie the feelings I'd been developing for Bryce for a long time, though I probably shouldn't be surprised that she saw right through me anyway.

"Is there anything you don't know about me?" I ask bluntly.

Allie laughs. "I'm pretty sure some things I know about you before you know yourself," she teases.

It's hard to deny. Especially when it comes to feelings. I've always been purposely obtuse, having completely closed myself off to even the possibility of love for the better part of a decade. Some hurts run so deep that they can take what feels like a lifetime to heal.

"Yes, I told him I love him too," I admit. I hear her clap her hands with glee.

"Yay!" she squeals. "I was so rooting for you two."

I laugh. It's good to hear her so happy. And I decide instantly that I'm not going to bring up what she's going through, at least not directly. If she wants to talk about the deep depression she's struggled to overcome since losing her first pregnancy earlier this year, she knows I'm here for her. But she sounds so normal, and I'm just glad we're both in a better place.

"Enough about me," I insist. "What's new with you?"

"I'm glad you asked," she replies perkily. "David

and I have decided to take that second honeymoon. We're going to Fiji!!"

"Holy crap!" I exclaim. "That sounds amazing. When? For how long?"

"We leave in two weeks, and we'll be gone for ten days," she replies. "I would love to see you next weekend before we go."

"Of course," I agree. "Sunday brunch again?"

"It's a date," Allie affirms.

Downstairs, the doorbell rings, heralding the arrival of food. And I suddenly realize how hungry I am.

"I've gotta go, Al," I tell her. "But it was so good talking to you. Talk soon, okay?"

"You betcha," she responds. "Bye, Sera."

∾

After lunch, Bryce calls to say he won't be back until dinnertime. Realizing that means I have no excuse, I call my mom. I decide beforehand that I'm going to keep things very high level. On top of already being emotionally exhausted, my mother and I have only recently forged a closer relationship. Most of my life she'd been passive aggressively critical and overbearing. But one of the few bright sides of my relationship with Alessandro was that it outed *why* —

that my father, who left when I was twelve, had cheated on her in a spectacularly awful way.

Still, when I manage to get her on the phone, I do share that I saw Alessandro and ended things officially and completely. I can tell she's relieved. She suggests coming for a visit, since we haven't seen each other in some time, but I bristle at the idea of revealing my new relationship with Bryce. She's already met him, but not as my love interest. And I just don't think I'm ready for that. So I make vague promises of a visit sometime in the future and steer the conversation away from me. Since she's always happy to talk about herself, it's not hard.

But once I'm done talking to her, I'm spent. And I have no desire to call my father. Having only recently spoken to him for the first time since I was a teenager, it just feels like a conversation I'm going to need more strength for.

Instead, I troop downstairs to the kitchen to throw together dinner. Bryce will be home soon. And the thought perks me up considerably.

⌒∿⌒

I'M JUST ASSEMBLING A SALAD TO GO WITH THE lasagna that's in the oven when Bryce returns carrying two large duffel bags. Tristan helps him bring them in, and Bryce sees him out before coming to me.

"Hey, you," he greets me, wrapping his arms around me from behind and kissing my neck. "Sorry I had to be away all day."

"I missed you," I reply, turning my head to kiss him.

As I wasn't quite done with the salad, I'd only intended a quick smooch. But he kisses me hungrily, holding my face to his with a strong hand. My body responds, and heat rises quickly in me. I drop the salad tongs and turn to face him without breaking the fervent dance of our lips.

His tongue gently teases mine as he slips his hands around my hips, pulling me toward him. I push into him hard, wrapping my arms around his neck for leverage. I can feel his readiness against my hip, and a small moan breaks out of my throat through our kiss. When he finally pulls his mouth from mine, we're both panting and aroused.

"I missed you too," he responds. He looks down at my frilly white apron. "And I'm going to fantasize about coming home to you making dinner in nothing but this apron."

"You're killing me with the dirty talk," I moan, pushing him away so I can finish making dinner. He grins and leans back against the counter opposite me.

"You don't like it?" he teases, his blue eyes bright and sparkling.

"I like it. Very much. You have no idea," I reply. "Now sit your gorgeous ass down so we can eat."

He laughs and moves to the dining room, popping open the bottle of wine I'd put on the table. "I'll keep that in mind," he responds.

I hand him the salad bowl over the counter and remove the lasagna.

"Anything else I do that you like very much?" he asks.

I shoot him a look as I bring the casserole to the table. "Plenty," I assure him. "But if I start talking about it, I just know I'm going to end up with lasagna on my back. So let's eat. Then I can *show* you."

Bryce laughs and concedes by sitting down. "I look forward to it," he replies suggestively, taking a sip of wine.

Dinner is full of silence and tension. But the best kind of tension. The feeling of Bryce's eyes on every inch of me as I eat is tantalizing. And I can't keep my eyes off of him either. Every movement is laden with suggestive undertones. By the time we are done, and the last dish is washed, I'm so turned on I can barely think straight.

Bryce leans back against the stove, eyeing me speculatively.

"That was good," he remarks casually, crossing his arms over his broad chest.

I shift my weight from one foot to the other. "Thanks," I reply softly.

His eyes drink me in, darkening as the tension builds.

"Damn, baby, if your eyes could talk," he mutters.

The corner of my mouth quirks up in a knowing smile. They'd be saying, *Take me already, damnit*, I think to myself.

"Mmmm," I reply noncommittally, unwilling to admit what I'm thinking. "Is this the part where we let things go at my pace?"

Bryce chuckles and pushes himself upright. "If we went at your pace, I have a feeling we'd already be done by now," he remarks. He saunters past me and I watch him slowly climb the stairs. He pauses before he gets too far and crooks a finger at me. "Coming?"

TWO

My heart pounds in my chest, my feet stubbornly refusing to move. Or unable. I'm suddenly very weak in the knees at his invitation.

I take a few deep breaths and find the will to move before slowly following him up the stairs and into the bedroom. I find Bryce stripping, until he's left in only a white T-shirt and his boxers. My eyebrows fly up, and I freeze in the doorway. He looks back at me, grinning while he tosses the clothing he's removed into a laundry bag.

He stretches out on the bed, lying on his side, and pats the other side of the bed invitingly. Slowly, I join him, lying down to face him.

After a few minutes of staring lustfully at each

other, Bryce reaches out and strokes my face gently. "I hope I didn't offend you," he murmurs. "I like your pace. But we've got all night. There's no need to rush."

I cock an eyebrow and kiss his finger as it slips by my mouth. "We do have all night," I agree. "So fast or slow, I bet you that we could easily manage twice." I kiss his fingers again as they pass. "Or maybe even three times."

Bryce laughs. "That's one way to go about it," he allows.

"Now you have me curious about the other ways," I reply.

He grins and slides toward me. "Oh, good, we're to the showing part," he responds.

He reaches a hand out and runs it down my temple, the side of my face, his thumb grazing my lip gently, then down my neck. He lightly brushes his fingers along my collar bone and back, then continues running his hand down my chest, over my T-shirt, stopping at the peak of my nipple visible through my shirt. He circles and pinches it, causing a moan to escape me. He does it again, harder, until I moan louder. He brings his other hand up, pinching both nipples simultaneously until it's a pleasurable pain that has me writhing and moaning. Seemingly satisfied, his leisurely stroking continues down my stomach, over my leggings, stopping on my hips.

He grips me tightly, pulling our bodies together. His lips meet mine for one hot second, his tongue doing a quick sweep of my mouth before he slides down me, his lips and nose grazing my nipples on the way. His head comes to rest at my hips, his hot breath mingling with the heat between my legs. He uses his lips and nose to caress at the spot while his hand roves over my backside, down my leg, and cups underneath my knee. He holds me there while he nuzzles me, breathing deeply of the scent of my wetness. I'm so turned on I can barely move as I watch him.

"You smell fucking amazing," he groans.

With his mouth still in contact with my body, his words reverberate through me in a way that makes me even wetter than I was before. As if he knows, he rubs two fingers along the seam of my leggings, sighing happily at the dampness he finds.

Slowly, he peels off my leggings and underwear. I'm so hot and wet, that when his tongue hits me it almost feels cool. Temperature aside, his slow, deliberate strokes send tremors through me. But unlike the previous night's steady acceleration, Bryce continues his gentle, methodically unhurried exploration. It feels so amazing that I can't even form words to ask him to go faster, harder. It's pleasure unlike anything I've ever experienced before. Pleasure for the sheer sake of pleasure. Not to hurtle toward the finish, but just to revel in it. And I find I don't want it to stop — but I do want to do the same to him.

"Bryce," I manage to whisper.

It works, and he stops, pulling back and resting on his haunches at the foot of the bed. I push myself upright, tugging off my shirt and bra in one solid movement. His mouth opens a fraction, his eyes fixed on my erect nipples. Remembering my mission, I lean forward and pull his shirt over his head, directing him with my hands to lay back on the bed. I tug his shorts off, his massive erection springing free. I groan with approval but focus through the lust screaming in my veins.

I kneel next to his head and he looks at me questioningly. "I want to do that to you," I explain. "While you do that to me."

"Oh, fuck yes," he breathes, his pupils dilating massively.

Smiling, I swing a leg over him, allowing him to pull me into position. He places my knees above his shoulders and pulls my hot, wet center back into range of his mouth. As soon as I feel the first lick, I take him in my mouth. He shudders beneath me as I slide him in as far as he'll go. Keeping him there, I work my tongue over him as I grab his sack with my free hand and pull it toward his shaft, massaging both as I swirl my tongue firmly around him. I feel his tongue stop, so I ease back, moving from root to tip with a light grip and feathery swirls of my tongue. He resumes, and we both gently work each other simultaneously until the feeling of utter hedonistic, numbing pleasure seeps through me completely.

Deciding he's been too quiet for my liking, I abandon my pursuit of simultaneous gratification and focus on taking him to a level where he'll forget his own name. My feathery swirls accelerate quickly to deep suction, my light grip to a slick pump, working him into a hard, quivering frenzy. Predictably, his head drops back as the change registers, and he moans loudly.

"Shit," he cries. "That's … oh, god …"

As he loses his words, I ease up and climb off of him. He springs up and knocks me over, his mouth consuming mine frantically. When he breaks free for air, I can't help laughing.

"Sorry," I chortle. "I know you wanted to go slow. I just couldn't help myself."

He wipes at his chin, chuckling with me. "Don't apologize," he replies. "That felt fantastic."

I run my hands over the well-developed muscles of his arms.

He nuzzles his nose against mine. "How can I make you feel fantastic?"

I bite my lip. "Take me from behind," I breathe, squirming to get enough room to roll over.

"Goddamn, baby, you know just what to say," he groans. He rears back and reaches one arm under my hips and, with one pull, simultaneously rolls me over and raises my hips into the air like I'm a doll.

As if I wasn't immensely turned on before, all of my nerve endings come alive and I'm acutely aware of every square centimeter of our flesh touching as his knees open my legs and he runs his hand along my dripping core.

I feel his tip nudging at my opening and the sensation makes me clench in anticipation. He eases in slowly, and my body quickly responds, like it wants the deep, full feeling of him just as much as I do. And he doesn't disappoint. Though I can't feel his hips against my backside, so I know he's not even fully in. I lift myself up so I'm on all fours, stretching myself out and buying him a little more room. It's enough, and he slips in to the hilt, causing us both to moan appreciatively.

I look back at him, and the sight of his amazing, muscular frame behind me, his exquisite features set in a mask of pure bliss, and his manhood buried completely in me almost makes me come on the spot.

Mastering myself, I reach an arm back to grasp his hand, to anchor us both for what comes next. He grips me back and takes the cue. His first thrust is painful, and not in the best way. But I don't make a sound. On the second thrust, I start to acclimate to his sheer size. And by the third, the pain is but a welcome compliment to the pleasure of his massive member stimulating every sensitive spot I have. It's not long before I want more.

I bite my lip and catch his eye. "Harder," I beg, whimpering.

He throws his head back for a moment, clearly unhinged by my plea. But he gets it together quickly and complies, ratcheting up the intensity of his thrusts. His eyes drop to my breasts, which are now shaking furiously under the force of our bodies colliding. The pure lust on his face drives me crazy.

So, I beg him again. "Harder, baby, please."

And this time, when he lets go, I have to turn away and use both arms to brace myself for the best fuck I've ever had. He slams furiously into me, and waves of pleasurable pain crash through me. It feels like only moments later when I feel the familiar tightening, each spearing thrust of his massive cock building to the ridiculously powerful climax that follows. He continues to thrust into me through the guttural screams that rip out of my throat and through my arms giving out. Through it all, he keeps my hips locked in his tight grip, riding me over wave after wave of incredible release that just keeps going and going. Finally, when I feel as if I'm about to black out from pleasure, he eases off slowly, sliding out so I can collapse onto the bed.

He lays down next to me and I look up at him. His cock is red and still alert, with no sign of his massive erection abating.

"You didn't finish?" I ask incredulously.

He shakes his head, sweaty and panting. Knowing that, plus the look of utter satisfaction on his face, and suddenly I have a second wind. I pull my shaking body up and climb over him, sliding him into me once more. He looks up at me, bewildered. But I ignore it and start riding him.

"You're incredible," he moans.

I'd laugh, but I'm too focused on his pleasure now. I take his face in my hands and kiss him deeply, but it slows me down. So I let him go, moving his hands to my breasts. He kisses and strokes them as I return to grinding my hips over him.

I run my hands over his hair, relishing the feeling of his lips all over me as I ride him. I should be sore and spent, but instead I'm finding it just as pleasurable as he seems to be. I look down into his eyes. And I've never seen anyone look back at me the way he does. Like he sees me. Adores me. Would do anything to please me.

"God, I love you," I breathe.

He trembles underneath me, pushing to encourage my hips to go faster as he approaches climax.

I pick up my speed. "I love you," I repeat.

His breathing accelerates to a fever pitch.

I brace my arms on him as I slam into him as hard and fast as I can. "I love you," I moan one, final time.

He bellows his release, and I feel him coming, warm and slippery, and it pushes me over the edge. I focus on continuing to ride him through our orgasms like he did me, and amazingly feel him continue to come inside me for far longer than should be possible.

As we both descend, I allow him to slide me onto the bed next to him. He holds me in his arms, placing light kisses on my lips, cheeks, and chin.

"You okay?" he asks.

I look up at him in awe. "Amazing," I admit. "Though I might be walking funny tomorrow."

He grins. "Ditto," he agrees, and we both laugh. "Seriously, though, that was …"

"The best fuck ever?" I offer.

"That's one way to put it," he agrees. "Though I thought most women liked to call it 'making love.'"

I consider that for a moment. "It was that too, I suppose," I finally allow. "But I've always associated that phrase with tender, sweet sex. Which, if it wasn't obvious, isn't really my preference."

"Just a good, proper fuck, then?" he asks huskily.

The question causes me to tighten, despite recent activities. "Even hearing you *say* it turns me on," I admit, grinding up against him.

He laughs. "I never would have guessed," he replies. "But I'm glad. It's what I like too, but I don't usually let go like that. I don't want it to be painful."

"It was, at first," I acknowledge. "But that didn't last long. And then it was amazing." I bite my lip and shudder with pleasure. "I've never had an orgasm like that."

He smiles, clearly pleased, and kisses my forehead. "Me neither," he agrees. "But then, I don't think I've ever lost myself in someone so completely for so long."

I look at him quizzically and roll my head back to look at the bedside clock. "Holy shit, we were going at it for more than two hours?!" I exclaim.

Bryce chuckles. "Didn't feel like that long, did it?" he asks, nuzzling my neck. "If we call it an early night we might be able to do it again in the morning." His lips trace a path up to my ear, his breath simultaneously tickling and turning me on.

"I both can't believe I have to wait that long and

am worried I won't be able to keep up with you," I joke.

"Something tells me it's me who will be keeping up with you," he replies suggestively. "So tell me how far this goes. Rough play? Bondage?"

"Why, are you into those?" I ask him curiously.

He shrugs. "Not really, but if you are, I'm willing," he replies.

I laugh and kiss him gently. "You are too much," I murmur, looking up into his eyes. "No, I'm not really into those either. Just a good, deep fuck. And you have a distinct advantage on both counts. But I hope you're ready to push the boundaries of just how deep and hard you can fuck me." And I'm incredulous when I feel his cock twitch between us. I look down in shock.

Bryce laughs. "I think that was him accepting the challenge," he offers. He stares at me for a minute. "I'm glad I didn't know about this before. Or I wouldn't have played it so cool all those months knowing I could be testing the limits of how hard a fuck I'd really enjoy, with the most amazing and gorgeous woman I've ever met."

"Pillow talk," I tease him accusingly. "Post-orgasmic exaggeration. But I'm glad things worked out too."

Bryce levels a serious look at me. "I mean it," he

insists. "You know I've been crazy about you from the start."

I can't help but be self-conscious. It's hard to believe someone like him would think that about someone like me. "You're lucky I know how smart you are," I tease, attempting to make light, "or I'd question your intelligence for that."

He shakes his head and huffs an unamused laugh. "You don't see yourself, Sera," he replies seriously. "So I'm going to keep telling you until you believe me." He hooks a finger under my chin, forcing me to look into his eyes. "Never forget how much I love you."

THREE

The next morning, as soon as I wake up I know my prediction was dead-on. Even rolling over to look at Bryce causes me to feel the rawness between my legs. It actually makes me giggle.

"Was I talking in my sleep?" Bryce asks, opening his eyes.

"You talk in your sleep?" I ask, sliding into his arms.

He kisses me on my head as he pulls me to him. "I like waking up next to you," he dodges.

I shove him playfully. "Uh-huh, way to avoid that one, tiger," I tease him. "I was laughing because I'm so sore I swear I still feel you in there every time I move."

He laughs. "Yeah, the sheets are kind of chafing me," he admits. "Guess we'll have to heal up before we give it another go."

"Now we just have to practice not looking like we fucked each other silly for hours," I giggle. Suddenly, something occurs to me. "Does Emily already know? About us?"

"No, I've been a little busy," Bryce replies with a smirk. "Why?"

"Well if she doesn't, she's going to the second she sees us both walking funny," I explain.

Bryce barks another laugh. "Oh, well," he replies. "Not much to do about it now." He sits up and slings his long legs over the side of the bed.

And I get a nice view of the firm, well-defined muscles of his back. I lean over and trace my fingertips over his lower back muscles. He looks over his shoulder curiously. I grin up at him.

"Sorry, couldn't help it," I say, letting my hair fall over my face to hide my embarrassment.

He turns around and flips me over, climbing on top of me. "You've got to stop looking so sexy. It literally hurts," he murmurs into my neck, kissing his way down to my chest.

"Mmmm," I groan. "Funny, because as it happens I hurt *less* when I'm turned on."

"Don't say things like that," Bryce moans. He

drops a hand between my legs, lightly skimming my sex.

Even the gentle touch is too much, though and I suck in a breath sharply. "No hands," I chastise him.

He raises an eyebrow. And I realize it was the wrong thing to say. His head drops between my legs and, before I can stop him, his silken tongue is pushing between my lips, stroking the extra-sensitive bundle of nerves hidden inside. It stings at first, but like last night's escapades, that melts into pleasure quickly. And he doesn't stop until I'm coming in his mouth. Again.

As we pull up to his mom's house a few hours later, I'm still pouting that he wouldn't even let me try to return the favor.

He kills the engine and looks over at me. "You're not still sulking, are you?" he teases me.

I feign a glare at him. "No," I snap jokingly.

He chuckles and gives me an amused half-smile.

And I can't keep it up, cracking a smile of my own. "Yeah, laugh it up, baby. You'll get yours later."

Bryce leans over to whisper in my ear. "I've already got everything I need," he murmurs, kissing my neck. It's unexpected sweetness. Usually when he's whispering in my ear, it's something dirty.

I find I like it anyway. He shoots me a grin and climbs out of the car, so I follow suit. As soon as I round the car, he takes my hand. Feeling his rough, warm grip makes me feel a whole other level of safe than I even used to feel in his presence when he was simply my overprotective, close friend. And I can't remember ever being so happy.

He leads me into the house. We can hear Emily talking before we even enter the living room. But a hush falls over the room as we walk in, still hand in hand. Three shocked faces take us in — Emily, their mother, Rebecca, and their Aunt Charlotte. And I don't know who looks more thrilled to see our obvious coupledom. Bryce smirks down at me, clearly amused by their astonished silence.

"Hi, guys," Bryce greets them, letting me go to kiss his mother and aunt on the cheek. He then sits down on the smaller of the two couches in the room, pulling me down next to him. He's so relaxed and casual, you'd think we'd always been showing up to brunch at his mom's house as a couple.

But Emily's having none of it. She tugs dramatically at her long, chestnut waves, her blue eyes brimming with excitement. "Yeah, hi, hey, nothing going on here," she intones sarcastically. "Just my brother.

And my friend. *Together*. Unless you've just started holding hands with all our friends."

"She was my friend first," Bryce reminds her, putting his arm on the couch behind me and crossing his legs.

I suppress a smile. I'd get on his case for torturing his sister, but she's meddled in our relationship so many times lately, it's kind of fun to watch him take a little revenge.

"How are you doing, Mom?" he asks nonchalantly.

His mother gives him a look that's somewhere between disapproving and amused. I imagine Emily drives everyone a little crazy. But I know she means well, and she's got a heart of gold. She's been a good friend to me since we met and became close while I was helping with their father's funeral. So I almost want to spare her. Almost.

"I'm fine, darling, thank you," Rebecca responds. "It's so nice to see you, Sera. How are things with you?"

"Oh, no," Emily insists. "Nuh-uh. First you have to tell us: Are you or aren't you together?"

I give Bryce an overly affected look of bemusement. "We did come here together, didn't we?" I ask innocently.

He can barely contain his smirk. "Yep. Seemed a waste to drive separately," he replies airily.

And I swear Emily looks like she's about to punch us.

"Oh, for heaven's sake, Emily Rose Hoyt," Charlotte chides her. "They're obviously a couple. Unclench."

Bryce laughs.

Emily doesn't. She pouts openly, pointing it my direction first. "Sera, you pinky swore to be my friend no matter what," she reminds me. "Don't leave me hanging."

"Em," I sigh dramatically. "If your boyfriend wanted to mess with his meddling sister a little, wouldn't you let him?"

She takes my meaning immediately, squealing loudly as she jumps out of her seat to hug me.

I laugh as she embraces me. "But I'm with Charlotte on this one, anyway. Wasn't it obvious?"

"Always get the story straight from the source," she responds. "I don't assume."

I mash my lips together, suppressing a sarcastic response about her gossipy tendencies.

"Speaking of stories," I say, diverting the subject away from Bryce and me. "Rebecca, would now be a good time for us to talk about Landon? I meant what I said a few weeks ago. I really do want to hear more about your husband. You've all come to mean so much to me, and I'm sad I wasn't able to know him before he passed."

I'd already discussed doing exactly this with Bryce a while back, but he still looks surprised. I give him a look, wondering if it was okay to ask. He pulls me toward him and kisses me softly on the cheek. And I know it was.

Rebecca smiles sadly but, to her credit, flawlessly maintains her composure. Her husband only having passed a month or so ago, even though it wasn't unexpected, I'm in awe of how well she's doing.

"I think I'd like that," she replies softly. "Let's go eat and we can all share our favorite memories of him."

The meal is exquisite, and the reminiscing flows well beyond brunch. When Bryce and I say our goodbyes late that afternoon, I feel more like a part of his family than I even do of my own. Not that that's saying much, about my family anyway. And I can see how happy Bryce is for it too.

As we descend the front steps, he wraps his hand around mine once more. He walks me to the passenger side of the car, where he gathers me into his arms.

"They all love you," he says, looking down at me adoringly.

"Good," I respond, wrapping my arms around his neck and going on my tiptoes to kiss him. "Because I love them too."

He smiles and nuzzles his nose against mine.

I look seriously into his eyes. "Now take me home so I can do naughty things to you."

Bryce laughs and releases me, opening the car door so I can get in. "Yes, ma'am," he replies, grinning as he closes the door behind me.

☙

BUT ONCE WE'RE HOME, WE ACTUALLY END UP ON the couch, laying down holding each other and talking about all sorts of things. It feels like now that I'm getting to know him as a lover and partner, I need to relearn everything I already know about him from that slant. And he seems to feel the same. Our talk is much more hopes-and-dreams oriented, and we're just as in sync as we were as friends. Though it's hard not to expect something to crop up that will make this come crashing down around my ears.

But I decide, as I lay in his arms, looking into his gorgeous blue eyes and talking about our future, that I'm going to try to just be happy. It's against my nature and what life has taught me so far, but I'm so ready for hope. And Bryce Hoyt, with his sunshine smile and fierce loyalty, is just what I need.

We talk late into the evening, not even stopping through a light dinner. It's not until we realize it's past our usual bedtimes that we head upstairs. But I make good on my promise, seeing to his pleasure just as thoroughly as he saw to mine this morning.

∾

WHEN I WAKE TO MY ALARM THE FOLLOWING morning I find myself alone in bed. But I can hear the shower running. Bryce must be done with his workout. Gleefully, I slide out of bed to join him.

The bathroom is steamy, but I can just make out his tall form. And as I get closer I can see more of his gorgeous body. I'm instantly as wet as his glistening skin.

I knock on the glass door. Bryce turns, looking not terribly surprised to see me.

"Did you wait to take a shower until you knew I'd be getting up?" I ask suspiciously.

One of his eyebrows waggles suggestively and I laugh, sliding open the foggy door and stepping in. He's on me immediately, pulling me into the hot stream of water, his mouth pressing into mine insistently. My hand slips to his cock to stroke him into readiness, but I find there's no need. He's already there. I groan softly into his mouth as my own wetness is made redundant by the moisture that's engulfed us.

"Good morning, gorgeous," he says into my ear. "If it's okay with you, I'm going to fuck you. Hard."

I groan, leaning into him. I can't even speak, so I simply nod. Bryce turns me around, pressing on my back until I'm leaned forward and braced against the wall. And with a tilt of his hips, he's pressed himself into me from behind. I gasp at the suddenness of our joining, and he gives me the smallest fraction of a moment to adjust before his hands grip my breasts and he begins thrusting roughly into me. It's only painful for a second before I'm moaning in ecstasy. With Bryce groaning behind me as he holds nothing back, and every part of me still sensitive, it's not long before we both come apart with pleasure.

I turn back around, returning my lips to his for a final kiss before I playfully shove him out of the shower. "Thanks," I say, waving at him as I close the door.

He laughs and shakes his head. "That's cold, Sera," he teases.

I shrug and start to lather up my hair, pretending to ignore him. He laughs again as he dries off. When he leaves to get dressed I watch his unbelievably smoking hot backside as he walks away. And it's all I can do to concentrate long enough to finish showering.

∿

IT TAKES ME UNTIL MID-MORNING TO FULLY GET MY head into work. Which is good, because I have a late morning meeting with Charles Sutton. I decide to drop in his office ahead of time to check in with him, given the understandable tension in the office these last weeks. Understandable because his son is pending trial for sexually assaulting one of my former employees. And the whole office has been buzzing with theories and gossip, to the point that I know even Charles must be hearing them by now.

I knock softly on his door.

"What?" his commanding, voice calls sharply.

Steeling myself, I poke my head in the door. "Good morning, boss," I greet him. "Mind if I come in?"

He turns from his place by the windows, his hands behind his back, a worn-out expression on his stern features. "Yes, of course, Sera, please," he replies, returning to his desk chair.

I take a seat opposite his desk, crossing my legs

nervously after I'm seated. "How are you, Charles?" I ask.

He drums his thumbs on the armrests of his chair. "Managing," he replies. His dark eyes meet my own, and I see a great sadness in them. "What about you, Ms. Evans? My company absorbed yours not quite two months ago. Even aside from the issues with my son, I know it's been a difficult time for you."

I huff an ironic laugh. It's hard not to feel like the drama in my own life has invited it into Charles Sutton's. Not that his son's behavior is in any way my fault, but our contentious relationship before that even came to light made the transition difficult.

But then, I'd run my own real estate consulting services company for nearly five years. And Charles Sutton brought me into the fold with the express, though undeclared, purpose of mentoring me to become his successor, having deemed his eldest son's disposition a poor fit for the job. In hindsight I should have expected the epic clash of wills between Daniel and me. And if I hadn't personally been going through so much, I might have been able to contain myself better.

I heave a deep sigh. "It's been tumultuous, to say the least," I admit finally. "But I can't help feeling there's a reason for everything. And I have no regrets about coming to work for you or about folding Evans

Realty Services into Sutton Developments. Being exposed to more of the industry, harnessing the power of our combined companies, I understand why you wanted this. I imagine it's what my grandfather would have wanted. For both of us."

Charles steeples his fingers under his nose, as he is wont to do, but I also notice tears in his eyes. And I realize they're in mine too. Perhaps it's the reminder of Grandpa Tyler, the bond that ultimately brought Charles and I together. He mentored us both, after all, and is the reason I became a real estate agent and started my own company. Not that I needed to with the immense fortune he left behind from his own investments, but because it's what I wanted. And working for Charles has been a natural extension of that journey. The bond we've already formed is irreplaceable, and perhaps also a contributing factor to my emotional response.

"No doubt," Charles responds softly, smiling. "Thank you for saying that. All of it. You are resilient as always, my dear, and I'm glad to hear you're happy to be here despite everything else."

"How is the rest of your family faring?" I ask curiously. I don't know much about Charles' wife or his other two sons. But I imagine this is just as difficult for them.

Charles gives a small shrug. "His brothers are, as I

was, unsurprised, given Daniel's past issues. My wife has been struggling," Charles admits, sighing deeply. "It's been hardest on her, I think."

"I can't even imagine," I murmur, looking down into my hands.

"I'd like you to meet them one day," Charles responds.

I look up, startled, though I shouldn't be. I know he has big plans for me so it would only be natural.

"But not now. For now, we have enough to be getting on with, I think."

I glance at my watch. "Speaking of which," I prompt him.

He looks at his own watch, nodding in agreement and rising from his chair. "Shall we?" he asks.

I smile widely, despite my lingering sorrow. "Lead the way," I reply.

He laughs, nods, and does just that. And perhaps it's my imagination, but the rest of the day seems to go more smoothly.

∾

When Tristan drops me home in the evening, Bryce is already there. And he's making dinner.

"The only thing that could make this better is if you were shirtless," I tease him by way of greeting.

He looks up from chopping carrots and smiles. "Hey, you," he replies, smiling back with his patented sunshine smile. "How was your day?"

I kick my shoes off and drop my bag on the counter, sinking into a chair at the bar. He leans across the counter to kiss me.

"Better than I expected it to be," I reply when he pulls away. "How was yours?"

He huffs a forced laugh. "A laugh a minute," he replies sarcastically. "I'm starting to get why you were over being the boss."

"That bad, huh?" I ask with a grimace.

He stops his chopping again to give me a look. "I probably shouldn't complain. Things are going surprisingly well, considering," he allows. "I didn't think I'd be as on top of things as I am after just a month of running the company without Dad."

"I told you. You're the most capable guy I know," I assure him. Then I add, with a sly smile, "But I think you need a massage after dinner. Full body."

He doesn't look up, but a smile slowly spreads across his face. "You're just trying to get me to chop off a thumb, aren't you?" he teases.

I put my hands up in defeat. "Fine, I'll leave you to it then," I accede. "I'm going to change." But as I head up the stairs, I can't help pausing and watching him work. And wondering how I got so damn lucky.

∾

AFTER DINNER, BRYCE IS SPLAYED OUT ON THE COUCH with his feet in my lap as I rub firm strokes up and down his soles.

"So I forgot to mention something," he murmurs, opening his eyes. "They set a trial date today. For Daniel Sutton."

My eyebrows shoot up. "And you're just now telling me? When?" I demand.

He shrugs. "Sorry, it slipped my mind. And then you started rubbing me," he smiles provocatively. "It starts in two weeks."

I continue working his instep as I process that. "I should check in with Heather soon," I murmur. I haven't talked to Heather Irving, my former employee and Daniel Sutton's victim, in a few weeks. I'm a little surprised I haven't heard from her actually, but I'm sure she's got enough on her plate.

Bryce nods. "Probably a good idea," he agrees. "But for now, I have other plans." He gently pulls his foot out of my grasp and sits up. He scoots along the couch until he's right in front of me. Slowly, he leans in and nuzzles his nose against mine.

I can't help grinning like an idiot. "Hi," I say shyly.

"Did you know your eye color changes from light

brown to hazel to pretty much full-on green?" he asks, looking deeply into my eyes.

I laugh. "It's like a mood ring," I reply. "Or a happiness scale, actually."

"I hope green means happy, because that's what they are right now," he says.

"It might," I say evasively, blushing.

"Hmmm," he says thoughtfully. "Let's see how green they can get." He kisses me softly, and the feeling of his mouth on mine wipes all thought from my brain. He pulls away and stares into my eyes again. "Not bad, but I think we can do better." Suddenly he grabs me, lifting me over his shoulder and rising from the couch. I squeal with surprise as he carries me out of the living room and up the stairs.

"Bryce! Holy crap!" I shout.

He smacks me playfully on the backside. "You know you like it, woman," he responds. But he sets me down at the top of the stairs anyway.

At first I think he's acknowledging my obvious displeasure at being moved bodily, but I quickly realize as he starts kissing me and pulling at my clothes as he pushes me toward the bedroom that it was a necessary step toward getting me naked as fast as possible. And that, I don't mind.

FOUR

When I get home from work on Tuesday, Bryce is still at the office, so I take the opportunity to check in with Heather as Tristan hovers unobtrusively near the window wall. I note that he seems to like it as much as I do as I listen to the line ring. Though who wouldn't — day or night, the view of downtown Seattle and Elliott Bay is spectacular. But as I continue to wait, Heather doesn't answer, and I eventually get dumped into her voicemail.

"Hey, Heather, it's Sera," I start. "Just wanted to check in and see how you're doing. I heard about the trial date. Maybe we can get together before then. If not, just let me know if there's anything you need, okay? Talk soon. Bye." Feeling awkward, I hang up.

Behind me, I hear the front door open and turn to see Bryce striding in, looking like hot business as usual in dark slacks and a baby-blue button front shirt. He gives me a huge grin, and I can't resist running to greet him.

He scoops me up gleefully and kisses me deeply. "Second best possible greeting," he murmurs, letting me go.

"What's the best?" I can't help asking.

Bryce's eyes flick up to where Tristan stands by the window and he mouths the word *apron*. I roll my eyes and shove him lightly. Tristan strolls casually toward us.

"You guys are disgustingly cute," he teases us. "I'm going to go home and throw up now."

I stick my tongue out at Tristan and Bryce calls after him, "Don't let the door hit you in the ass on the way out."

Tristan throws up a final wave without turning around. "'Night, boss."

We both laugh as the door closes behind him.

"Now, about that apron," Bryce says, turning to me.

I shake my head and huff a laugh. "Can you eat an apron? Because I'm hungry," I reply airily, heading for the kitchen.

And though Bryce doesn't say anything more on

the subject, I can tell just how much he's salivating to see me in *just* that apron.

⁓

I LEAVE WORK EARLY ON FRIDAY TO PUT OPERATION Apron into effect. I prepare an elaborate dinner and have it all laid out on the table before I get a call from Bryce's assistant that he's headed home.

Grinning like the cat that ate the canary, I let Tristan know that Bryce is on his way home. And that I'd like him to wait outside the front door until Bryce gets here, and then he can leave. Tristan laughs and shakes his head but does as I ask. And I go upstairs to change. Or strip, as it were.

So when Bryce walks through the door not quite fifteen minutes later, his look of confusion due to Tristan's unusual position rapidly disappears as he catches sight of me next to a tableful of food. Wearing sky-high red heels, a matched red lip, and the apron. And nothing else.

His jaw drops as he takes in the small sheet of fabric that's by no stretch of the imagination covering my generous curves. Free of a bra, my breasts topple out the sides, and it only just skims the bottom of my hips. I hold out a glass of whiskey.

"Welcome home, baby." My voice is husky with

desire. Being mostly naked and waiting for a gorgeous man has made me as ready for what comes next as he is.

But instead of the pouncing I expected, he methodically sets his keys and wallet on the table by the door. As he slowly advances on me, he undoes the top two buttons of his shirt. He stops in front of me, casually accepting the proffered glass and taking a measured sip. And even though I'm wearing four-inch heels, he still towers over me.

I discreetly take a deep breath and I cock an eyebrow at him, marveling at his control. It's all I can do not to shake with anticipation. "How was your day?" I ask as nonchalantly as I can. And I manage to sound much calmer than I feel.

Bryce carefully sets the whiskey down on the table behind me and rolls his broad shoulders. "It's about to get a whole lot better," he murmurs, looking deeply into my eyes. His gaze is fire itself, burning me from the inside out.

My lips part and a small breath escapes me.

A smile flits across his features, and he uses his thumb to stroke firmly from my bottom lip, down my chin, to my neck and chest. "Where do you want me to fuck you, Sera?"

My whole body tightens in anticipation, heat pooling between my thighs. I don't trust myself to speak, so I simply look over at the couch. He gives a small nod. Grabbing my hand, he leads me the few steps into the living room and sits down on the over-stuffed white behemoth. His eyes never leave mine. With a tug he spins me around and pulls me into his lap, so my back is pressed against his chest.

He brushes the hair away from my neck, his breath hot on the sensitive flesh. Tilting my head with one hand, he presses his mouth into the place where my neck meets my shoulder, then runs his tongue up to my ear. I gasp in surprise and lean back into him. His other hand reaches around, firmly grasping my breast under the apron, my nipple pinched between his unforgiving fingers. As he sucks and twists at me, I writhe against him, racked with desire. I grab at the hand working my breast and pull it out from under the soft fabric. I guide it under the bottom of the apron, between my legs.

His mouth breaks away and a low moan escapes him. My hips buck at the sound and he tames them with his hand. His fingers slide down and into the soft mound of flesh between my legs, finding their target quickly. And he works the vulnerable nub between two fingers just as he did my nipple. As my breath quickens and I loudly affirm my enjoyment, his other hand works under me, undoing his pants. And I feel it when his cock springs free, hard and hot.

I turn my head, my lips finding his, and our tongues do a feverish and lust-filled dance for a few moments before he pulls away, sucking my bottom lip on the way. He wraps an arm around me and lifts me slightly, then uses the other hand to slip himself inside me. And I can't help but gasp loudly and spasm at the sudden filling, my whole body tight and quivering in response.

Determined to be his every fantasy tonight, I push his pants to the floor, then spread my legs for leverage and brace my hands on the couch between his open knees. And I put all my concentration into raising and lowering my hips over him. At the first thrust, both of Bryce's hands drop to my hips and he groans loudly.

"You feel …" he pants through the words, "… so fucking good."

I pump again and this time he rises to meet me.

"Yes, Sera. Don't stop. God, don't stop."

I put everything I have into managing the almost overwhelming feeling of him inside me, every nerve ending screaming with pleasure. And I focus on the ride, up and down, and again. Until I'm sweating, shaking, screaming. Or perhaps it's just him screaming as his hands grip my sides, his hips rising to meet mine hard on every thrust, crying out loudly with every gratifying plunge into my slick center.

When I feel like my arms will give out I lean back

with him still inside me. He turns my head roughly, the fire of his passion erupting as his mouth roughly claims mine. His hips slide downward, off the couch, and his hands slide under my thighs, holding me in place. Using his arms to support me in position, he uses the freedom of his lower half hovering off the couch to start thrusting wildly.

And it's pleasure like I've never known, with me totally at his mercy as he balances me over him, spread open as he plunges deeper than I thought possible. A low ache begins to build and a desire to shatter into a million pieces pours through me but is just out of reach. I suddenly remember a move he made our first time, and I slip a finger between my legs. With a small touch I find the catalyst I was looking for. So I press harder, faster, until I'm keeping rhythm with him. Until I'm coming so hard that I've lost control over myself. But he doesn't stop, and the orgasm continues until Bryce can't hold the position anymore.

He sinks carefully onto the floor, laying me on the plush rug between the couch and the coffee table. He hovers over me, panting and just as slick with sweat as I am. His mouth descends on my nipple, his teeth pulling at it through the thin fabric. And then the other. I'm so spent that I can barely arch my back into the pleasure, but my hands pull at him nonetheless, desperate to have him inside me again. He smiles down at me.

"So impatient," he teases, sliding into me slowly.

I groan and wriggle under him.

"You just." He thrusts slowly. "Need." Again. "To." Again. "Relax." He keeps the rhythm, running his nose up my neck and kissing me as softly as he takes me.

I do as he says and relax into it. And I'm not sorry. The slow, sensual pace allows me to feel every inch of him and he of me. I close my eyes and bite my lip, intent on savoring the drawn-out ascent.

It's not long before I notice him speeding up. And not long after that I hear his breath hitch, and he nuzzles his face into my neck before his final shift back into an earth-shaking, orgasm-inducing frenzy. His thrusts are as shallow and fast as his breathing, and I focus on letting my climax wash over me before he loses it. And when it does, I grip him to me and tighten around him, pulling him in with me. His guttural groans spur on the continued contractions of my muscles as I ride the peak, causing him to shudder and quake over me, in me. I feel his release, hot and wet, spilling into me. Almost crying with gratifica-tion, I release him, and he rolls off of me.

He laces his fingers tiredly in mine, and we lie there in silence for a long while. When I feel like the world has stopped spinning with mad desire and lust, I roll toward him onto my side, propping my head on my hand.

"So did that live up to the fantasy?" I ask, tracing a finger down the muscles of his chest and stomach through his shirt. His answering smile is one of pure, exhausted bliss. He fingers the ruffled edge of the apron fondly.

"It turned the fantasy on its back and fucked it seventeen ways from Sunday," he responds matter-of-factly.

I chew my lip thoughtfully. "Do you have any other fantasies?" I ask curiously.

Bryce's eyebrows shoot up and he rolls onto his side to face me. "Four months," he says.

I look at him questioningly.

"That's how long I've know you. Wanted you. I could write a book — maybe even several books — about all of the fantasies I've had of you."

I press my lips together to suppress my amused smile. "For instance?" I prompt.

His eyes flick to the window wall behind us.

"Ah, yes, you mentioned that one recently."

He leans in and kisses me softly. "We can take mine one at a time," he replies. "How about you? Did you ever fantasize about me?"

I can't help giving him an incredulous look. "Um.

Yeah," I say in a tone that implies that should've been obvious. "Have you seen yourself?" I poke him in his ridiculously large bicep. "I even had a dream once about us having sex that gave me an actual orgasm," I admit.

Bryce looks impressed. "Damn, that's pretty awesome," he says. "Well, whatever I was doing in that dream, I'd be happy to make it a reality."

And it hits me again. This man. Over and over he's proving to me that I've made the right choice. That I can trust him completely. That he adores me completely.

"My fantasies. Your fantasies. I want to do all of it," I admit. "I trust you, Bryce. Completely."

His face is inscrutable for a moment until he presses his lips to mine tenderly. He of all people knows how much that means for me. How closely I guarded my heart for so long.

He breaks the kiss but moves only far enough away so he can look into my eyes once more. "And I trust you completely," he replies. "No matter what life brings us, Sera, never forget how much I love you."

∿

BY SATURDAY AFTERNOON WE STILL HAVEN'T MADE IT out of bed for more than a few minutes here and there. I know it won't always be this way, this new and exciting. So I want to enjoy every moment of wanting and being wanted so badly that things like food, sleep, and the outside world don't seem all that important. But even on top of that, there's a depth to being with Bryce that I've never experienced. And I know it's borne of the solid friendship we've created over the last months. So it's hard to regret anything that's happened to lead me here.

But I'm somewhat brought back to reality when Heather returns my call late that afternoon. I slip into a robe and leave the bedroom, going downstairs so I can talk to her in private. But she sounds distant and doesn't want to talk much, though we do manage to make plans to have dinner next Wednesday. When I hang up, I feel perturbed. I stare out the living room window wall into the grey mist of the day, wrapping my arms around myself for warmth and comfort.

"Everything okay?" Bryce asks from behind me.

I turn to see him sauntering toward me from the stairs, finally dressed in grey sweats and a white T-shirt. It doesn't make me want him any less. Though the sense of discomfort that still lingers from my brief chat with Heather puts a pretty big damper on my libido.

"I don't know," I reply honestly, sinking into my favorite chair.

Bryce takes a seat on the couch next to me and silently waits for me to explain.

"It seemed like Heather was doing so well for a while there. Her new job has been going well. She's getting therapy and has plenty of support leading into Daniel's trial. But she sounded off. I can't quite put my finger on it."

"Scared? Nervous? Doubtful?" Bryce offers patiently.

"Yes," I reply sweepingly. "All of that." I shake my head sorrowfully. "I just hate that one heinous, unspeakable act can continue to victimize her. And probably will for the rest of her life."

Bryce considers me thoughtfully for a moment. "Well," he starts carefully. "You of all people know what that's like. If anyone can help her through this, it's you."

I meet his concerned gaze. We don't talk much anymore about how, three months ago, he saved my life from a deranged employee with a massive grudge against me. How she kidnapped me, beat me, and almost shot me before Bryce showed up, Alessandro in tow, causing her to turn the gun on herself.

I rub my eyes as if it'll remove the image of the back of her skull exploding from my mind. "I don't know what I'm supposed to do," I admit. "I still have nightmares myself. Elevators still scare me sometimes." Once you've been kidnapped at gunpoint in one, it's hard to forget. "But even that pales in comparison to being violated the way she was. I can't even begin to imagine what she's going through."

Bryce leans forward with his arms resting on his massive thighs. He looks into his hands for a long while. Finally, he looks up at me seriously.

"Between serving in the military and running a company that profits off the vulnerability of others, I've seen a lot of different kinds of pain," he says. "But I've also seen hope. And perseverance. It's normal to have doubts, to wonder if it'll ever get better. If continuing down a path is worth the cost. The ones who make it through have a good support system. It's the ones who try to pretend like bad things aren't happening or refuse help that suffer the most in the long run. Heather has her parents, us, her therapist, and hopefully other friends and family who are helping her through this. She's dealing with this and moving forward. But I think even she knew that path was going to be harder in the short term than doing nothing. But Daniel *will* be convicted. And Heather *will* get through this." He reaches out and folds his hand over mine. "And so will you."

His words strike such a chord in me that my eyes fill with tears, and it takes me a moment to figure out why. I blink back the tears as I finish putting my thoughts into words.

"The day I called you, when we hadn't spoken in more than three weeks," I say softly, looking to him to see if he remembers. Though I'm certain he does.

"Yes, after I'd stupidly yelled at you for not dealing with things that were difficult. Like the attack. Our feelings for each other. Your trust issues." His expression is grim and remorseful. "I should've called you first." He leans back into the sofa, running a hand over his hair.

"I didn't accidentally call you that day," I admit.

He huffs a dry laugh. "I know," he replies with a wry smile.

I shake my head. "What you don't know is how low I was," I respond. "Alessandro had stopped calling and was doing god-knows-what in Italy without any sign of ever returning. Daniel was making my transition to Sutton Developments hell. My half-brother decided he didn't want to meet me. Allie had lost her baby and crawled into her cocoon of depression. And you were hurting, and I *was* denying that I had feelings for you. When we stopped talking, and all of that was going on, I almost gave up hope."

Bryce looks at me quizzically. "But you didn't.

And you got through it. And Heather will too, with your help," he reiterates.

I shake my head. "I didn't get through it. *You* got me through it. Before you came along, I didn't know what it was like to be loved by someone who was always there for me, even when their own world was falling apart. Not even my parents, for fuck's sake," I admit. "Whether I wanted to admit my feelings or not, I always knew you would be there for me. Even when we weren't speaking, I knew if I needed you, you'd be there."

"I was," he agrees, smiling at me sadly. "I am."

I nod, pulling my knees to my chest. "I know."

We stare at each other for a few moments, an understanding passing between us, a recognition of how truly deep the bond we share is.

"What does this have to do with Heather?" he asks, tilting his head.

I can't help but laugh. "Nothing," I admit. "What you said just made me realize that I'm no longer an island. And I'm glad for that. That on some level I always knew how much you love me. And that's what got me through everything I went through. Even if I wasn't ready to love you back. So thank you. For that. And you know, everything else." I give him a sheepish smile and he laughs.

"Anytime, gorgeous," he replies. "To that end,

think of the Heather and Daniel situation from that slant. You'll do what you can to support Heather. And the whole thing will be difficult for you too. But we'll get through it, just like we've gotten through everything else."

"Yes," I agree, my eyes once again sparkling with tears — this time of joy. "*We* will."

FIVE

On Sunday morning I find it insanely difficult to tear myself away from Bryce to meet Allie for brunch. But since it has been three weeks since I've seen my best friend, I know I need to dig deep. Bryce doesn't make it easier, lounging half-naked on the sofa as I look for my keys, then begging for more kisses as I try to depart.

But finally, I manage to get myself there, where I find Allie already waiting at the restaurant. In stark contrast to the summery outfit she wore last time, she now wears a charcoal grey long-sleeved tunic over thick black tights, her strawberry blond hair hanging in loose waves around her shoulders. And she looks really happy.

"Sera!" she squeals when she sees me, pulling me into a tight hug.

"Hey, babe," I reply grinning and squeezing her back.

She presses me away to arm's length and scrutinizes my face. "You're glowing," she remarks suspiciously. "I'm guessing things are going well?"

My grin turns maniacal as I follow her in to the restaurant. "You could say that," I reply coyly.

"Oh lord, you're going at it like rabbits, aren't you?" she asks, rolling her eyes as we're seated at a booth.

I cackle. "Maaaaaybe," I admit.

She shakes her head and laughs. "I forget what that part of the relationship is like," she responds. "At least I can relive it vicariously through you."

"Won't you be *actually* living it pretty soon in Fiji?" I tease her.

Allie smiles shyly from behind her menu. "As it happens, even the thought of a romantic vacation has made things a little more exciting recently," she admits.

"Oh, really?" I ask. "How *much* more exciting?" I'm teasing her mostly, since I know she's too shy about that sort of thing to actually tell me.

She laughs and waves me off. "It's probably not as exciting as I'm making it sound. Mostly things are back to how they were before," she replies. "When you live with someone and have regular access, it's just not as interesting, even at the best of times."

I suddenly realize I didn't tell Allie that Bryce and I are living together. And unfortunately, I'm not able to wipe the guilty look off my face before she notices.

"What are you hiding?" she asks sharply.

"God, Allie, I forget what a bloodhound you are," I mumble.

Thankfully, the waiter shows up to take our orders, so I have a moment to regroup.

When he's gone, I sigh heavily and approach the subject cautiously.

"You know how I told you I had personal security because the people who are after Alessandro are trying to get at him through me?"

"Yes," she replies, clearly unsure of where I'm going with this.

"And how having them around made me isolate myself?" I continue.

Allie nods, but waits for me to continue with a wary look on her face.

"Well, Bryce agreed to let me back off the security to just to and from work, but only if he moved in with me." I brace myself.

"So you and Bryce are living together. And going at it like rabbits," she deduces drily.

I nod.

She looks at me disapprovingly for a moment before sighing and shrugging. "Well, at least that gives you easy access."

"It's not permanent," I hedge.

"Pfff," Allie responds. "We'll see." She looks at the nervous expression on my face. "Oh, Sera, don't worry about what I think. As long as you're happy, that's all that matters to me. You know that."

"Thank you," I reply. "But in some ways, it even feels fast to me."

She levels a look at me. "You know, don't you."

It's not really a question, and I'm not sure what she means. I give her a puzzled look. "I know a lot of things," I reply slowly. "To what, exactly, are you referring?"

"That he's The One." She says it matter-of-factly, like she's just remarked that I know he likes to wear blue shirts.

I chew on my lip, trying to decide if I should attempt a denial. But in true Allie form, she sees right through me before I can even get that far.

"If you haven't realized it yet, that's fine," she replies airily, sipping the glass of water in front of her. "But I've known for a long time."

And I can't help but laugh at that. "Seriously? You knew that I wanted to spend the rest of my life with him before I did?" I reply sarcastically. And then realizing what I've just admitted, I clap a hand over my mouth.

Allie grins triumphantly. "See? That wasn't so hard," she says with a wink. "I'm happy for you."

"I'm happy too," I admit. "Ridiculously, rainbows-sunshine-and-unicorns happy."

Allie laughs, though her attention is quickly diverted as our food arrives.

After a few minutes of silently stuffing our faces, Allie swallows enough of her food to continue the discussion.

"Is he as hot with his shirt off as he is with it on? No wait, of course he is. I'm sure he's even hotter. How much hotter are we talking here?" she presses.

"It hurts thinking about it," I reply with a lascivious grin.

She lets out a frustrated groan. "What's wrong with this guy then? Is he ..." she leans forward and lowers her voice, "lacking in the size department?"

"Allie!" I reply, shocked. "I've never heard you talk about this stuff, much less ask those kinds of questions." I examine her for a moment. "What happened?"

She blushes furiously. "I went off the depression meds at the suggestion of my therapist," she admits. "And it's been great. I'm great. I feel alive again. So I guess things have just started working again." She grins like a school girl.

I almost want to cry with happiness. "That's so great," I breathe. Then after a pause, "Does this mean you might come back to work?"

She presses her lips together. "I think so," she replies. "After vacation, David and I are going to decide."

I want to jump up and hug her, or clap, or dance. But I hold it in, not wanting to pressure her. But I think she gets how happy that makes me anyway.

"Now, are you going to answer the question or what?"

A shit-eating grin splits my face. "Exactly the opposite of lacking," I reply, biting my lip thinking of it. "His only flaw is being too fucking perfect."

Allie laughs. "Yeah, we'll see about that. Let this phase wear off and every time he forgets to replace the toilet paper roll or pick up groceries on his way home, you'll be ready to tear his head off," she assures me.

I laugh in return. "Probably," I agree. "And not that I've ever been in a relationship long enough to know, but I'm sure you get past that phase too."

Allie nods sagely. "Oh, yes. Once he's realized that everyone is much happier if he just stops doing things that piss you off," she replies.

I look at her skeptically. "Seriously?" I ask.

Allie bursts out laughing. "Hell, no. You just give up after a while and stop giving a shit," she chortles. "And it's great."

"Ah, such high praise and hope for the romantic future I have ahead of me," I reply with feigned wistfulness. But then, dropping back into my usual tone, "Consider me warned. I'm going to enjoy the going-at-it-like-rabbits phase while I can."

"Then you better finish those waffles," she replies looking pointedly at my mostly uneaten food. "Sounds like you're going to need your strength."

⌇

AT HOME LATER THAT EVENING, WHILE BRYCE AND I are lazing in bed — dressed and watching television, for once — my dad calls. I show Bryce the caller ID.

"You going to answer?" he asks curiously, stroking my thigh reassuringly.

I shrug. "Might as well," I reply.

While I feel readier to deal with it now, I'm not sure when, if ever I'll be totally comfortable talking to my father, as he was absent for so long and for some reason has picked this tumultuous time in my life to want to reconnect. The single lunch we shared was awkward enough. I'm not sure how many more uncomfortable conversations I can handle.

"Want me to leave?" Bryce asks considerately.

"No, it's okay," I reply with a smile. I take a deep breath and pick up the call. "Hello?"

"Sera," Kent Evans' voice breathes in a sigh. "I'm so glad you answered. I was starting to get worried about you."

I roll my eyes. "I'm fine," I reply. "There's just been a lot going on. How was your business trip?"

"Productive. But I'm glad to be back home," he replies genially. "What's been going on there?"

I glance over at Bryce, not sure if I want to get into it with both men able to listen. "You know, I was just getting ready for bed," I fib. "How about we have lunch next weekend and we can talk about it?"

"Yeah? Are you sure? I mean, I'd love to see you, but I was worried after Hunter and I cancelled at the last minute before."

As if I needed a reminder that my half-brother clearly has no interest in meeting me.

"It's okay, really," I interrupt. "I'd probably have done the same in his shoes."

"He feels bad about it," Kent replies.

I'm shocked, and skeptical, but he sounds sincere. So, he believes it, anyway.

"He said that he'd come next time, but only if you were okay with it."

I frown at the obviously manipulative tactic. Because if I say no, now I'm the asshole. And I'm sure he expects me to say no, or he wouldn't have made the offer.

"Of course I'm okay with it," I lie.

Bryce gives me a look. I know he can't hear Kent's side of the conversation, but Bryce knows a lie when he hears one.

"Well! That's great, Sera," he replies, sounded beyond happy and relieved. "Same time and place?"

"Yep," I respond, eager to hang up. "See you next Saturday at noon."

"Goodnight, Sera."

"Goodnight, Kent." I hang up and groan loudly.

Bryce smirks unreservedly. "So I'm meeting your dad next weekend, huh?"

I shoot him a glare. "I'm going by myself," I respond snappishly. And I immediate feel bad for it. "I'm sorry. I don't know why I suggested we have lunch. Ugh. But it really is something I'd rather do on my own."

Bryce gives me a patient look. "I hate to break it to you, but I'm either meeting your dad, or you get to explain why Tristan has to stand within three feet of you at all times," Bryce replies. "Your call."

My eyes widen with realization. "Why did I get to go by myself to meet Allie today then?" I ask petulantly.

"Because it was three blocks away, and it's Allie," he replies drily. "But I can't let you go across town to meet a man I don't know by yourself."

"Fuck," I swear.

Bryce laughs. "I'll behave, I promise," he says, still chuckling.

"They're probably going to like you more than they like me," I grouse.

Bryce smiles his sunshine smile, and I immediately find it's impossible for me to be cranky any longer.

I pick up my pillow and whack him with it. "Stop." *Whack.* "Being." *Whack.* "So." *Whack.* "Perfect." *Whack.* "Damnit!"

Bryce shields himself half-heartedly from each blow, and on my last swing captures both me and the pillow. He throws the pillow off the side of the bed and pins me under him, planting kisses all over my face. I squeal and wriggle in protest, ultimately dissolving into indignant giggles.

But he abruptly pulls away after a moment. "Wait. They?" he asks.

I sit up, adjusting my camisole. "They," I confirm. "My father and my half-brother."

Bryce leans back into his pillow with his arms behind his head, considering that. "Well, that ought to be interesting," he replies thoughtfully.

"You promised to behave," I remind him.

He shoots me a sly grin. "Oh, I'll behave. At lunch anyway," he replies. "But I make no promises until then."

I only have a split second after I realize he plans to resume his attack to get away, but I'm not fast enough. Not that I mind since, as always, it quickly evolves into much more naked and pleasurable play.

SIX

I also find I don't so much mind the dawning of the workweek anymore now that Bryce is living with me. Shower sex after his workout has become the norm, and it leaves me happy, if not a bit distracted, for most of the day until we can get back to it before bed.

Work itself has slipped back into a steady, drama-free rhythm. Though without Daniel, I'm far more loaded with responsibility than I'd like to be. But it's still mostly manageable, and I'm just not as easily fazed these days, being at a zero stress level physically and emotionally.

But on Wednesday I get a one-two punch that knocks me back. First, Bryce calls to tell me that Daniel's trial has been postponed until further notice, mentioning something about a procedural error. Not long after, I get a text from Heather saying she can't make dinner and she'll let me know when she's able to reschedule. I text her back asking if she's okay, knowing that she's likely not in light of the news, but get no response. And for the rest of the day, I can't shake my concern for her.

Predictably, Bryce encourages me to let it go, that only she can decide to reach out, and to give her space if that's what she needs. It doesn't make me any less worried, but I decide that he's at least partly right — there's nothing I can do about it. So I bury myself in my new routine of work and Bryce, and by the end of the week it's mostly stopped niggling at me. Mostly. But when I realize that's happening, it starts niggling at me that it's not niggling at me, so I decide to just go back to worrying. Even though there's nothing I can do. Understandably, it drives Bryce a little crazy but, as with everything, he takes it in stride with immeasurable grace and patience.

When Saturday dawns, and I mentally prepare for lunch with my father and half-brother, I wonder briefly how far Bryce's Zen will go. Not that I know exactly what to expect, but I'm bracing for the worst. Though still hoping for the best.

I'm a little surprised when Bryce comes downstairs in dark slacks and his favorite cerulean blue button-front shirt that makes his eyes look the same, bright shade. He looks ridiculously handsome, of course, but he's normally a jeans and T-shirt kind of guy on the weekend. I'm wearing my usual uniform of shirtdress and leggings, opting for a deep purple long-sleeved dress with black leggings. So I don't look underdressed next to him, per se, but it does make me wonder.

"Why so fancy?" I ask him teasingly.

He cocks an eyebrow. "You don't think I look nice?" he asks, running a hand over his chestnut hair. I stand up and reach up to do my own pass, noting that it's long enough to really run my fingers through again. He sighs happily and slouches to let me massage my fingers along his scalp.

"You're gorgeous and you know it," I murmur. "But it's just lunch, at a bistro. There's no dress code." He straightens up and runs his fingers along my arms.

"Maybe not for the restaurant," he allows. "But there's an implied meeting-the-father dress code."

I laugh. "You're worried what my father will think of you?" I ask incredulously.

He shrugs. "Doesn't hurt to look nice," he replies.

I have to bite my lip to contain myself. "You are too cute, Bryce Hoyt," I respond.

He frowns exaggeratedly. "Not cute," he replies,

deepening his already low voice. "Manly." He kisses me ferociously, his hands pawing at every inch of me, his hips pressing into mine.

When he pulls away I'm gasping for breath. "Careful there, tiger, or your manliness will be a little *too* obvious," I joke.

His eyes sparkle mischievously as he lowers his mouth to my ear. "Wouldn't want that. It might be …" he runs his nose down my ear and neck, causing that entire side of my body to tingle, "distracting." He kisses my clavicle softly, then pulls away, grazing a nipple with his fingertips as he goes. And then he walks nonchalantly to the kitchen bar to grab his wallet.

It takes me a full minute before I'm composed enough to move. He grins back at me over his shoulder, perfectly aware of the effect he's had on me.

"Ready?" he asks, turning back to me.

I shake my head at him. "If you're ready to start behaving, I'm ready to go," I qualify.

He laughs. "Fair enough."

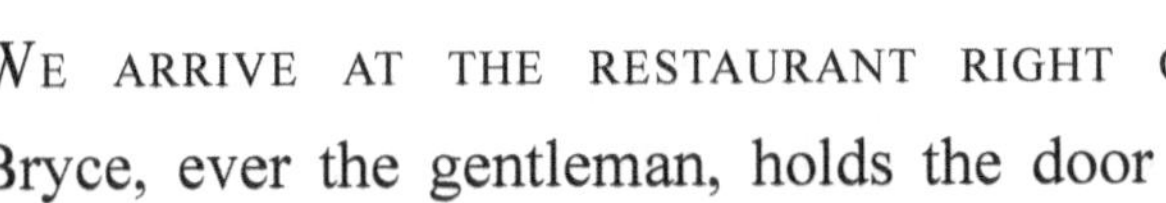

WE ARRIVE AT THE RESTAURANT RIGHT ON TIME. Bryce, ever the gentleman, holds the door open for me. He's practiced at discretion, but I've started to notice how he scans a room whenever he enters it. And I'm glad we don't go out more often, because it's a reminder of the still present potential for danger. I sigh inwardly, wondering how we'll ever know to stop looking over our shoulders.

But I'm quickly distracted from my own thoughts as I spot my father waving at me from a table off to one side of the restaurant. I can see the appraising look he throws Bryce as we approach, and I realize I'd forgotten to tell him I wouldn't be alone. But, since he isn't either, he'd already gotten a table that could seat four.

And for the first time, I notice the half-brother I've never met. The product of my father's secret other "wife." A wife only in practice at the time, as he was still married to my mother. But all I know about my sibling is his name — Hunter — and that he's seven years younger than me. And, at around twenty-three years old, he still looks mostly like a kid. At least to me. And I can tell by the look Bryce is giving him, he feels the same way. I remember suddenly that Bryce, in his once nonstop quest to gather intel on everyone I associated with, mentioned Hunter having anger issues, and I regret never asking what he'd meant.

As we arrive at the table and they both rise to greet us, Hunter looks even younger as my eyes flick from him to Bryce. Bryce, at thirty-four years old, has a distinct air of commanding confidence. It helps that he towers over all of us, broad and strapping, his hard body still completely evident under his well-tailored clothing. He's the epitome of the manly protector. Hunter looks like a man-child in comparison. Though he actually also looks much like my father, with the same sturdy but otherwise unremarkable build and the same light brown hair as both my father and me. Hunter is also only a few inches shorter than my father's six feet, putting him right around my height. It all contributes to the air of youth about him.

"Sera," my father greets me. "It's so nice to see you. I didn't know you'd be bringing someone."

"Sorry," I reply sheepishly. "I forgot to mention. This is Bryce Hoyt. Bryce, this is my father, Kent Evans."

Bryce extends a hand, which my father shakes firmly. "Nice meeting you," Bryce says, his voice low and measured.

"And you are?" There's a challenge in my father's eyes that irks me.

"Bryce is my boyfriend," I interject.

The corners of Bryce's mouth twitch as he takes in my irritated tone.

I reach a hand out to my half-brother. "You must be Hunter."

He glances down at my hand before taking it. His handshake is surprisingly solid. "Yeah," he says dismissively. "Nice to meet you."

My father shoots an annoyed look at Hunter. "Please, sit," he offers, taking a seat himself.

Hunter sits down next to him, so Bryce and I take the seats across from them. There are only three menus, but having been here before with my father, I already know what I want, so I pass mine to Bryce. Likewise, while Hunter peruses his menu, my father's stays folded in front of him. And he's staring at Bryce.

"I'm sorry it took me so long to get back to you," I say to my father, attempting to draw his attention away from Bryce before he notices.

Kent's eyes jump to mine, and he seems to snap out of it a little. "It's okay, I'm just glad we were able to get together," he replies. "How did everything go with your, er, merger, was it?"

"Yes, the merger," I confirm, loosing a breath. I hadn't realized how long it's been since we saw each other. And so much has happened since then. Not that he needs to know about most of it. "It was rough going for a while there. But things seem to be mostly in a good rhythm now. I've taken on a lot more responsibility, but I'm also learning a lot."

"More responsibility than running your own company?" he asks skeptically.

I smile vaguely. "Well, no," I admit. "It's just different, I guess. When it was my company, I had to do a lot of tasks I didn't really enjoy but were necessary. Now I mostly get to stick to the real estate-related stuff — project selection, negotiation, goal setting, that sort of thing."

I think hard for a minute trying to remember what my father actually does, if he'll even understand where I'm coming from. He used to change jobs a lot when I was a kid, and I know he talked about his current job at our last lunch, but I'm having trouble recalling exactly what it was. I seem to remember it being related to the legal field, but for some reason it's eluding me at the moment.

"What do you do for a living, Mr. Evans?" Bryce pipes up, and I want to kiss him for asking.

I hadn't noticed, but his menu is now folded on the table in front of him and he's leaned back in his chair casually, one hand resting on my knee. I also note that Hunter is still studying his menu, though I'm beginning to think it's to avoid participating in the conversation.

My father shifts imperceptibly under Bryce's cool gaze. "I'm a process server," he replies.

Ah. Yes. That. Bryce suppresses a smile and

purposely avoids looking at me. He obviously finds that funny, and I'm not sure why.

"What is it that you do, son?"

"I run a corporate security firm," Bryce replies matter-of-factly.

My father frowns. "Hoyt, did you say? That wouldn't be Hoyt Corporate Services, would it?" he asks curiously.

And I'm sure the surprise shows on my face.

"You've heard of us," Bryce replies with an amused smile. "How nice."

"Yes, well, your company has been around a long time," Kent hedges. "You seem a bit young to be running the operation, though."

I can't help the indignant look that breaks across my face. "Um, hello? I ran my own company for years, and I'm younger than Bryce," I pipe up.

"Sera, I apologize," my father replies, blushing. "Obviously, you were doing very well. It's just Hoyt Corporate Services has quite a reputation. And some very high-profile clients."

"What he means is, my company protects some of the largest and wealthiest companies in the Seattle area," Bryce interjects. "And those companies are run by people with high standards. They expect their affairs to be handled by someone who knows what they're doing. Someone with experience."

Now my father is beet red. And I notice that Hunter has put his menu down and, while still silent, is watching with amused interest.

"Well, yes," my father replies, clearly beyond embarrassed. "But I didn't mean to imply anything bad about you, Bryce."

"It's all right, Mr. Evans," Bryce responds in a calm tone. "I didn't expect to be running the company so soon, either. But my father recently passed away, so that's just how it went. I have both undergraduate and graduate business degrees, had been training under my father for the better part of two decades, and was deployed multiple times as a Navy SEAL security specialist. So I assure you I'm more than qualified."

And Bryce is such a humble person, that he says it as if he were simply talking about the weather. But I can't help giving a smug grin. And Hunter looks positively gleeful.

"Badass, dude," he says seriously to Bryce, raising a fist.

Bryce laughs and reaches out to reciprocate the fist bump. "Thanks," Bryce replies, still chuckling.

My father is spared responding as the waitress arrives to take our orders.

"How long have you two been dating?" my father asks after she's gone.

And while I'm thankful he's moved on from questioning Bryce's qualifications, I'm not sure I like where this new line of questioning is going, either.

"Well, we've known each other for months," I reply carefully. "But we've only been dating a couple weeks now." Lordy. Saying it sounds odd. It feels like we've been together for so much longer.

"Oh, well, that's nice," my father responds, clearly relieved that Bryce wasn't just a secret I'd been withholding from him.

"What about you, Hunter?" Bryce asks, leaning forward onto his arms. "What do you do with your days?"

Hunter shrugs noncommittally. "Haven't been able to find a job since I graduated," he replies, sounding bored.

"Translation: he plays video games when he isn't out vandalizing public property with those —"

"God, Dad, could you please not?" Hunter interrupts my father. Our father. Hunter doesn't look mad, just embarrassed.

"What did you get your degree in?" I ask Hunter kindly.

"Art," he replies simply, finally looking me in the eye.

And I'm extremely surprised. I look over at Bryce to find him studying Hunter with an appraising look.

This was news to him too. And that kind of amuses me, considering Bryce usually knows that kind of information. Again, at least when it comes to people I might spend time with.

"Also known as a 'Would you like fries with that?' degree," my father jokes.

But nobody laughs. Hunter shifts uncomfortably in his seat. I almost ask Hunter what kind of art he does and what sort of job he is looking for, but I don't want to give my father more opportunity to make jokes at his expense, so I opt for changing the subject instead.

"I'm sure he'll find something great," I respond to my father. "I don't think you ever mentioned what your wife does." I suddenly realize I have no idea what Hunter's mother's name is.

"Barb is a beautician," Kent supplies.

"Oh," I respond, not quite sure of what to say. "That's great."

Awkward silence descends upon the table for a moment until Bryce breaks it.

"You guys 'Hawks fans?" Bryce asks.

Hunter shrugs, but my dad lights up. "Hell, yes," he responds vehemently. "I can't wait to watch us kick Dallas' ass tomorrow."

"I don't know, we're pretty evenly matched," Bryce replies. "Should be a good game."

"Evenly matched? Please!" my father scoffs.

And for the bulk of the rest of lunch, they proceed to break down each team's strengths and weaknesses and make predictions on tomorrow's game. I'm not a huge football fan, but frankly I'm just glad there's something to fill the conversation. And by the time we're done eating, whatever tension that existed between my father and Bryce is long gone.

I also realize I didn't really get much of a chance to talk to Hunter. So as we are leaving, and my father and Bryce are still chatting animatedly about all things football, I slip Hunter my business card.

"My cell number is on there," I explain quietly as we walk a bit behind the others. "I'd like to get to know you better, but I don't think we'll get to do that with these two around. Give me a call sometime, okay?"

Hunter turns the card thoughtfully in his hands before carefully slipping it into his pocket. "Sure thing," he responds. While his response is as taciturn as he has been all afternoon, he at least seems less bored and standoffish than he had at the beginning of lunch, so I take it as a win.

Once Bryce and I are alone in the car, I'm quietly processing the afternoon when he touches me lightly on the knee without taking his eyes off the road.

"You okay?" he asks gently, returning his hand to the steering wheel.

"Yeah, definitely," I assure him. "Though I think it's going to take me a while before I can get a good enough read on things to decide how I really feel about it all. What did you think?"

Bryce laughs. "It doesn't matter what I think," he replies with a grin.

"Oh, please," I respond. "Of course it does. You're the best judge of character I know. I take it you weren't impressed then?"

He looks over at me briefly, obviously flattered by the praise. "I don't want to say anything negative about your father. You've probably heard enough of that to last you a lifetime," he says carefully. "And in general, it seems like he honestly wants to make amends and get to know you."

"But?" I prompt.

Bryce presses his lips together and shakes his head.

"Spill it, Hoyt. Does this have anything to do with him being a process server? I saw that look on your face."

Bryce bursts out laughing. "Yes and no," he admits. "I don't have anything against process servers. But given your father's history, it just cracked me up. Because it totally fits."

I give him a bemused look. "And why is that?"

"Process servers deliver, or serve, legal documents and summons to people. Often people who don't want to be served. So they have to be, let's say, *creative* at times," Bryce explains. "So it's funny because your father has always been a sneaky bastard, but now he's actually getting paid to be one."

"That is strangely appropriate," I agree. "I notice you didn't mention having anything negative to say about Hunter. I thought you were concerned with some sort of anger issue he supposedly has."

Bryce glances askance at me. "So you *do* listen to me occasionally," he jokes.

I give him a sharp look.

"Okay, okay. I may have been wrong about Hunter. The kid seems harmless. In fact, I'm surprised he's not more of an ass given what a jerk his dad is to him. So whatever happened, I think there's some serious context missing."

"What happened?" I ask.

Bryce doesn't answer for a moment. "If I suggested that you wait until he tells you, would you be upset?" he asks tentatively. "Like I said, I think it needs context, and I don't want it to negatively affect your opinion of him if it's what I think it is. And it looks like he could use you in his court."

"When you put it that way, I guess I can wait," I

agree. "Do you get sick of being right all the time?" I want to be grumpy about it, but his answering laugh is all sunshine, and I find it hard not to smile.

"Baby, I wish I were," he replies. "But we're all wrong sometimes."

SEVEN

I don't have to wait long to satisfy my curiosity about Hunter's past. On Wednesday morning, in the middle of a rather unremarkable workweek, I get a call from an unknown number on my cellphone that turns out to be my half-brother.

"Hey, Sera, it's Hunter," he starts, sounding awkward and uncomfortable.

"Hunter!" I say, trying not to sound as surprised as I feel. "I'm glad you called. What's up?"

"I'm catching a ride with a friend into Seattle for a thing tonight," he replies. "I thought we could hang out. Or whatever."

"Ah, well, that sounds good and all, but I have to work until around six," I reply apologetically. "And I don't want to interfere with your plans for the evening."

"Oh, no, that's not until, like, way later," he replies. "Like ten or eleven tonight at least."

Ah, to be young again.

"Well in that case, we can grab some dinner. Or you can come over to my place," I offer. "I usually cook anyway. The more the merrier. You can even bring your friend if you want."

"My friend has other plans today. If you text me the address I can walk or take the bus there," he says.

"Where are you coming from?" I ask, curious.

"Uhhhh, I think we're staying at a place in Burien?" he hazards.

"That's not really walkable. In fact, it's even kind of far to take the bus," I inform him. "How about I have my driver come get you before they pick me up?"

"You have a *driver*?" he asks incredulously.

"Heh, yeah," I admit. "It's, um, kind of a thing. I can explain later. Just text me your address and I'll let you know when they'll be there to get you."

"Awesome, sounds good," Hunter says agreeably, sounding much more enthused. "See you later then."

"Yep, bye," I respond.

After hanging up, I sit at my desk wondering if inviting him over was the best idea. Because it'll give him a front-row seat to a number of things I'm not sure I want my dad to know. Like the fact that I have round-the-clock protection. Though, since Bryce is half of that equation, maybe it won't be so noticeable. But it'd be hard to miss that Bryce lives with me. I shake it off as, for the most part, I realize it doesn't much matter what my father knows. It won't change whatever I decide I want our relationship to be.

I call Tristan and Bryce to let them know the change in plans for the evening and text Hunter with the arrangements. And then I do what I do best and ignore my reservations by burying myself back in my work.

JUST AFTER SIX THAT EVENING, I'M EXITING THE building when I get a text from Tristan that they'll be about ten minutes late due to traffic. I sigh resignedly as I step out into the autumn chill. Since it's not raining at the moment, I have a seat on the wooden bench in front of the building.

The late September air is crisp and moist. With sunset less than an hour off, the light has begun to dim and glow around the bright green leaves of the cherry tree I'm sitting under. It's really quite beautiful.

A flash of movement in my peripheral vision catches my attention, and I swing my head around. A tall, dark man exits a dark blue sedan not thirty feet away. And he's staring at me. And approaching quickly. On gut instinct, I rise and bolt back into the building.

"Penny," I pant as I dash into reception.

Penny Westchester's blond curls bounce as her head snaps up, her brown eyes filled with concern at the obvious alarm in my voice. "Sera, everything okay?" she asks, rising from her desk and coming around to meet me.

I glance over my shoulder, but there's nobody there, inside the building or in front of its wide, glass façade. But I see the tail end of a dark blue sedan turning out of the entrance to the parking lot, and a shudder rolls through me.

"It is now," I reply tensely, giving her a forced smile. "I just got spooked waiting for my ride. But everything's okay."

Penny looks at me skeptically. I don't know her well, and she certainly doesn't know about my protective detail or the circumstances that necessitated it.

"Okay, well, if you're sure," she responds. "If you need anything, just let me know."

I nod gratefully. "Thanks," I reply. "I think I'll just wait for my ride in here."

Penny nods and returns to her seat, glancing up at me regularly, probably to make sure I'm not continuing to spiral into panic.

I sink into a black plastic chair in the waiting room where I can see the front curb and focus on breathing normally. Thankfully, it's not long before the black town car pulls up.

I give Penny a small wave and stride purposefully out to meet Tristan as he unfolds himself from the front seat. I'm out the door and jogging to get to him before he can open the back passenger door to admit me. I know Hunter is back there, and I don't want him to hear what I have to tell Tristan.

Tristan looks at me questioningly as I throw a hand up against the door, blocking his path.

"Hey, Sera, everything all right?" he asks, suddenly on alert.

I shake my head and blink back tears I hadn't realized were there. "Someone was here," I say tensely, in a low voice. "I came out to wait for you and they approached from a dark blue sedan, just there." I gesture to the spot the car had occupied.

Tristan's eyes widen at the closeness. "Why were you even out here by yourself in the first place?" he demands, clenching his fists in frustration.

"I'm sorry, Tristan, I wasn't thinking," I respond. "Things have been quiet. I just forgot for a minute. Please, don't say anything around Hunter, okay?"

"What did he look like?" Tristan asks, ignoring my plea.

I sigh heavily. "He was tall. Maybe six-three. Short, black hair. Dark eyes. Thin build. Menacing looking. Probably Italian," I admit.

Tristan looks at me somewhat skeptically. "So he just approached you? What makes you think he was actually after you?"

"Because when I bolted, he turned tail. I saw his car leaving the lot as soon as I was inside," I reply with thinly veiled anger. "And no, I didn't get a look at the plates. But he was here for me, Tristan. I know it."

I hadn't even stopped to consider I might have been paranoid. I *felt* that this guy was coming for me. But it's the first time I've gotten a look at one of my pursuers. Well, it's Alessandro they're after, really. I'm just a fucking pawn. It all makes me so angry. Apparently, even not being with him anymore hasn't changed anything, which he himself predicted. It's maddening.

Tristan considers the information grimly. "Get in," he finally replies in a clipped tone. "I'll talk to Mr. Hoyt when we get you home."

Which means Bryce is already back at the

condo. Fuck. I'm not sure how to keep this from turning into a shit show in front of Hunter. I shake my head, still angry, and allow Tristan to open the car door for me. As I slip in, I put on my best game face.

Hunter is sitting behind the driver's seat with a bemused look on his face. I give him my best "everything is great" smile.

"Hey, Hunter," I greet him.

"Hey, Sera," he replies. "I like your ride."

I laugh. "Thanks," I reply shortly. "How was your drive down from Bellingham?"

Hunter shrugs. "Fine."

I smirk. It's like talking to a surly teenager. "So what's this thing you're here for?" I ask him.

Hunters looks at me but flicks his eyes away quickly. "It's an artist thing," he replies vaguely.

"Oh, like a gallery opening?" I ask curiously.

His answering smile is amused. "Something like that. So like, what about you? What do you do again?"

I consider how to explain it simply to Hunter without making him think I think he's stupid. "I work for a company that builds stores, apartments, that sort of thing," I respond. "Upscale ones, usually. They bought my company since we have a lot of expertise in putting together those sorts of deals." It's the barest bones explanation I can think of to avoid confusion or overexplaining.

"Do you have people that design the aesthetics of the spaces?" he asks. "You know, to make them feel upscale?"

I smile at the shrewd question. "We do," I reply. "Several, in fact, and we work with a lot of companies on interior and exterior visual design and materials. It's not something I'm particularly involved in the details of, but the finishes on the spaces we build are very important to the perception of our brand."

Hunter nods knowingly.

"Is that the sort of thing you're interested in doing?"

"Not really," Hunter replies. "I'm more into freestyle art."

"What does that mean?" I ask.

Hunter smiles cryptically as the car pulls to a stop in front of my building, effectively halting the conversation.

Hunter is quiet on the way up because, well, he's just kind of a quiet guy, it seems. Tristan is quiet too, but I can feel the tension rolling off him in waves. And I'm quiet because I'm dreading how this will unfold when we get inside.

We enter the condo to the amazing smell of barbeque and Bryce in the kitchen, clearly slaving on whatever masterpiece of meat and sauce he's created. He comes to meet us in the entryway, wiping his hands on a towel. He's already changed into jeans and a white T-shirt. He looks so handsome, and so happy, that it's all I can do to keep myself from collapsing tiredly into him.

"Hey, baby," he greets me with a perfunctory kiss. "Hunter, nice to see you."

"Hey, man," Hunter responds, looking around the condo in awe.

Tristan gives me a pointed look. "Sera, why don't you show Hunter around while Mr. Hoyt and I touch base?" he suggests.

I nod and lead Hunter to the window wall.

Hunter glances back over his shoulder. "Is Bryce that dude's boss?" he asks observantly.

"Yes," I reply. "Bryce's company does private security."

"Ahhh, so that's why you have a driver and a bodyguard and stuff," he replies, following me through the living room.

I cock my head, intrigued by the opportunity. That's as good an explanation as any. At least, besides the actual explanation. But I don't like lying, so I just let the assumption hang in the air.

"Make yourself at home," I encourage Hunter, gesturing to the couches. But I brought him to this side of the living room because it's impossible not to be drawn to the panorama behind us. And I'm not disappointed.

"Shit," Hunter swears, looking out over downtown and Elliot Bay. "People actually live in places like this?" He shakes his head, dumbstruck by the view.

While he's distracted, I glance back nervously at Tristan and Bryce, who are still standing in the entryway. Bryce is now glowering, staring at a spot on the floor while Tristan speaks lowly. He's rolling his massive shoulders anxiously, the muscles of his back clearly tensed. And as if he senses me staring, Bryce's clear blue eyes snap up to meet mine. And his gaze is so filled with love and concern that I have to look away before I cry.

"I actually didn't live like this until recently," I admit to Hunter. "But I couldn't help myself. I just fell in love with it."

"I can see why," Hunter murmurs, continuing to stare silently out the window.

I hear the front door open and close. "Hey, I need to go talk to Bryce for a minute," I tell Hunter. "Be right back."

Hunter nods mutely and I slink away.

Bryce is still standing in the same spot, waiting

for me. "You okay?" he asks, gently gathering my hands in his and kissing them lightly.

"I was a little shaken at first, but I'm okay," I admit. "We knew this could still be an issue."

Bryce nods grimly in agreement. "I was starting to hope it was passed, but it is what it is," he replies somberly. "What do you need?"

I close my eyes, letting my emotions wash through me for just a moment, searching for the answer to his question. With startling clarity it hits me. I open my eyes, staring boldly up into his. I lean in so only he will hear me when I answer.

"I need you to fuck me up against the windows tonight," I reply huskily glancing over at the window wall. "Until I can't think of anything but riding you until you're screaming my name."

And what I've learned about my man is that his stillness in moments like these is a sign of his deep well of self-control. Because I can see in the slight flare of his nostrils and his dilated pupils that he likes it. No. He fucking *loves* it.

He takes a step forward so he's calmly towering over me. "I think that can be arranged," he promises with a glint in his eye. "Oh, and don't think I didn't notice that you hung that frilly little apron in the kitchen. It gave me a hard-on just looking at it." His words send a jolt through me, and I bite my lip to suppress the lustful grin threatening to break across my face. His eyes keep hold of mine for another heartbeat before he steps away, breaking the spell. "Hey, Hunter, you hungry?" Bryce's head snaps up to look over at my half-brother, still standing by the windows, and the vibe in the room mellows into casual relaxation.

I shiver lightly at the power of Bryce's emotional control over not just himself but everyone around him. And finally I feel safe again.

I saunter into the kitchen to get what I need to set the table and am joined shortly by Bryce to finish the usual trappings of dinner. It's not long before we're all seated and diving into Bryce's self-proclaimed "best barbeque ever."

"You know, I thought you were full of shit," I mumble through a mouthful of the ridiculously delicious meat. "But this is amazing."

Bryce smiles happily and leans over, using his napkin to wipe sauce off my chin.

Hunter laughs, and we both turn to him, a little surprised. "What?" he asks, shrugging. "It is good."

I shoot Bryce a furtive look but say nothing. We continue to make small talk, and Hunter progressively comes out of his shell. Finally, Bryce asks the same question I did earlier.

"So what exactly is it that you came here for?"

Hunter considers Bryce for a moment. "A bunch of artists are getting together to make an … installation of sorts," he admits.

Bryce raises an eyebrow. "Is this the kind of 'installation' that's created at night because it's done publicly, and," Bryce clears his throat, "not exactly legally?"

The look of shock on Hunter's face is priceless, and Bryce's instincts pay off once again.

"How could you possibly know that?" Hunter asks in disbelief.

Bryce smiles and I know what's coming. He points his thumbs at himself. "Security consultant."

And I can't help but bust up laughing. Hunter gives an embarrassed smile.

"But seriously, Hunter. I think you know how I know. Do you want to tell her or should I?"

My brother rolls his eyes and squirms uncomfortably in his chair. "I was arrested twice last year," Hunter admits. "The first time for vandalism and resisting arrest." He pauses, frowning. "The second, for assault."

"Do I want to know why?" I ask, looking between the two men.

Bryce shrugs and leans back in his chair, with a distinct air of staying the hell out of it now that he's opened the flood gates.

Hunter heaves a sigh. "I'm a guerrilla artist," he explains. "I was part of a team, actually. We did location-specific perception-altering pieces."

"English, please?" I ask, looking helplessly at Bryce.

"They go outside and make everyday things you see on the street look like something else," Bryce explains. "Sometimes intended to cause public harm."

"No," Hunter protests. "We didn't pull that kind of shit."

"So you didn't paint a wall to look like an alley? And then lure a cop car toward it at night so he rammed it at thirty miles per hour?" Bryce asks sharply.

Hunter pales at the depth of Bryce's knowledge.

"In case you hadn't noticed, you shouldn't attempt to lie to this man," I inform Hunter.

Hunter's eyes shift from Bryce to me. "My crew didn't do that," he insists.

"I'm listening," Bryce says patiently.

"I don't owe you any explanations," Hunter says tightly.

Bryce smiles indulgently. "No, I suppose you don't," he agrees. "But where you end up tonight may depend on it. See, I'm close, personal friends with at least a third of the police force in this city. One phone call and you and your friends may have a much more difficult night than you planned."

"*Bryce*," I gasp, surprised. I'm still reeling as Hunter's world is a whole new beast to me. But I don't want to scare away the only sibling I have and make him feel like he was lured to my house only to be threatened.

Bryce sighs and picks up our dinner dishes, ferrying them into the kitchen. "Look," he says on his way back. "I don't want to get you and your friends in trouble. I'm pretty sure you're not lying. But I want to know what really happened, so I know for sure I'm not turning a blind eye to dangerous criminals."

"That's a little harsh, don't you think?" Hunter asks accusingly. "That was just a prank. That my crew *didn't pull*."

Bryce's eyebrows shoot up. "If you think vandalism, destruction of public property, and endangering the well-being of a police officer are *funny*, then you've got a lot to learn," Bryce says dangerously quietly.

Hunter, at least, seems to get finally that he's walking a precarious line as it's a while before he responds.

"We did shock-value pieces," he finally admits. "We would draw people hanging out of high windows that looked realistic from the ground. We'd put down fake blood trails leading to cemented-in pieces made to look like bodies. That sort of thing. We didn't hurt anyone or destroy property." He glares at Bryce.

"Then who did you assault?" I ask softly. I want to ask *why*. Why do they do what they do at all? It certainly doesn't make any sense to me. But odd, random art in public places isn't the end of the world. Assaulting someone, however, is a whole other matter.

Hunter leans forward on his arms, twisting his fingers together. "My crew wasn't the only one in our neighborhood," he replies quietly. "The other crew, they were the ones that would go for destruction and chaos. We ran into them one night. Words were exchanged. One of their guys called me … well, he said something pretty bad, then pushed me from behind. I turned around and lashed out. But I had a crowbar in my hand. I practically took off half his face." Hunter shakes his head sadly. "In case it doesn't go without saying, I didn't mean to hurt him like that. It was a horrible mistake."

I'm so mesmerized by Hunter's story that I don't realize until he stops speaking that my hand is clamped over my mouth in horror. He nearly took off a guy's *face*. Bryce's expression is ominously blank.

"Wait a minute," I pipe up. "You said that all past tense."

Hunter smiles vaguely. "That's right. Both crews disbanded after that night," he replies.

"Then who are you meeting tonight?" I ask.

"It's a gathering," he explains. "Of all of us in western Washington, to do one, huge piece together. Peacefully, and not to cause harm." He glances reassuringly at Bryce. "But I haven't done anything public since that last time we were out. And I probably won't again after tonight. I just feel like I need the closure. And this is huge. I guess I wanted to be a part of it all one last time." His expression is so forlorn I want to hug him. But I'm still so appalled by everything I've heard.

"Does dad know?" I ask, my voice barely above a whisper.

"No," Hunter responds sadly. "Not really. He thinks I'm in a gang, or a drug dealer, or a drug user, or all of the above. He thinks I'm just a violent, vandalizing thug. A lost cause. Worthless."

And this time I can't help it. I rise from my chair and go to him, leaning down and wrapping my arms around him from the side. I don't say anything, I just squeeze him with everything I've got. After a moment he lays his hand over mine, squeezing it gratefully.

"So you gonna call your cop friends on us?" Hunter asks Bryce warily.

Bryce shakes his head. "No," he replies. "I think

you've had enough trouble with the law to last you a lifetime. Just be smart tonight and stay safe. And call us if you need anything."

The relief on Hunter's face is obvious. "Thanks, guys," he replies.

I finally let Hunter go and sink back down into my chair. "Thanks for being honest," I respond. "Brother."

Hunter's eyes lock with mine, and my heart shifts. And I see in his eyes that he feels it too. And that neither of us are used to having a real family. But looking between Hunter and Bryce, I'm thankful to be making my own.

EIGHT

Once Hunter is gone I sink into Bryce's lap on the couch. I rest my forehead against his as he traces light circles on my thigh with his thumb.

"Heavy night," Bryce murmurs, his eyes probing mine. For what I'm not sure. Signs of cracking, probably.

"Yes, but it wasn't all bad," I reply thoughtfully. "I think my brother and I have a real shot at getting to know each other. To be there for each other like our parents haven't been for us."

"You called him your brother," Bryce points out.

"So?" I ask, frowning. "That's what he is."

Bryce's strong fingers run over the length of my

leg. "You've only ever called him your half-brother before," Bryce responds.

"I guess I'm feeling like I'm surrounded by family now," I explain. "Real family. The family I'm choosing."

Bryce looks at me, his eyes sheening in the moon-light now trickling through the windows. He wraps his arms around me, laying me on my back on the soft cushions. His arms braced by my sides, he hovers over me, hungrily drinking in my face with his eyes as if he wants to memorize every pore.

I gaze up at him, slightly confused, but tingling with anticipation. "I thought you wanted me up against the windows," I tease him.

His mouth swoops down to mine, his lips like wind on the fire building in me. He pulls back before I'm ready to let him go and I whimper in protest. He smiles down at me indulgently.

"Some other time," he promises. "Tonight, I'm going to make love to you right here."

My breath catches in my throat at his husky tone, his tender words.

He undresses me slowly, his tongue and lips tenderly caressing me as he goes. When I'm naked and trembling beneath him, he sheds his own clothes much more quickly, and I note he's already full and long. And if I was ready before, the sight sends a rush between my legs that has me aching and approaching the edge already.

His mouth reaches for mine and his torso sinks into mine. I wrap my arms around him, desperate to pull him onto me completely, into me. As his tongue dances with mine, he finally allows it, sinking into me slowly. We both moan into the pleasure before our hips dance, same as our tongues, slowly stoking the fire.

I run my hands down the strong muscles of his back, feeling him flex into me with every thrust. His lips drop to my neck, and I'm free to unleash my moans into his ear. I feel him harden sharply in me, his breath quickening. I dig my heels into his sides, encouraging him. But the sharp press has an altogether different effect, and he slides his hands under me, rolling over abruptly so I'm pressed on top of him.

He holds me to him, his mouth at my ear. "I love you, Sera." He drops his head back, so he can look into my eyes. "Never forget how fucking much I love you."

I lean into him, pressing my lips to his briefly, sweeping my tongue over his bottom lip as I rear up. "I love you too," I breathe, sinking him back into me.

With hands clasped, I tilt my hips over him, softly

at first, then harder and harder, building methodically until we're both approaching climax.

"Come for me, baby," I encourage him.

My words are like throwing gas on the fire. His face and body contort with pleasure, and he bucks wildly beneath me as he explodes in fiery passionate bliss. I feel his seed, hot inside me, and the combination of hot, wet, and writhing sends me tumbling into ecstasy. My screams of pleasure outlast his, the fire in me finally quelled. And when I look down at him, he's half laughing, half dizzy with gratification.

I sink onto the sofa next to him, nearly swooning from the effort of bringing us both to climax. My hand finds his and our fingers intertwine.

"Let's buy a house," Bryce's voice abruptly cuts through my post-orgasmic stupor.

I shoot upright, aghast. "Excuse me?"

Bryce sits up next to me, leaning back against the cushions. "You heard me," he replies. "I love living with you. But this is *your* place. We should have an 'our' place."

"Bryce, we haven't even been dating a month and you want us to make one of the biggest commitments people can make?" I ask incredulously.

"I'm not proposing," he clarifies.

I laugh. "I don't mean to be blasé, but real estate

is a much bigger commitment than marriage. Especially these days," I remark.

"I hadn't thought about it like that," he admits.

"I don't think you thought about it much at all," I reply. "If it's all the same, I think we should chalk that suggestion up to after-sex stupid."

Bryce arches an eyebrow at me. "Call it what you want, but there are other reasons it's a good idea," he replies stubbornly.

And I get the sense that I've offended him. "Such as?" I prompt.

"Well, we've determined you're not out of the woods yet. Moving would be a good opportunity to make you safer," he responds. And I have to admit to myself that he's not wrong. But it's a shit reason for us to buy a place together.

"We've already demonstrated the security here is good," I remind him. "So I don't think they'll try anything here again."

Even Bryce can't argue with that. But he still pouts nonetheless.

"Baby," I plead. "I don't want us to take such a big step just because something like this is hanging over our heads. Again. And it's not something I'd want to do until we're married."

Bryce cracks a smile. "You said 'until,'" he replies, slightly mollified.

I crawl between his legs, pulling his arms around me. "I did," I agree, looking up into his eyes. "I can't believe I'm the old-fashioned one here."

Bryce laughs, his sour mood gone. "I just can't bear the thought of wasting one minute of our new life together," he replies huskily. "But you're right. We're going to do this the right way. You deserve that."

"*We* deserve that," I correct him with a smile.

He nuzzles his nose against mine in agreement, and I sink happily back into his embrace.

∽

ALMOST A FULL WEEK FLIES BY WHEN, THE following Tuesday, I hear from Allie, who is back from her vacation. She wants to meet for brunch as soon as possible, so we schedule for the coming Saturday. She sounded so relaxed and excited that getting to today was torture.

But as I go to meet her for brunch, I work on containing my own nerves, my imagination having gotten somewhat away from me over the last few days. For some reason I've settled on expecting to hear that they are moving to the tropical paradise. That it's best for Allie's stress levels and David will just work remotely. I know it's a silly and irrational fear, but I can't imagine what else would have her so excited to come *back* from vacation.

For once I'm thankful Bryce had to go into work today, so I couldn't nag him all morning with my fears. Because somehow it's easier to be a neurotic mess in front of Tristan. Not that Bryce doesn't handle it well, but I hate troubling him with it. Tristan … well, it's kind of his job. And he'll get to go home at the end of the day.

I get a booth for Allie and me even though she hasn't arrived yet because it's starting to get busy. Tristan requests a separate, small table within sight distance, insisting his presence will just keep us from talking about "girlie things." I don't give up, but he continues to insist. He hasn't relented by the time Allie arrives, so I just leave him to his lonesome meal.

And Allie looks ridiculously fantastic. She's lean, tan, and beaming with happiness. After giving me a greeting hug, she slides into the booth with a satisfied sigh.

"So I'm guessing Fiji was everything you'd hoped for," I tease her.

"Oh, Sera, you have no idea," she replies dreamily. "I could have happily stayed there for the rest of my life."

I freeze for a moment.

"What? What did I say?"

"Nothing," I reply, dismissively waving my hand. "You just sounded like you had news and …" I trail off, unable to admit to my fear.

"And?" she prompts inquisitively.

"I got it in my head you wanted to move to Fiji," I admit, blushing furiously.

Allie laughs. "Oops, sounds like I stepped right in it then, didn't I?" she asks, beaming. "I'm not moving to Fiji, Sera."

And I shouldn't feel as relieved as I do, since I knew it was silly to start. But I do. "Thank God," I breathe.

"But David and I did agree to start trying again. For a baby," she responds candidly.

"Allie! That's fantastic!" I exclaim. "I'm so happy for you."

"Thanks," Allie replies sheepishly. "Also, I'm not going back to work. I'm quitting permanently."

That stops me short. I'm torn between supporting her and missing her. "Oh, Allie, you know I love you, babe," I reply sincerely. "And if that's what's going to work best for you, then that's great."

"I appreciate that," Allie responds just as sincerely. "I realized that I started working for you not knowing where it would lead, and in the end, it just isn't what I want for a career. Though I'll be honest — I'm not sure what I *do* want."

"That's totally fair," I concede. "And I'm sure you'll figure it out. Now. Tell me all about Fiji."

"Sun, beaches, sparkling clear blue water, blah, blah, blah," she jokes. "I'd really rather hear about what's new with you. How are things with Bryce?" A shit-eating grin splits across her face.

I glance furtively at Tristan across the restaurant, but I'm confident he can't hear me. Not that it really matters.

"Amazing," I reply with a sigh. "It feels like we've always been together."

"Do you think you always will be?" she asks shrewdly.

"It seems like it should be too early to talk about that kind of thing," I respond tentatively. "And yet we have. Several times."

"How so?" she presses.

I shrug. "When it happens, it's always a given. When. Not if. And it feels so natural, honestly," I admit. "I feel like I should be scared. Or I should have reservations about moving too fast. But Bryce and I have always connected on another level. And it's like now that's complete, and nothing can stop it or take its place."

"Wow," Allie says slowly. "That's intense. Great, but intense."

I nod. "I agree completely. But, I'm also happier than I can ever remember being. He feels like my family, same as you." Talking about it this way I feel laid bare and vulnerable. And it's finally making me a little uncomfortable.

Sensing that, perhaps, Allie changes the subject. "Hey, I meant to ask you what you want to do for your birthday," she says with a mischievous glint in her eye.

I groan loudly. As usual, I'd forgotten that was coming. But she's right. Next Friday I'll turn thirty. "Nothing," I grouse. "We don't even need to tell anyone it's my birthday."

"Awww, don't spoil my fun," Allie insists. "At least let me take you out to dinner or something? You're turning thirty. Before me, thank God. We need to celebrate. Say goodbye to your twenties. Preferably with booze. And cake."

I can't help but laugh. "I'm down with the booze and cake," I admit. "Or maybe a booze cake. But nothing too crazy."

Allie claps her hands giddily. "Yay!" she squeals, bouncing in her seat.

"Already too crazy!" I warn her jokingly.

She quiets and bounces lower, clapping softly.

And it makes me laugh again. "You're nuts. I missed you."

She smiles brightly. "Missed you too, babe," she responds.

∾

A FULL MEAL AND MORE THAN AN HOUR AND A HALF later Allie has gone home, and Tristan is walking me out of the restaurant.

"You look happy," he remarks as we round the corner to the small parking lot sandwiched between the restaurant and the building behind it.

"I am," I admit. "It's great seeing Allie, well, Allie again. She …" I'm stopped short as we approach the car.

A man leans against the trunk casually, picking at his fingernails. He's medium height and build, with dark hair and olive skin. Tristan follows my gaze and, before I can so much as blink, he's shuffled me behind him and drawn his gun.

"When I tell you to, run back to the restaurant and call Bryce," Tristan instructs in hushed tones.

The man leaning against the trunk of the car catches sight of us and stands.

Tristan raises his gun and addresses the man. "I'd advise you to leave. Now."

"Nobody is going anywhere."

My skin crawls. The voice comes from behind me. I turn, my back against Tristan's, to find a second man, with his own gun drawn and pointed at me. It's the man who tried to approach me last time just outside of my work, once again staring me down menacingly. Tristan keeps his gun trained on the first man and glances back at the second.

"Drop your gun now or I will shoot," Tristan instructs.

My heart is beating so loudly in my ears that I barely hear him.

The second man laughs. "Not unless you want her dead," he scoffs.

But even I hear the bluff. Though even if he was the best liar in the world, I know they'll want me alive if they plan to use me against Alessandro. Not that I intend to be taken. But Tristan is already ahead of me. He doesn't say another word or give any further warnings. His foot finds mine and I know what to do. When he steps down on my toes, I drop to the ground. Tristan swings around, lightning fast, and shoots the second man between the eyes. And just as quickly points his gun back at the first man.

"Run," Tristan commands me without looking back.

So I do. And I don't look at the crumpled body as

I jump over it. But I do notice the blur as the first man bolts and Tristan follows. Not that that stops me — I do exactly as Tristan instructed and run back into the restaurant.

The hostess looks shocked as I burst through the door, clearly terrified.

"Call 911," I insist, searching my purse frantically for my phone. "Someone has been shot in the parking lot, and my bodyguard is in danger."

The hostess pales and nods, picking up the phone on the podium and placing the call. Finally locating my phone, I frantically call Bryce.

∾

As I sit in the back of the squad car, Bryce paces the bit of pavement next to me for the thousandth time.

"He's okay," I assure him. "I know it. You didn't see how fast he moved. There's no way that guy got the drop on him."

Bryce waves a hand in the air, frustrated. "I know he's fast. But he shouldn't have pursued. He should have stayed with you."

Ah. So Bryce isn't worried for Tristan's safety. He wants to yell at him for leaving me.

"But I'm fine," I insist. "Thanks to him."

Bryce stops abruptly and squats in front of me. "You're not fine," he seethes. "These motherfuckers are coming after you head-on. No more subterfuge, no more stealth. They approached you directly, in daylight, with guns. They must be pretty fucking desperate to be this bold, this careless. It's *dangerous*, Sera."

A police officer appears at the back of the squad car and Bryce stands up, facing him. "They've found Mr. Thomas," he informs Bryce. "He lost the suspect and is on his way back now. And the body has been removed. Scene is clear. We'll meet you down at the station."

Bryce nods to the officer and extends a hand to me. He silently leads me to his car, putting me in the passenger seat and leaning against the door in wait. It's not long before Tristan appears.

"Get in the back, we're going to the police station to give a full statement," Bryce instructs Tristan sharply, without so much as asking if he's okay.

Tristan does as instructed and, before Bryce can get in, I turn to Tristan and mouth, "Are you okay?"

He nods briefly, his eyes on Bryce as he opens the driver's side door.

I mouth "thank you" as discreetly as I can before facing forward again.

～

We spend far longer than I'd like at the police station. I get the feeling it's because Bryce feels like it might be one of the only places in the city that I'm truly safe. My suspicion is confirmed when we're given a police escort home.

As we quietly enter the condo, I can't find words that I think will make any difference. I know Bryce is furious, and not really with Tristan, but with his inability to fix this. To end the danger I'm in. We're in. And there's nothing I can say or do that will help.

I go upstairs to take a shower. As I strip off my clothes, it feels like the armor I've had to sheath myself in to keep it together falls away with them. Exhausted, emotional, and naked, I sit on the floor of the shower and let the water flow over me. But it doesn't soothe me, and soon hot tears join the stream as my body shakes with sobs. I feel, rather than hear Bryce approach, but I don't look up.

I do, finally, hear a broken cry escape him as he realizes I've come apart. He climbs in with me, fully clothed, and wraps his arms around me. His body shakes with mine, despairing with me. I unwrap my arms from where they held my legs against my chest and slide them around his soaked shirt. And we hold each other like that until the water starts to run lukewarm.

We don't speak even as we dry off and, both naked and exhausted, climb into bed and know no more.

NINE

Sunday morning arrives, and for early October there's far too much light in the room for my liking. But then, my eyes are puffier and more sensitive than usual. And the reasons why come flooding back. I breathe deeply, fighting down the tide of emotion. I roll over, not really expecting to find Bryce still abed this long after dawn, but he's there nonetheless, awake and contemplating the ceiling, one arm tucked under his head.

He turns his head to meet my gaze and gives me a small smile that doesn't reach his eyes.

"Good morning, sunshine," I greet him, attempting my own half-hearted smile.

He rolls toward me, stroking along my arm with

his free hand. He leans in, touching his lips softly to mine.

"Hey, gorgeous," he replies. "How'd you sleep?"

My instinct is to assume I didn't sleep well after yesterday's events. But I realize that I actually did. I slept hard, and for a long time. And had not a single nightmare. I'm struck dumb, as nightmares were such a constant companion for so long as I went through these last months. But they've stopped. And it occurs to me that that's been true since I've shared a bed with Bryce.

"Surprisingly well," I admit. "How about you?"

He strokes my face gently and smiles sadly. "I always sleep well next to you," he replies. "Oh." He looks as though he remembered something, and he rolls to reach the nightstand on his side of the bed. He pulls something out of the drawer and turns back to me, something tucked inside his large hand.

"What's that?" I ask warily.

Bryce smiles, much more openly this time. "It's a gift. For you," he replies. "I'm not usually one to remember this kind of thing, but this is different. We're different. Because one month ago today, you changed my life forever." He lays his palm flat to reveal a small, black velvet box.

And the girlie girl inside me wants to squeal with excitement. But I settle for an eager grin. "Oh, baby, you didn't have to do this," I chastise him. I didn't even realize the date, or think to commemorate such a thing, but I know he wouldn't want me to feel self-conscious.

"I know," he allows. "But because you're not the type to expect it, it's all the more reason to give it to you. I'd give you the world if I could, Sera."

I snuggle up next to him and press my lips softly to his. "You're my world, Bryce Hoyt."

He kisses me passionately for a moment before pulling away gently. "I'll just take these back then, I guess," he replies airily, leaning back to put the box back on his nightstand.

I playfully smack his chest. "You'll do no such thing!" I admonish him. "Gimme."

He laughs and hands me the box. I open it gingerly, part of me wanting the anticipation to last, like I'm a little girl at Christmas again. But the reveal is just as satisfying. Even in the dim daylight, light bounces off the dazzling square gem earrings. They are delicately beautiful in their simplicity, and absolutely breathtaking.

"Diamonds?" I ask in shock.

"Diamonds," he confirms. "Though they're still not half as gorgeous as you are."

I don't even have words to express to him how thoughtful he is, how sweet, how wonderful. So I put the box on the nightstand behind me and show him instead.

AFTER BREAKFAST, I'M SITTING IN MY FAVORITE chair, wrapped in a blanket and sipping coffee. Bryce sits at my feet, leaning against the chair and reading a book. It's such peace after the chaos of the day before. But I still turn the day over and over in my mind, looking for clues. I also spend a considerable effort trying to think of ways to end it. But I come up wanting.

"What if we went somewhere?" I ask abruptly, breaking the quiet. Bryce slips a bookmark into his book and closes it onto his lap, turning to look up at me.

"Where?" he counters.

"I don't know," I admit. "Just away. For a while. So they can't find me. Until enough time has passed, and they just stop trying."

Bryce sighs heavily. "I'm all one for a good vacation, but I can't just leave for long periods of time, Sera," he replies. "I have a company to run. And you have a job here. We have lives here."

"You're right. I just don't know what else to do. But after yesterday, the thought of just going on with my life as usual seems impossible. I feel like I'd only just stopped looking over my shoulder," I explain, tears welling in my eyes. I wipe at them angrily.

Bryce climbs to his knees, taking my face in his strong hands. "I'm going to do everything in my power to keep you safe," he says, looking me squarely in the eye. "Know that." He pauses, looking somewhat hesitant to say what he's thinking. "I've started my own investigation. I am going to get to the bottom of this, no matter what it takes. But it's going to take time. And it will be dangerous. And while I don't want us to be apart, if you'll feel safer away from here, I can make arrangements."

My mind swims with questions, but moreover the suggestion that I leave him is unbearable, and I feel the need to shut that down first and foremost.

"I don't want to leave you, either," I respond.

A look that's half pained and half adoration crosses Bryce's face. "I figured you'd say that," he replies. "And part of me wants to get you away from all this. But the thought of you being somewhere I can't be, where I can't protect you …"

I press a finger over his lips and shake my head. "Stop worrying," I say. I remove my finger from his mouth and pull his face to mine. When I kiss him it's full of sorrow and angst, but most of all love. Always love.

༄

THE NEXT MORNING I HAVE TWO GUARDS accompanying me into work. And they don't leave for the day like Tristan normally would. The new guard takes a desk near my office while Tristan takes a desk near reception. It's all been cleared through Charles, but I'd asked that nobody else be told the details. Needless to say that doesn't stop the office gossip. Especially as the new guard, Marcus, follows me around silently all day, never more than ten feet away.

When I talk to Bryce at lunch he has news. Daniel's trial has been rescheduled for two weeks from today. I frown, wondering if Charles has already heard. If he had, he showed no sign of it this morning, though I may have been too distracted by my own problems to notice. I decide to check in on him again just in case.

Charles' assistant, Anabelle, waves me past, looking furtively at Marcus as we pass. I knock and wait for Charles' invitation to enter, asking Marcus to wait outside.

Instantly, I know Charles has heard that Daniel's trial is, indeed, back on. In the privacy of his own office, his face is drawn, his shoulders slumped. He rises as I enter, and I can't help but going to hug him.

"Thank you," he says huskily. He gestures to the

chair opposite his desk, which I take.

"It looks like we're both having a pretty shitty time," I reply honestly.

Charles chuckles drily. I'd given him a high level overview of my situation, but there wasn't time to discuss it in any depth. And despite my own feelings, I am curious to hear what my mentor thinks of it all.

"I've been through much worse, my dear," he responds. "But you can't seem to catch a break. How are you holding up?"

"Honestly? I'm terrified. And so over it," I grouse. "I wish to hell I'd never got involved with the bastard who brought this on me." But despite my rancor, I don't really mean it. Part of me still loves Alessandro, even. I'm just so angry.

"I'd love to reassure you that everything happens for a reason," Charles parries wearily. "But honestly, bad things happen all the time to good people who've done nothing to deserve them. Only you can choose how you handle it. Whether to press through and overcome it or succumb to self-pity."

I blush furiously. He's right, I'm wallowing.

"Well, when you put it that way." I sigh. "You know me. I'll get through this. Some days are just harder than others."

"Indeed," Charles agrees.

"What would you do, if you were in my shoes?" I

ask curiously. His eyebrows shoot up.

"I'd be hard pressed to truly understand what you're going through, Sera," he hedges. "But the most important thing is safety. If it were me, I'd do whatever I had to, whatever I could to make myself, my loved ones, safe."

~

FOR THE REST OF THE DAY, CHARLES' WORDS SEEP into my consciousness. And by the evening, the beginnings of a plan have formed in my head. Realizing how selfish it is to keep everyone else in harm's way, I know I must remove myself. Go somewhere nobody knows where I am. Who I am.

I could never forgive myself if something had happened to Tristan, even though it's a known risk of his job. Or, God forbid, Bryce. I can't even think about that possibility. And with the new investigation he's launched, the odds are so much higher that something will happen to him. That thought pushes me over the edge, and I know I must disappear.

And while I have the means to do so, I don't have the connections. And it's obviously not something I can ask Bryce to help with. I'm sure he'd have the kinds of contacts that could create a new identity under which I could travel, but I'm also sure he'd never let me go alone. And I don't want anyone to catch wind of my plan, to try to stop me.

Thankfully I have enough knowledge on how to be untraceable online to find the answers I need. So that night I go looking for someone who *can* get me what I need. It doesn't take long to find. It takes longer to arrange untraceable payment, actually, and to arrange a way to receive the documents and other items I'll need without tipping off my bodyguards or Bryce.

But by Friday I've managed it, though not without laying out considerable sums of money in the process. As it's also my birthday, I've gone home early under the guise of getting ready for my birthday dinner with Allie, which Bryce will, of course, also be accompanying me to. But my real plan is to finish my preparations. Because once Bryce is asleep, I'm leaving.

I stow my small packed bag behind some boxes in the coat closet downstairs. I don't take much. I can always buy what I need once I reach my destination, and the less I pack the easier it will be to leave unnoticed, to travel unnoticed.

I take the letter I've written Bryce explaining everything and bring it into the bedroom. I settle on placing it in his nightstand drawer, as he rarely uses it. In fact, the only time I've seen him use it was when he pulled my "anniversary" gift out of it.

I slide it open. Only one object sits in the drawer — another small, black velvet box. It only takes me a moment to realize it's probably my birthday present, and that I'll need to find another place to hide my letter. I start to close the drawer, but curiosity gets the better of me. I set the letter aside and slowly pick up the box.

I hesitate, not usually the type to snoop, feeling guilty for potentially spoiling Bryce's surprise. But my inquisitive nature gets the better of me, and I open it anyway.

A diamond engagement ring sparkles back at me. Princess cut, just like the earrings, but much larger, and perfectly beautiful in its simple, platinum setting. My vision clouds as tears fill my eyes. And my resolve is hardened knowing I can't possibly put someone who loves me this much in danger. I close the box and return it to its exact place in the drawer. I decide I'll put the letter on the kitchen counter as I leave.

I dress carefully for dinner, donning the gorgeous earrings Bryce gifted me. Then silently, I master myself and descend the stairs. I shove all of the emotions the sight of that ring brought up deep back down. I can feel it all later. Bryce will be home soon. And I need to play the delighted birthday girl. The happy girlfriend. If only for just a little while longer.

TEN

We get to the building where the restaurant is, but we have to take an elevator to the twenty-first floor. Exiting to the top floor restaurant, we wait just outside the entrance for Allie and David. I can tell it makes Bryce nervous to be out in public with dangerous people still out there looking for me.

Having gotten home late, he didn't have time to change, so he's still wearing the khaki slacks and black button-down he wore to work. He catches me looking at him and pulls me close. His normal smell of evergreen and summer, mixed with his natural musk from the day, fills my senses and makes me a bit heady. He brushes my hair back from my face and looks searchingly into my eyes.

"You're wearing the earrings," he murmurs approvingly. "They look fantastic on you."

I finger the sparkling gems lovingly. "They remind me of you," I reply fondly.

He smiles, not quite his sunshine smile. He's still worried. "Then you should wear them all the time," he responds. He leans in close, nuzzling his nose against my ear and dropping his voice. "And I'd like to see you wearing nothing but those earrings later." His hot breath on my ear and neck, along with his words, sends shivers down my spine.

I relish it, trying not to think about it being one of the last times for what may be a long time.

I'm saved from the bittersweet moment by Allie and David's arrival. Hugs or handshakes are had all around, along with loud birthday wishes. Blushing, I duck into the restaurant, eager to get to the part where there's cake and booze.

Allie teases me the whole way to the table, making sure to loudly remark that we are here for my birthday. She knows how much it embarrasses me, but that's clearly part of the fun for her. Thankfully, once we're seated and looking at our menus, it dies down.

"You okay?" Bryce leans in to ask.

"I'm fine," I whisper. "It's only going to get worse once she's gotten some drinks in her, though."

Bryce laughs. "Then we should get a few drinks in you, so you care less," he teases.

And now I laugh.

"What are you two lovebirds tittering about?" Allie demands from across the table.

Bryce and I snap back upright, grinning. "Oh, you know, where would be the best place in the restaurant for a quickie," I joke.

David laughs, but Allie pulls an unamused face.

"At least David thinks I'm funny."

Allie sticks her tongue out at me and I return the gesture. The men roll their eyes at each other conspiratorially.

As we make small talk about our workweeks, I realize I never told Allie what happened after she left the restaurant last Saturday. And I don't think now is really the time. But she's going to be more surprised than most when I leave. And mad, of course. Not for the first or last time tonight, I suppress my thoughts and try to focus on the conversation.

And the food, which is amazing. As total carnivores, Allie and I had agreed a steakhouse was our only option. And as I dive into my ridiculously melt-in-your-mouth filet mignon, I know we made the right choice. Everyone seems pretty happy, in fact, and it's one of the only times everyone sinks into truly companionable silence.

But the inevitably of the birthday song arrives. And Allie, predictably, sings the loudest and most off-key. I can't help laughing, though, as I feel the love of those closest to me. There are worse ways to turn thirty, I decide. And the chocolate bourbon cake doesn't suck either, making good on Allie's promises of booze and cake. And booze cake.

All in all, as the dinner wraps up, I decide it was the perfect birthday get-together. Small, low key, good food, and the people I love. And blessedly few jokes about aging. What more could I possibly ask for?

Bryce and I stick around for a few minutes, lingering in the lobby so I can enjoy the view. The city lights twinkle around us spectacularly. And I know my dawdling is making Bryce even more nervous, but I feel like I need to take it all in one last time. He waits beside me as patiently as he can, though, his fingers entwined with mine. And I can feel him staring at me.

I glance over at him leaning with his back against the windows, simply taking me in. He doesn't look worried or impatient right now. He's exquisite in this moment, perhaps more so for my desire to drink in my last looks at his handsome face.

"What are you thinking about?" he asks.

I wonder if it's a general question or if he senses

what I'm preparing to do. Probably the former, or he'd be a lot less calm.

"How grateful I am for this life," I reply honestly. It's part of the truth, anyway.

He's silent for a moment, his blue eyes bright and shining. And I know exactly what he's thinking, so I beat him to it.

"Never forget how much I love you, Bryce Hoyt."

And his true sunshine smile splits across his face, melting my heart even more than it already was. "You stole my line," he teases. His eyes darken with intensity. "I love you too. Now let's go home."

"What, no dirty things you want to whisper in my ear first to drive me crazy?" I tease, letting him lead me to the elevator.

He glances around at the empty lobby. "It's not as much fun when there aren't other people around," he remarks.

I laugh, and it feels good. "You're incorrigible," I chide him as we step into the elevator.

Once the doors close behind us, and we're completely alone, he presses me roughly against the back of the elevator, towering over me. A thrill shoots through my body, warming me from my core to the tips of my fingers and toes.

"You have no idea," he murmurs, finally dropping

his lips to mine. The force of his kiss takes my breath away.

I wrap my arms around his neck, drawing him into me as close as I can get him. But the elevator doors ping open before I expect them to. Never one to be rude, Bryce pulls away, turning to face forward.

But we're both stopped short at the three large, dark-haired men facing us in the elevator as the doors slide closed behind them. I can feel Bryce stiffen next to me. The one closest to the panel pulls the elevator's red "stop" switch, and Bryce steps in front of me as the man in the middle takes out a gun. I try not to throw up as panic overtakes me. All I can think is, *Not again*. Not another gun, in another elevator, another kidnapping. But Bryce wasn't with me last time. I watch him slip his hand under the back of his shirt and wrap around his own gun, flicking off the safety.

"Don't do anything stupid," the man on the left says. "Just give us the girl and neither of you will be hurt."

"You're not taking her, so get out now. That's my only warning." Bryce's voice is full of quiet, barely controlled rage, and I've never heard him sound so terrifying.

And large though these men are, none of them are as big as Bryce. But while he's got the intimidation factor going for him, there are still three of them. I press my lips together, trying to stay silent and will away the tears threatening at the back of my eyes.

The man in the middle with the gun laughs. He turns his head to the man who spoke first. "This guy thinks he can …"

Bang! The loud sound of a gunshot goes off in the small space and the man in the middle drops. Before I can even process what happened, another deafening crack reverberates through the elevator and the man on the left drops. As I start to register the pain in my ears, I realize Bryce's gun is drawn and is trained on the third man. Like the now-dead men, I wasn't fast enough to notice Bryce draw and fire his gun. Twice.

But the third man, the one who'd stopped the elevator, apparently did. Because he now has a gun that is pointed back at Bryce. A very large gun. Bryce eyes it tensely but doesn't shoot.

"I think you know what happens if I fire," the man says calmly.

Reluctantly, Bryce nods. Leaving me to assume he knows we'd both be dead if the guy got off a shot. Because I know Bryce would sacrifice himself in an instant if he thought I'd be safe. And at that thought I can't fight the tears back any longer, letting them spill silently over.

"Good. Now, I assume you also know that I have

no desire to kill her. She's of little use to me dead. So let's get this over with quickly before we have company. Drop your gun now or I shoot."

Even before Bryce complies, I know he will. And based on the speed of his first attack, I also know what's coming next. But so does the dark-haired brute with the big gun. Bryce opens his hand, dropping his gun, and attacks simultaneously. But the bastard is already pulling the trigger. Given the proximity, though, Bryce manages to cross the short distance in time to knock the gun upward, deflecting the shot into the ceiling.

But our attacker seemed to be prepared for that, too, as his knee is already flying up, dislodging Bryce from the grasp he has on the gun. It's not enough for the man to keep his own grip on the weapon, however, and the gun tumbles out of his hands onto the floor. Bryce's attack continues relentlessly, his fist swinging for the man's stomach, chest, and head, only to be blocked each time. I can only watch in horror as the two, dangerously evenly matched, trade attempted blows.

My eyes flick to the ground, to the pools of blood spreading and joining under the two bodies. Fighting another wave of sickness, I try to concentrate on finding one of the guns on the floor. But before I can focus long enough, Bryce grunts in pain, causing my eyes to snap back up to the fight. The third man looks to have landed a hit to Bryce's face. Bryce is reeling back, blood spurting from his nose as the man dives for his gun.

"No!" The cry escapes my lips before I can stop it.

It's all happening so fast. Too fast. I throw myself to the ground, desperate to get my hands on one of the fallen weapons as I watch our attacker reel back up with his own, spinning around on a dazed Bryce. But he's too close to shoot as Bryce lurches at him, catching him in his midsection and pushing him hard into the side of the elevator.

Unfortunately, the humongous gun is still dangerous. I watch in horror as he brings it down on Bryce's skull. A loud *crack* echoes as it makes contact, and Bryce slumps to the floor, unconscious. The man huffs a short, satisfied laugh. And then kicks Bryce in the head with enough force to flip his large body away. I tuck my head down, into the floor, unable to look at the blood streaming from Bryce's face, and the reality of what just happened. My stomach lurches and my head spins. I can feel darkness tugging at me, and I know I'm close to fainting. My hand finds something hard and cold under my midsection. I grip it, trying to anchor myself to the feeling, to awareness.

"Well, ain't this a pickle," I hear the man murmur through the ringing in my ears. "It's gonna be tricky getting you out of here fast enough."

I feel the elevator jolt and resume its descent. A hand grips the hair on the back of my head hard, drawing me to my feet. The man's cold, dark eyes meet my own.

But I look down at my hand, still holding whatever it is I'd picked up from the floor. I want to weep with relief when I see that it's Bryce's gun. He looks down too. But too late. I fire into his face. The recoil throws me back, but I know from the warm, coppery spray that hits me that I didn't miss. And I at least have that satisfaction as I rapidly lose consciousness.

ELEVEN

Waking up in the hospital this time is much different from the last time. The first thing I see is a trio of concerned faces. Allie, David, and Emily all peer expectantly at me. But I can only think of one person.

"Bryce," I croak, my mouth dry. "Is he okay?"

Allie rushes to my side, slipping her hand in mine. David steps up beside her and gives my leg a reassuring squeeze.

"He's alive," Allie offers. "But he's not in good shape, Sera. They won't know more for a while."

I reach my hand out for Emily, knowing she must be as heartbreakingly worried as I am. She rushes to me, her eyes filled with tears, and Allie and David step aside to let her embrace me.

"Oh, Sera, I'm so glad you're safe," she murmurs, embracing me carefully and stroking my hair.

When she pulls away, I look down, trying to figure out why she was so particular in the way she held me, to see if I'm injured. But while there is a good amount of blood on my dress, I can't feel any pain. And knowing I'm whole makes my worry for Bryce all the more pressing.

"What's happening, Em? Why don't they know?" I ask, tears streaming desperately down my face.

"They said he sustained severe head trauma," Emily replies, the tears slipping down her face now as well. "He's still in surgery."

"How long have I been here? When …" I'm interrupted by a nurse bustling in through the door.

"Okay, everyone, let's please stop upsetting the patient," she snaps testily. Everyone takes a huge step away from the bed and gives her a wide berth. "Ms. Evans, I'm Nurse Kettleman. You don't appear to have sustained any physical trauma, but you were brought in unconscious approximately two hours ago. I'll need to check your vital signs now, okay?"

I note that the ringing in my ears is gone, and though tired and emotional I think she's right. I think my trauma is purely mental. So I nod, too tired to resist, and knowing I won't get answers from a hospital bed anyway. After a few minutes of questions and poking, she declares me fit to be released and hustles out the door to get the doctor.

I sit up and swing my legs over the bed, hopping down. "What else do we know about Bryce's condition?" I press, looking hard at Emily.

She shakes her head sadly. "Just that it's too soon to know," Emily replies. "That's it. Mom and Aunt Char are in the waiting room. They didn't want to overwhelm you."

"Has anyone spoken to the police?" I ask.

Allie and David share a look at my sharp tone.

"Of course," Emily responds. "And they're already on it. They know what happened from the video feed in the elevator, and they're trying to identify the bodies."

"That's good, but is there a police officer here now?" I demand.

While I'm terrified for Bryce, I haven't forgotten the reason we're here. And why I'd planned to leave. But with that out the window, and the boldness of tonight's attack, I know I'm more vulnerable than ever, but leaving is out of the question.

"Yes," Allie replies. "There are two in the waiting room. But the bad guys are dead, aren't they?"

I sigh heavily, not wanting to answer for fear of making them worry more. "Let's talk about this later.

Right now, I need to get out of this damn hospital room," I reply.

"Well, then it's a good thing I'm here," a voice answers from the door.

I look up to see a fit, middle-aged man in scrubs.

He extends his hand. "I'm Dr. Miller. And from your chart and your attitude, I'd say you're fit to be released. If you have any trouble or black out again, please come back, okay?"

I don't take his hand, but he smiles warmly at me nonetheless, and instead signs and offers up a copy of my paperwork.

"Thank you, doctor," I respond. "But I'm not actually leaving the hospital." I take the proffered discharge slip and storm out the door.

Allie, David, and Emily follow, directing me to the surgical waiting room. I stop on the way to clean myself up as best I can. There's blood spatter on my face and chest, and a little in my hair, that I'm able to remove. The stains on my clothing will just have to wait.

Continuing into the waiting area, we find Rebecca and Charlotte, who stand as we enter. I go to Bryce and Emily's mother first, wrapping her tightly in a hug.

"Rebecca," I breathe as she embraces me in a way

that only a mother can. "I'm so sorry." I bite back the guilt, the tears, and I let her go.

"I'm just glad you're okay," she replies, her eyes shining with tears. "Don't worry, Sera. Bryce is strong. And stubborn. Always has been. He'll be okay. I can feel it."

I don't respond, but hug Charlotte instead. She gives me an encouraging smile as well. At a different time I'd be saddened by how warm and reassuring Bryce's family is, as opposed to my own selfish and critical parents. But right now I'm laser-focused on what I can do. What I must do.

I step away from the women and over to where Allie and David are.

"Thank you, guys," I say. "For coming. I know this is probably scary and confusing. But I'll be okay. You can go home."

"Are you sure?" Allie asks skeptically. "We can wait here with you until Bryce is out of surgery. Or as long as you want."

I smile sadly and pull them both into a hug. "There's no need, really," I reply. "I should talk to the police and be here for Bryce's family. I'll let you know if I need anything, though, okay?"

"If you're sure," Allie responds, still obviously unconvinced.

I grab her hands in mine and squeeze them, giving

her my best impression of calm confidence. "I'm sure. Love you guys," I say. "I'll let you know when we hear something."

After a few more reassurances, David finally manages to pull a clearly still uncertain Allie away. Once I'm sure they're gone, I approach the two police officers on the opposite end of the floor. I recognize one of them from the night I was attacked outside Bryce's apartment. And as I approach, I see the clear glint of recognition in his eye as well.

"Officer Abbott," I greet him. "I need your help."

"Ms. Evans," he responds. "I'm so sorry to meet again under these circumstances, but I'm at your disposal. We've actually been waiting to see if you needed us. What can we do for you?"

"Is there a detective assigned to the case yet?" I ask.

"There is," he replies slowly.

"Good, then I need to talk to him. Here. As soon as possible," I insist.

He considers me for a moment. "Sure thing, ma'am, I'll call him right away," he finally agrees. "And please know that all of us on the force are going to do everything we can to help," he glances at his partner, who nods in agreement. "Bryce is practically one of us."

"I appreciate that," I respond softly. "I'll be in the

surgical waiting area. I need to make another phone call."

As I return to Bryce's family, I call the next person I'm going to need for my plan. Given the hour, I'm not surprised when he doesn't pick up right away. But eventually he does.

"Sera?" Tristan's voice is laden with sleep. "Everything okay?"

I look up at the ceiling, blinking back tears and concentrating on speaking as calmly as I can. "No. Bryce and I were attacked tonight. I'm okay, but Bryce is in surgery. And I'm afraid we're still in danger. I need your help, Tristan."

"On or off the books?"

His question brings a grim smile to my face. Because I know he's asking if he should ditch his GPS tracker. The loyalty his question demonstrates, at any other time, would warm my heart. But right now all I feel is cold fury.

"I would never ask you to do something off the books, Tristan," I respond. "But thank you all the same. Just come down to Swedish First Hill and we'll talk."

"I'll be there as soon as I can," he assures me.

⌒

BRYCE IS STILL IN SURGERY, AND I'M GIVING A FULL history to Detective Jacobs when Tristan arrives. He waits patiently while I finish filling in the tall, wiry detective on the situation. He's seen the police reports from my previous issues where I was followed twice and attacked on two separate occasions as well, including the attack of last weekend, but I'd never brought up Alessandro in my reports. Never hinted that there could be something bigger behind it. Until now. And now I've told him what I know, damn the consequences. Including that Bryce himself had launched an investigation. I can only hope it's enough.

But if it's not, I have a Plan B. Which is where Tristan comes in. As soon as the detective is gone, I find a quiet corner of the waiting room.

Tristan gives me a brief hug, which I gratefully accept. And I catch Tristan up too. Because he's only been told bits and pieces here and there, and if he's going to help he needs the whole story.

"Wow," Tristan murmurs as I finish. "That's a lot, Sera."

I close my eyes and give a brief sigh. "I know, but I need to focus right now," I reply. "Or I'm going to fall apart. I need to find Alessandro and get him to put a stop to this. And the only way I can think of to potentially reach him is through Marco Rossi, who took over his company here in Seattle. They're practically family, so Marco will almost certainly know where Alessandro is. Unfortunately, the number I have for Marco isn't working anymore. But honestly, I want to do this in person anyway. So I need you to find him for me and take me there once Bryce is out of surgery."

Tristan considers that, then nods. "Okay," he agrees. "I'll let the officers know that someone should stay here with you until I get back. And I'll get another guard to join me for first shift. I don't want to take any chances."

"That's probably a good idea," I reply.

And for once, none of my reservations about having the guards around matter — the thought of not having them is far worse. I can only hope this gets resolved quickly. And I'm furious with myself for letting it get to this point before going on the offense.

With Tristan gone, I return to the waiting room with Bryce's family to, well, wait. And hope.

It's several hours before a surgeon emerges, looking grim. We all jump up, snapping abruptly out of our half-asleep stupors.

"Mrs. Hoyt?" the surgeon asks.

Bryce's mother steps forward. The surgeon

extends a hand, which she takes timidly, clearly terrified.

"I'm Dr. Barnes. Your son made it through surgery and is in recovery. We were able to repair the damage. Now all we can do is keep an eye on him to make sure the swelling goes down. The rest is up to him. Chances are good he'll wake up, but with this kind of head injury, it's impossible to know what the aftereffects will be."

"Thank you, doctor," Rebecca manages. "But what does that mean?"

"A traumatic brain injury often affects speech, cognitive function, mobility, and so on," he admits.

We all exchange horrified glances.

"But," he hedges, "as I said, there's no way to know if he'll have any of those issues or to what extent. And with rehabilitation there is a high success rate for recovery."

"When will he wake up?" Emily asks, gripping my hand tightly.

Dr. Barnes shakes his head. "We don't know. But we will keep him sedated for a while longer to give him time to heal. I'd recommend you go home and get some rest. We will call you if there are any developments," he replies.

I let out a frustrated gasp. "We can't see him?" I ask.

Dr. Barnes' eyes meet mine, and I see the compassion there. "I'm afraid not," he responds softly. "Not with this kind of injury, and the type of surgery that was done. Once the antibiotics have had a chance to take hold, you'll be able see him."

I try to fight back the rage and sorrow brewing in me before saying anything more. But Charlotte beats me to it.

"And when exactly will that be?" Char snaps uncharacteristically.

Dr. Barnes is clearly used to dealing with distressed loved ones, as he takes it fully in stride. "Twenty-four hours," he replies.

I sink into the chair behind me, no longer able to stand. Emily sits next to me and wraps an arm around me. I look up through tears at the doctor.

"So there's a chance he won't wake up?" I ask thickly.

The doctor looks down sadly at me. "There's always that chance, but I believe he will," he replies.

"But if he's fighting for his life, won't it help to hear our voices?" I press. I don't even think of asking what happens if he starts to lose that fight, if we'll be permitted to say goodbye, or even have time. But thankfully my question seems to have given Dr. Barnes pause.

"I'm a firm believer that that's true," he finally replies. "Come back this afternoon. If you're willing to go through the sterilization process, you can see him and talk to him, one at a time."

I jump to my feet and hug him before I can stop myself. "Thank you," I breathe.

He gives me a small, reassuring pat before stepping back. "Just check in at the nurse's station if you have any questions and to leave your contact information," he responds, then disappears through the swinging doors behind him.

I turn to the other ladies. "I hate to have to bring this up, but someone should notify Bryce's company of what's happened," I say tiredly.

Rebecca nods. "I already did, dear, don't you worry about anything," she replies.

I look at her in surprise. Having so recently dealt with the death of her husband, I finally realize how calm she's been through this so far. And I'm grateful, as that makes it easier for me to keep it together. I reach out and squeeze her hand.

"Thank you," I reply sincerely. "But unfortunately there are other matters I *will* need to worry about this morning. But please call me the instant you need me, and I'll drop everything. Okay?" I look at each of them in turn and they all nod. Out of the corner of my eye, I see Tristan and Aiden, one of my other former bodyguards, hovering. I embrace each of the women and say my farewells.

When I make my way over to Tristan and Aiden, I'm surprised when Aiden hugs me warmly.

"Thank you, Aiden," I say in surprise.

He gives me a sad smile. "My pleasure, ma'am," he replies. "What news?"

I sigh deeply. "Bryce is out of surgery and in recovery. We won't be permitted to see him until this afternoon, but the doctor sounded relatively optimistic at his chances," I reply, leaving out the part about potential issues and recovery. I just can't right now. "But there are other pressing matters at hand. Tristan, did you get the information I asked for?"

Tristan nods grimly. "Yes, ma'am," he replies.

I press my lips together, determined. "Good. Let's get moving, then. I'd like to stop home and change, and then go directly there," I instruct.

Tristan glances at his watch. "It's just past six a.m.," he points out softly.

I give him a sharp look. And never mind the fact that he's five inches taller than me and is far stronger, he wisely snaps his mouth shut in response.

"He'll be up. Or I'll wake him up. In either case, I'm not concerned," I spit angrily. And I can only hope Tristan knows I'm not angry with him, nor with

Marco, really. And not even with Alessandro. I'm just angry with the world right now, for doing this to Bryce. He doesn't deserve it.

I turn heel and march out of the emergency room, my two guards scrambling to keep up behind me.

TWELVE

It's not quite seven a.m. when, freshly showered and changed, I bang on the door of Marco's tiny house in Fremont. Tristan and Aiden flank me, exchanging a nervous look behind my back. I don't think either of them have ever seen me on the warpath, but I don't much care.

Marco answers the door, looking casually bewildered in blue flannel pants and a black T-shirt.

"*Buongiorno*," I greet him. "I'm sorry to show up like this, Marco, but I need to speak with you."

"Sera, *buongiorno*, of course, please come in," he replies, bemused as he stares at the two men with me. He steps back, allowing us all to cross the threshold into the small living room behind him.

Marco pulls a few stray papers off the couch,

gesturing for us to sit as he takes a chair. His wife, Angela, pops her head in from the kitchen.

"Serafina! *Buongiorno*! *Come stai*?" she greets me.

How am I? I suppress an ironic laugh as I rise to hug her.

"Angela, *buongiorno. Sono stato meglio. E tu*?" I return. "I've been better" is probably the understatement of my year.

"*Bene, bene*," she assures me.

Well, I'm glad at least one of us is good.

"Cappuccino? Espresso?" She looks around at each of us, but we all shake our heads.

"I only need a word with Marco, *per favore*," I reply.

"*Sì, naturalmente*," Angela responds kindly, smiling and ducking back into the kitchen.

Marco shifts nervously in his chair. "Well, it must be something very urgent if you've come to see me. What can I do for you?" Marco asks with a note of suspicion.

"Where's Alessandro?" I ask bluntly.

Marco squirms, and I don't miss his eyes darting to the small set of stairs in the entryway.

"You've *got* to be kidding me."

"Sera, you must understand …" Marco starts, but I cut him off with a growl.

"I must understand nothing," I reply tartly, rising and going to the bottom of the stairs.

Tristan hops to his feet, clearly unsure of whether or not to follow. Marco eyes the gun now exposed as Tristan's jacket shifts.

Ignoring them both, I yell up the stairs as loud as I can. *"Alessandro Vittorio Giordano, you'd better get your ass down here right —"*

He appears at the top of the stairs before I can even finish. But he's not the man I remember. Thin and pale, his dark hair hangs long and limp around his face and unkempt beard. Even from this distance I can see the dead look in his dark eyes. And his tired sweats and T-shirt look like they could use a good washing. He's a far cry from the dynamic, fiery, and well-coifed man I loved.

"Buongiorno, mio tesoro," he replies in greeting, his voice hollow and tired. He starts slowly descending the stairs as if every step is painful.

Marco appears at my side. "Be kind, Sera, you don't know what he's suffered," Marco says softly.

I bite back an angry reply, knowing it will do no good. He ascends the stairs, Angela following behind him as Alessandro finally makes it down.

"I'm glad to see you're safe," Alessandro remarks, taking note of Tristan and Aiden's presence.

And I can't help it. My hand flies up and I smack

him across the face. Hard. He runs a hand over his lip, not even looking angry.

"I deserved that," he admits.

"And so much more," I seethe. "I may be safe for now, but Bryce wasn't so lucky." I practically choke on the words.

Alessandro raises an eyebrow. "I thought you said the giant was out of the picture?"

"No, I said it wasn't an option for me to go to him when I last saw you," I retort. "But he's very much in the picture. Assuming he survives. We were attacked last night, and not for the first time. And now Bryce is lying in a hospital bed, fighting for his life, because of *you*." My eyes fill with angry tears. "*Why?* Tell me why, goddammit, and what you're going to do to stop this before they take everything from me."

Alessandro doesn't answer. Instead, he trudges into the living room, sinking defeatedly into the chair Marco just vacated.

"Did you realize that you loved him before or after he was hurt?" Alessandro asks.

I'm dumbfounded at the seeming indifference of his response, but I answer anyway. "Before."

Alessandro huffs a small, unamused laugh. "Lucky him, then," he murmurs. He rubs his hands roughly into his eyes. "I don't know where to begin, Serafina."

I look to Aiden and Tristan. "May we have privacy, please?" I ask them softly.

They rise and head out the front door. "We'll be on the porch. If you call out, we'll hear you," Tristan assures me as he leaves.

"Thanks," I reply. As soon as they're gone, I sit on the couch nearest to Alessandro's chair. I consider him carefully for a moment.

He's a shell of the man I knew. What could rob someone so strong-willed, so vital, of their spirit, their hope, and their health in such a short time? I almost don't want to know. But unfortunately right now I need to. Because if he can't, or won't, I need to be the one to figure out how to stop this.

"I'm sorry," Alessandro finally offers into the silence. "I've failed everyone."

"What are you even still doing here, Alessandro? Have you been here since I last saw you?" I press.

He shakes his head sadly. "No, *amore*. I went back to do what had to be done. But it wasn't enough. So I came back to make sure you were okay. For all the good it did," he spits venomously.

"Clearly, they didn't need me to accomplish your undoing," I reply sharply.

He looks up and catches my eye. "True," he agrees. "But that's not really what they were after, unfortunately."

"It's time to tell me the truth. It's time I know what's going on. If you can't end this, I'm going to help you to," I push. "So tell me: Who is after you, and what do they want?"

Alessandro sighs heavily. "What do they always want? Money," he replies, dodging my first question.

I tap my fingers impatiently on my knee. "How much money?" I ask.

"Nearly three million dollars, at last count," he replies.

I can't help but huff a dry laugh. "That's all?" I ask incredulously.

He levels a tired look at me. "That's all that's left, yes," he replies. "But for all I've already given." He looks at me miserably, and suddenly, somehow, I know he's still trying to protect me. Even now, in his seeming impotence, from whatever it is that has brought him to this state.

And it's hard to forget how much I still care for this man. Sliding off the couch, I sink to my knees in front of him and take his hand.

"Unfortunately, I'm not exactly in a position to seduce it out of you this time," I tease him gently. "So you're just going to have to tell me on your own."

He smiles, and it makes him look more like himself. "As you wish," he consents. He takes a deep breath. "You asked me once why I left Italy, and I'm afraid my answer wasn't very satisfying."

I nod, recalling the conversation.

"I went into real estate because it's what my father did. But I wanted to make my own way, so I didn't join him, and it angered him. My older brother was already working with him, though, so I didn't understand until much later why. But he more or less disowned me. It was not the best way to start out in life, but it made me work harder, and I think it's part of the reason I was so successful." He pauses to rub a finger along his chin.

"What did your mother think?" I ask curiously.

His sad eyes meet mine for a brief moment. "My mama wouldn't have cared, I know, but once he stopped speaking to me, she couldn't either without angering him," he replies. "It was bad, for everyone. But as the years went on, and I started to do well, I thought about it less. Until my brother started coming to me for money, with this excuse and that."

I raise my eyebrows delicately. "And you gave it to him?" I infer.

He nods. "I'm not usually one to suffer wastrels, but I was already at odds with my parents. I couldn't stand not being there for my brother," he admits. "But as I earned more, he asked for more. So, at some point, I stopped. But my mentor, he jumped in with my brother to guilt me, to say I had no loyalty to family."

"You mentioned your mentor changed," I recall. "You said he was limiting? Is that what you meant?"

"Ah, that," Alessandro responds. "No, that was something else entirely. He started steering me away from certain projects and toward others and throwing his weight around when I disagreed. It was quite strange at the time. Between all of it, though, I'd just had enough. So I left. I went somewhere I could make my own way."

"San Francisco," I supply.

He nods. "*Sì*, San Francisco," he agrees. "And it wasn't long before I met Peyton there. Which, as it turned out, wasn't a coincidence at all."

"How's that?" I ask.

He shifts uncomfortably in his chair, and I give his hand a reassuring squeeze to settle him.

"When Peyton was in college, she studied for a year abroad in Italy, which I knew," he responds. "What I didn't know is that during that time she met and fell in love with Antonio, my brother. It was he who first mentioned San Francisco to me, as a land of real estate opportunity. I remembered that when I learned he'd sent her after me, to do whatever was necessary to keep my money flowing back to him."

"Holy shit," I gasp. "Why did he need your money so badly?"

Alessandro closes his eyes, but the tears still find their way through, sliding slowly down his hollow cheeks. "They were all *Cosa Nostra*," he replies quietly. He opens his eyes to my confused expression. "Made men, as Americans say. You even joked once, about my having mob ties, and I laughed at you. Turns out it wasn't so funny after all. My father had gotten into it when we were little, when his business was struggling. And he brought my brother in when he came of age. That's why he was so angry — he knew I was smart, and that I'd help him do well. And then I refused him." Alessandro shakes his head sadly. "They made a bad investment with mafia money. Lots tens of millions of euros a few years before I moved to the States. That's why my brother needed money. And why my mentor was even my mentor in the first place — he was one of them, sent to watch me, make sure I was doing everything I could to make back their money and give it to my brother. So as long as my money kept coming, through Peyton, everything was fine."

I stare at him, open-mouthed, in utter shock at the situation. In the last months he's learned that his father and brother are mobsters, his ex-wife only married him out of love and obligation to his brother, and his mentor is a mob goon only there to see a debt repaid. And I'm starting to understand the change that has come over him.

"So the divorce …" I start.

"Yes, the divorce. It stopped the money. And they weren't used to having to make their own anymore, or perhaps were never all that able. So they got desperate, and their debtors anxious," he replies. "They were given a deadline. And when they didn't meet it, they killed my father." More tears slip from Alessandro's dark eyes.

"Oh, Alessandro, I'm so sorry," I reply. "What about your mother? Your sisters? Are they okay?"

"They are," he confirms. "The older of my two younger sisters, Adriana, is *Carabinieri*. Military police. She is trained in hiding. She fled the country with my mother and my youngest sister. So at least I know they are safe."

"When did it happen?" I ask softly.

"Just before I went back," he replies. "While I was following Peyton. So it's no surprise that after tipping my hand to get more information once I arrived in Rome, my brother found me quickly. He told me everything and begged me on behalf of their unborn child to help them."

"She was actually pregnant?" I ask, surprised.

"So he said," Alessandro replies dubiously. "The

web of lies was so great, there is really no knowing. But I highly doubt it. In all the time I was watching her, she showed no signs."

"If she was pregnant and they needed money so badly, why did she agree to the divorce?" I ask, confused.

Alessandro smiles vaguely. "Because she's not very bright, Serafina," he responds. "She didn't realize I could push it through if she didn't answer my petition. And she thought she could plead her sob story to a judge."

"Oh, god, what did she say?" I ask.

"That I abused her, was a cheating bastard, and that I was in love with another woman," he rattles off. "In the heat of the moment I admitted to, at least, being in love with another woman, but of course denied her other lies. She was happy to have me out of her life not long after we married, and now I know why. But none of that mattered. Even if the judge didn't see right through her, which he did, she'd had her chance to respond to the paperwork and didn't. So it was done."

My hand flies to my mouth as a horrible realization dawns on me. "That's how they found out about me, isn't it?" I whisper.

Reluctantly, Alessandro nods. "My brother used that. Told me they'd come after you too if I didn't help him," he admits. "So I had no choice. I gave them everything I had. But it was not enough. So I promised to help Antonio find or make the rest of the money. But the timeline was short. And we weren't fast enough." Tears fill his eyes again and he presses them away angrily.

And I know whatever it is that happened next must be horrible, but I can't help asking. "What did they do?"

His dead eyes meet my own. "They killed Peyton. Right in front of us. And they told me they'd found you. And if they didn't get the rest of their money within a month, they'd kill you in front of me too. That's when I came back for you."

I gasp, doing the mental math quickly. "Alessandro, that was six weeks ago."

He leans forward, gathering both of my hands in his now. "I know," he replies. "And when they stopped hearing from me a couple of weeks ago, I knew it would get worse. Much worse. But I've been paralyzed. Too afraid to go back, too afraid to tell you. And my inaction cost my brother his life." His tears flow unreservedly now, dropping on the light carpet between us.

I slide a hand out of his grip and lift his face so he's looking into my eyes. "Your brother was responsible for his own life," I say firmly. "And you should have told me all this sooner. Much, much sooner." I let him go and rise to my feet. "If we pay them, will this stop? Will it be done?"

Alessandro looks up at me skeptically. "Yes, I believe it will," he replies uncertainly. "They have no use for me, and everyone else is either dead or out of their reach. But if I had that much money left, it would already be done."

I pause and wonder, did I really never tell him? Exactly how much money I have, the extent of the legacy my grandfather left? A great sadness wells in my heart knowing this could have been over long ago. That Bryce didn't have to be affected by this. That my and Alessandro's safety didn't have to be at risk. I stop myself from thinking about the others. Who knows what would have been changed if I'd just known the truth from the start.

"Call them. Ask them how much they need today to end this. And that it will be done," I instruct him.

"Serafina, I can't ask …" he starts.

I whirl on him furiously. "You're not asking. I'm telling you what's going to happen. The man I love is fighting for his life right now because of this, Alessandro. And neither of us will be safe until the debt is paid. So make. The. Fucking. Call."

And for once, he does as I ask.

❧

By midday, it's done. All of it. The money transferred, vows given that release us from the unknowing hell we've both been hostage to. I'd feel relieved if I still wasn't so worried for Bryce.

We drop Alessandro back off at Marco's. While Tristan waits to escort Alessandro to the door, he turns to me.

"I hope Bryce is okay," Alessandro says sincerely. "Truly. He protected you when I didn't. And for that I'll always be grateful."

I fight back the tears, not wanting to spend any more emotion on this man. "Take care of yourself, Alessandro," I reply stoically.

He looks at me as if he wants to say something else, but wisely doesn't. And then he's gone. Maybe someday we'll be friends again. But not today.

As soon as Tristan climbs back into the car, I give the order to return to the hospital. And then I let myself fall apart quietly in the backseat, while I can, knowing I'll need to keep it together again too soon.

THIRTEEN

When I arrive at the hospital I find Rebecca, Charlotte, and Emily in the waiting room, their faces shrouded in worry. I embrace them each in turn, trying to project an air of assurance that I don't really feel.

"When do we get to see him?" I ask by way of greeting.

Rebecca and Charlotte exchange a glance, and Emily pulls a nasty face.

"What? What's going on?" I can feel the blood drain from my face at their taciturn response.

"They say only one of us can go in," Emily pouts.

Charlotte throws her a sharp look.

"We've decided it should be you," Rebecca addresses me softly.

I'm taken aback. "I appreciate that, but you're his mother. I really think you should go," I reply.

Rebecca shakes her head. "I gave him life. But in his thirty-four years I've never seen him love someone the way he loves you. You're his life now," she says to me. "And I'm thankful for that. If he's going to fight for anyone, it will be for you."

Any hope I had of maintaining composure crumbles at her words, and I melt into her arms, sobbing. When I'm able to collect myself, I nod gratefully. "Thank you," I whisper.

They lead me to the nurse's station, and a short wisp of a woman in scrubs leads me to a room to undergo the sterilization procedure.

I emerge into the clean area a while later, scrubbed, stinging, and wrapped in garments that keep my bodily elements out of the environment around me. I feel like I'm wearing a space suit, but at this moment I don't care. I'd dress like a giant hot dog if it meant seeing Bryce.

I follow the directions I was given around the corner and into a room with no door. There's only one occupant, lying in a hospital bed, surrounding by tubes, wires, and machines that hum softly in the otherwise silent space.

I approach as close as I dare, stopping inches from the edge of the bed. There are tubes from his head, nose, mouth, and arm that snake over the great expanse of his chest and the side of his bed. I'm afraid to even be near them, should I accidentally bump anything.

When the initial fear has passed, I spend a minute just looking at him. His head has been partially shaved toward the back, his handsome face obscured by the tubes and tape. But I can see the bruising that spreads over his nose, chin, and cheek. Tears fill my eyes remembering how he got them.

I take a deep breath, fighting hard to stay calm. So that when I speak he hears me, and not my anguish.

"Hey, baby," I greet him. "I'm here. I'm sorry I couldn't come sooner. You had surgery, and they didn't even want to let anyone see you until tomorrow. But I couldn't wait that long. You know me, always impatient."

A flash of memory of the last time he called me that slips through my defenses. We were both naked. I blink the tears away hard and breathe deep to suppress the memory.

"The doctors say you're going to wake up. And that there's a good chance that you'll fully recover. And I'm going to be here for you every step of the way. But there's something else you should know."

I pause, not sure how much I should say, if it could somehow stress him further. So I couch my words carefully and explain how the threat against me, against us, is over. His face, his limbs, and his long frame are still throughout, not a hint of change in the beeping of the machines around him. But I persist.

"We're safe now," I conclude. "Even if it was too late to stop this. I'm so sorry, Bryce." My voice cracks at saying his name. I'm saved an imminent breakdown when a small speaker by his bed crackles to life.

"Ms. Evans?" the nurse's voice floats softly into the room. "Time is almost up."

I nod mutely, even though I know she can't see me, and my throat constricts with everything I want to say to him.

"I've got to go," I say apologetically. "But starting tomorrow I'll be able to visit more. We all will." Throwing caution to the wind, I step forward and slip my gloved hand over his, squeezing gently. "Never forget how much I love you, Bryce Hoyt." I turn and leave, barely holding back the tide of emotion.

❧

EVEN THOUGH WE AREN'T ALLOWED TO VISIT BRYCE until the following morning, we spend most of the time at the hospital anyway, sharing shifts in case there is news or he wakes up. Once they transfer him out of the clean area, his family is allowed to visit a fair amount, but non-family visits are more restricted. Still, I spend as much time as I can by his side, quietly reassuring him and calling him back to me.

As Sunday draws to a close I realize there is no possible way I'm going to be able to work while he's in this state. I call Charles to let him know and, thankfully, he completely understands, sends his best wishes and tells me to call if I need anything.

But I forget even my most basic needs until Allie shows up, all but forcing food and rest on me. I'm exhausted, and though I'm not hungry, I notice the impact of not eating much. The copious amounts of coffee I consume hit my stomach like lead, and my head pounds. By Monday night, I start to wonder how much of this I can take.

And by Tuesday morning the sentiment has spread, as I can sense the nurses and doctors are tiring of reassuring us that it's not abnormal for someone to be unconscious this long under the circumstances.

But on Tuesday afternoon, when I'm getting my umpteenth cup of coffee for the day, Emily comes shooting down the hall.

"He's awake!" she cries as she approaches.

And thankfully the cup of coffee is still filling in the machine, or I would have dropped it in my haste to get to him.

But before I can get far Emily has planted a hand firmly on my chest. "We can't see him yet. The doctors are with him now."

I pull back, frustrated. "Were you there? What happened?" I demand.

Emily shakes her head. "It was Mom. I don't know. She said he seemed disoriented, and she called for the nurses right away. They asked that she leave while they tend to him and get him checked out," Emily replies.

I frown and turn to get back to the waiting room, to talk to Rebecca directly. I find her beside a pacing Charlotte, both women twisting their hands together frenetically.

When Rebecca spots me, she approaches and wraps her arms around me. "He's awake. Focus on that," she says. Her tone worries me, but afraid to ask, I say nothing and we all take seats in tense silence.

What feels like hours later, a doctor asks Rebecca to go with him to see Bryce. Another long, anxious, stretch of time passes before she emerges, white-faced.

"Well?" Emily demands.

Rebecca looks up at her dismally. "Physically, he's doing quite well. He has all of his motor functions," Rebecca responds carefully. "And he seems in decent spirits, despite still suffering a considerable amount of pain, even with the medications he's on. So they're adjusting those doses."

"But?" I press, knowing there's something she's not saying. Something big.

"He seemed confused. He asked for his father," she admits. My heart sinks in my chest. "The doctors told him he needs more tests, and rest, before he sees *anyone* else. The privately told me not to break any kind of news to him right now, that they need time to assess the extent of his issues."

I start clutching my midsection as sharp pain shoots through me like I've been kicked. Rebecca reaches out and grabs me by the arms.

"Don't worry yet, Sera, please," she begs. "It's too soon. He's awake. And I can tell you right now, he's still our Bryce. Let the doctors look at him. One step at a time."

I should feel comforted. Because she's right. So even though I can't help but worry, I sniff deeply and nod. Rebecca and Charlotte step to the side to talk quietly, and Emily approaches me, wrapping me in a tight hug.

"I'm here for you, Sera," she assures me. "Remember, we pinky swore. No matter what happens."

I can't help but laugh. "Thanks, Emily," I reply. "Ditto."

She lets me go and we sink into the hard, plastic chairs in the waiting room. And we wait.

No news comes, and not long later a nurse lets us know that we should go home and come back tomorrow.

I return home reluctantly, and without my security guards for the first time. There's nothing to fear anymore. Well, nothing outside of the hospital, anyway.

∽

THE NEXT MORNING, I PACK A BAG FOR BRYCE WITH some sweat pants, shirts, his house slippers, and some hygiene items. As I pass the kitchen, I'm momentarily tempted to pack the frilly white apron that still hangs by the fridge. I resist, but somehow it gives me hope. Because it reminds me how much he loves me. And in love, there's always hope.

I meet Rebecca and Emily in the waiting room by eight per our usual routine, but Charlotte has gone back to work with the worst of the danger passed.

"I brought him some of his clothes and things," I say. "I didn't know how long he'd be here."

Rebecca smiles warmly. "The nurse says the doctor has some information for us. He'll be out shortly," she replies. "So hopefully we'll know soon."

I nod meekly, nervous. Thankfully, we're not made to wait long. A shorter man in a lab coat and glasses comes out and heads straight for Rebecca.

"Mrs. Hoyt?" has asks kindly.

She nods.

"I'm Dr. Farber."

"Call me Rebecca, please," she responds. "This is Bryce's sister, Emily, and his girlfriend, Sera."

"Ladies," he replies with a dip of his head. "Bryce is doing quite well, physically. But we are still a little concerned with his cognitive functions and his memory. Despite the reduction in swelling, he's still struggling with both. But please be assured that that's completely normal. He should make a good deal of progress in the next few weeks, but it could be up to a year before his recovery is complete."

"When can we see him?" I ask.

"He's perfectly fit for visitors, but be aware that he's currently unable to remember anything within approximately the last eighteen months."

We all three of us let out a collective gasp. None of us imagined it was that extensive. I try my best not to panic, but it's practically impossible.

Bryce won't remember me. My ears ring as the conversation continues, and I have to push myself hard to listen.

"Eighteen months?!" Emily spits out incredulously. "Will that get better?"

Dr. Farber holds up a hand. "As I was going to say, he should not be pressed to remember anything he can't at this time. He's been made aware of it, but nonetheless it's dangerous for his healing to push him. And we're going to keep him for a few more days to make sure the swelling continues to go down and he's weaned off of the majority of the medicines we've had him on," Dr. Farber hedges. "But yes, his memory should improve. Though there's no telling how much. Regardless, until his cognitive functions return to normal levels and his short term memory is repaired, he should take it easy. No work, no major decisions, no trying to force progress."

"And, on average, when do you expect to see that kind of improvement?" I ask quietly.

"He could be ready for work in a matter of weeks, months at most," Dr. Farber responds. "But he'll need to work with a rehabilitation therapist to aid his healing. After a year, whatever progress he's made is likely to be where he stays."

I rub the back of my neck, unease creeping through every pore in my body. "I've only known him for five months," I admit. "Is it okay if I go in? Just in case it jogs something?"

Dr. Farber looks like he wants to say no, and I

press my lips together, willing him to at least let me see him. If for nothing else than to see for myself that he's himself, mostly. That's he's okay.

"Normally, I would advise against it," he hedges. "But if you don't introduce yourself as his girlfriend, and you respond to his lead, I can allow it. He can't be subjected to strong emotion right now, though, so if you need to, please leave the room rather than upset him."

I nod, simply thankful for the opportunity. "I can do that," I agree.

Dr. Farber looks around at all of us. "That really goes for everyone, until he's improved. Let him lead. Watch him carefully for signs that he's had enough. Know when to back off. The nurses will help you," he assures us. "Any other questions?"

Rebecca looks to Emily and me, and we shake our heads. "Not right now, doctor, thank you," she responds.

"Then follow me," he responds. He grabs a nurse along the way and leads us to Bryce's room.

Emily pulls me aside as Rebecca enters with Dr. Farber and the nurse. "I'm here if you need me, Sera. Just remember the long game," she encourages me. "Even if he doesn't remember you right now, that doesn't mean anything. It's early."

I nod, swallowing hard. "I just want to know he's okay," I respond.

Emily nods, and slips her hand in mine. The warm, soft reassurance is more than welcome.

Dr. Farber exits, eyeing us as he goes, but saying nothing. I take a deep breath and let Emily lead me in.

The nurse stands by Bryce's bed, checking his vitals. Rebecca sits on the edge of his bed, holding his hand. And he's sitting up, completely free of tubes and wires. And he's smiling. My heart almost breaks with relief and gratitude. Because even if he doesn't remember me, he's *alive*. And he's going to be okay.

When he sees Emily, his smile widens into his classic Bryce sunshine smile, and I have to blink back bittersweet tears.

"Em!" he exclaims opening his arms to her. She drops my hand and rushes forward to embrace him warmly.

"Bryce," she replies. "I'm so glad you're okay." She pulls back. "Love the haircut, bro."

He laughs and runs his hand gingerly over the partially shaved patch. "I'll just shave the whole thing later," he assures her. "Nothing can stop these good looks, though."

Em laughs. "Boy, a traumatic brain injury can't even dent your ego," she teases. "Is it wrong that that makes me feel relieved?" Emily rounds the bed, dropping into one of the metal chairs on the other side.

And Bryce looks up and sees me for the first time. He does elevator eyes over me, and a shiver runs through me. He turns and looks questioningly at Emily, realizing I came in with her.

"Who is this?" he asks blankly.

And I can't help it. Even though I was expecting it, my heart breaks at his question, and I have to work to keep myself calm and my expression neutral.

"That's my friend, Serafina Evans," Emily responds carefully.

"Oh," he responds happily. "Nice to meet you, friend Serafina Evans." He extends a hand and something in me shifts again.

I identify the feeling this time — it's like a tiny death of a fraction of my hope.

I extend my right hand, shifting his duffle bag to my left. "You can call me Sera," I respond as evenly as I can.

His hand is rough and warm, and wonderful. He lets go far sooner than I'd like. "I take it we've met before," he responds drily.

I look at him in shock. "Yes, actually," I admit. "But how did you know that?"

He smirks and points at the duffle bag in my hand.

I blush furiously. "Oh. Yes, that. Sorry. I brought

some of your things. Sweats, shirts, slippers. And your toothbrush and shaving kit. Probably a few other things. I don't know." I hand over the bag dumbly, embarrassed by my verbal incontinence.

Bryce raises an eyebrow. "You brought those, huh?" he asks, confused. "Do I want to know why you had them in the first place?"

We all freeze for a moment, and it's all I can do to keep my jaw off the floor. He sure as hell doesn't seem like he's got any cognitive issues. He seems just as observant as ever.

"Um, it's a long story," I reply. "I'm sure Emily will tell it to you later."

Bryce nods, obviously placated. So maybe he's not as sharp as usual.

Bryce turns to his mom. "Has anyone told Madison I'm here?" he asks innocently.

A brief hush falls over the room as we all realize if the last thing he remembers is a year and a half ago, he's still the Bryce that was with Madison. The Bryce that was about to *propose* to Madison, if I remember the timeline of the downfall of their relationship correctly. Suddenly, I feel like throwing up.

Rebecca shoots me a furtive glance. "No," she admits. "We can worry about that later."

I swallow a lump in my throat. Rebecca and Emily continue shooting me sympathetic looks. And I know I need to leave. So I don't fall apart, and their response to me doesn't tip Bryce off that something is amiss. Especially if Madison is going to come parading in here soon.

And the thought of her being here while he's in this state makes me want to punch something. But I shove it all down.

"I should go," I interject. "Bryce, I'm really glad to see you're doing so well. I hope you keep getting better, okay?"

He nods happily. "Thanks, Sera, it was nice to … er, see you," he chuckles.

I catch Em's eye. "I'll talk to you soon, right Em?" I ask.

"Count on it," she assures me quietly.

"'K. Bye," I reply, ducking out as quickly as I can. And before I completely lose it, I call Allie and ask to come stay with her. Because I know being alone in the house I shared with Bryce is a recipe for a complete breakdown.

FOURTEEN

Staying with Allie was a good call. Since she's still not working, she's around constantly to be a sounding board, distraction, and source of comfort as needed. Especially since I decide to take the rest of the week off, unsure whether I'm in control enough of my emotions to make it through a workday.

Emily calls on Saturday to let me know Bryce is being discharged and will be going to stay with their mother. She blessedly doesn't mention Madison. She does say that Bryce has slowly started asking questions about his life these past eighteen months, and that they're carefully answering them. Since it was kind of difficult to avoid, they did have to break it to him that his father had passed, which has forced them to back off everything else as he absorbs that news.

It's the only thing she tells me that plunges me back into despair. And not for myself, for Bryce. Because I was there when he dealt with it the first time, and I remember how much it affected him. He needed me so desperately then, and it caused the chain of events that led me to realize how deeply I cared for him. But it's also what drove him back to his conniving ex, Madison, if only temporarily. I can only hope they're encouraging him to be cautious on that front. Because despite repeated attempts at suggesting I visit, they've made it clear that Bryce's mental state is still too delicate.

I return to my own home and to work the following week and bury myself deeply in the myriad of development projects I'd dumped on Suraj's desk with my absence. It's a reminder of how lucky I am to work with Charles, Suraj, and everyone at Sutton Developments. My absence would have had a much bigger impact had I still been running my own company.

It's not until Tuesday evening, when Heather calls, that I'm reminded Daniel's trial started yesterday.

"Heather," I answer. "Hi. I'm so glad to hear from you."

"Hey, Sera," Heather replies. "Sorry I've been out of touch. With the trial coming up I just needed some time to prepare myself, I guess."

"I totally understand," I reply. "How is it going so far?"

"Slow," she admits. "But being in the courtroom with him isn't as hard as I thought it would be."

"I'm glad to hear it," I respond, unsure of what else to say. I want to be there for Heather, but I've had to shut down my emotions so much lately it's hard feeling anything, for anyone.

"Officer Ramirez told me what happened to Bryce," Heather says. "I'm so sorry, Sera. Are you okay?"

"I'll be fine," I assure her. "You have enough to worry about. Is there anything I can do for you?"

"Oh, Sera," Heather sighs. "I'm an expert at deflecting, so I know it when I hear it. You don't have to do that. I have a great support system. Don't worry about me, or the trial. I'll let you know how it goes, okay?"

I breathe a sigh of relief, though part of me feels guilty. I've always been in the role of boss or mentor for Heather. It feels odd to have her looking after me. But I almost have no other choice than to accept it. I don't think I could handle being involved with Daniel's trial right now, even if I wanted to.

"Thanks, Heather," I respond gratefully. "I'll talk to you soon."

"Bye, Sera."

Once she's hung up, I realize Charles hadn't said a word about Daniel's trial these past two days, either. As his father, I can imagine this is almost as hard on him as it is on Heather, though obviously in a very different way. I vow to check in with him the next day and call it an early night.

~

CHARLES IS UNCHARACTERISTICALLY UNAVAILABLE for the remainder of the week. I take the hint and leave him alone. I myself, having perfected the art of burying my emotions in work, can hardly fault him for it.

But I'm shaken from my own determined head-down stance on Friday afternoon when Emily calls.

"Hey, Em, what's up?" I answer warily.

"Hey, Sera," Emily replies, already sounding reluctant. "Would it be possible for you to bring the rest of Bryce's things to Mom's tomorrow?"

Something tugs sharply inside my chest. "Of course," I reply. "Am I going to be able to see him?"

"That's actually kind of the point," she responds. "Bryce has started asking about the accident. There's so much that opened up, and he wants to talk to you."

I freeze in my chair. "What does he know?" I ask tensely.

"That he was protecting someone in an elevator when he was attacked," she responds. "Naturally, he wanted to know who. So we told him it was you. He actually seemed more satisfied by that answer than I thought he'd be. I think he thinks that's why you were at the hospital last week. That you were a client."

I laugh humorlessly. "Well, technically speaking, I was," I reply. "You really didn't tell him anything else?"

"Not yet," she admits. "He's still taking a lot longer to process things. We've been careful not to overwhelm him. But the doctors say he's already improved a ton, so I think he can handle more."

"Has he been seeing Madison?" I ask bluntly.

"Do you really want to know about that, Sera?" Emily asks timidly.

"I need to know where he's at if I'm going to talk to him," I reply snappishly.

Emily doesn't respond for a long while. "They've talked a few times," she finally discloses. "But he's agreed not to jump into anything. Or back into anything, from his point of view."

"Okay," I say, trying not to die inside that he's

talked to Madison multiple times, but I haven't been allowed anywhere near him. "I'll talk to him. What time?"

"Ten?" she offers.

"Fine. I'll see you then," I respond tersely.

"Thanks, Sera," Emily replies, sounding relieved. "I know it won't be easy for you. I appreciate it."

"I love you, Em, but I'm not doing it for you. I'm doing it for Bryce," I say tiredly.

"I know," she agrees.

When I hang up, I find going back to work impossible, so I trudge home to pack Bryce's things. And that night, the nightmares return.

❧

ON SATURDAY MORNING I FIND MYSELF TOO NERVOUS to eat. And tired as I am, I try to limit my coffee intake so as not to be a shaky mess. Though coffee or not, I end up a twisted ball of nerves as I unload the duffel bags from the car, lugging them individually to the door before ringing the bell.

Emily answers, looking as nervous as I feel.

"Hey, Sera," she greets me, pulling me into a warm hug.

I squeeze her back hard, gratefully accepting the last shot of comfort and warmth before I enter the house. We each drag one duffel bag into the foyer, leaving them there to be dealt with later.

"Where's your mom?" I ask curiously as she leads me into the living room.

"She's out shopping with Aunt Char," Emily responds. "She thought it might be less overwhelming if there were fewer of us here."

I sigh inwardly, unsure of whether I agree, but realizing ultimately it doesn't matter. "And where is he?"

"In his room," Emily replies softly as we settle on the small, grey-blue settee in the lush living room. "Are you really up for this?" Her blue eyes look probingly into mine, and I avert my gaze quickly.

"Yes," I reply tersely, unwilling to admit exactly how much I *need* to see him. How much I miss him. "How is he doing?"

"They were way off on his cognitive skills," she responds. "Or he just recovered that quickly. He has trouble with complicated sequences, but if they weren't testing him I'd never know there was anything different. Except the memory thing, of course."

"Of course," I allow. "And how is that?"

Emily gives me a heartbreakingly sad look. "Still no change," she replies. "He accepts whatever we tell him, but as far as he's concerned, it's July of 2017."

"Wait, I thought he was eighteen months behind? That's only fifteen," I respond, confused.

Emily shrugged. "We were wrong. He's been able to be more specific about his last, complete memories, and they end around July of last year," she replies.

"Is that better?" I ask.

Emily shrugs. "The doctors say yes, a little. Less to get back anyway. But still not enough," she acknowledges.

"No," I agree. "Still not enough. Anything else I should know?"

Emily eyes me warily. "He gets pretty agitated when we tell him too much at once. When he can't remember important things. It's why we haven't tried to get you two talking again. So just be careful, okay?" she asks.

I nod and take a deep breath. "Well, let's do it then," I say.

She leans over and gives my hand a reassuring squeeze before rising and striding purposefully from the room.

In no time at all, a heavier set of footsteps approaches. I don't dare look, holding my composure around me like a shield as long as I can. I only look up as he settles into the larger settee across from me.

He looks so normal. His chestnut hair has been

buzzed down, and he's leaned out a bit. I'm sure they're not allowing him to exercise yet. But he looks healthy, and more relaxed than I'd expect given what he's learned recently. His blue eyes fix on mine, but with none of the fire and warmth I'm used to seeing in them. It hurts, on some level, but I ignore it.

"That's your mom's spot," I say reflexively.

His mouth tugs up into a small smile. "You've been here before," he responds. His smile quickly fades, and I can see the air of grief about him.

The sunshine around him when he woke has been dulled by his expanding awareness of reality. Of the loss of his father. But he's nowhere near as devastated as he was the first time. Though there was so much else going on then.

"For your father's funeral," I admit in partial truth, baldly addressing the elephant in the room. "I'm so sorry, Bryce."

"Thank you," he responds quietly. He runs a hand over his buzz cut in such a Bryce way that there's another sharp tug of pain at my insides. "It's a lot to take in, even outside of everything else that's going on."

"How are you doing with all of this?" I ask him, gesturing around me metaphorically.

He shrugs. "In some ways, it's fine. I'm a roll-with-the-punches kind of guy. But knowing something and accepting it are two different things," he responds. And instinctively I realize he's talking about his company. That he'll once again need to accept running Hoyt Corporate Services at some point.

"Bryce, not only do you not have to, but you shouldn't worry about anything right now," I say, catching his eye. "Dealing with the loss of your father is enough. You don't have to think about everything that follows. I talked to your mom. The company is in good hands — your VP seems perfectly capable. I think everyone understands you need time to heal and figure out what's right for you in this new life of yours."

Bryce looses a deep breath. "Thank you," he replies. "That actually helps." He looks at me curiously. "How did you know that's what I was worried about?"

I consider that and decide to be as honest as I can. "Because I was around when you dealt with this the first time," I admit. "And I knew you pretty well, once."

"Really?" he asks skeptically. "Because I couldn't have known you more than a year or so."

I huff a dry laugh. "We've actually only known each other for five months," I admit. "I hired you during a rather difficult situation at my own company."

"Ah, so you are a client," he responds. "And not a friend of Em's."

"Oh, I'm friends with Emily," I correct him. "But yes, I'm a client of yours. Or was, anyway."

"So I stopped the bad guys?" he asks with a grin. "I'm glad it wasn't for nothing then."

"You protected me," I agree. "More than you know. And I'll be forever in your debt."

Bryce leans forward, his smile mellowing into something more thoughtful. "We were dating, weren't we?"

His expression is still so casual, I know it's not a memory. Just Bryce, putting the pieces together like he always does. In a way it's reassuring. In a way, another small fragment of hope dying.

"Yes," I admit.

Bryce nods. "Every time I asked Emily where my things were, she dodged the question. And then you show up with them, again. So I figured as much, but thank you for being honest with me," he responds.

"You're welcome," I reply slowly. "But I don't know any other way to be."

Bryce laughs. "That's refreshing. Everyone around me right now seems to want to shield me from the truth," he remarks. "Don't get me wrong, I under-stand why, but it gets old fast."

I smile vaguely in response, and at the knowledge of all I'm not telling him. "I can understand that. But being honest and telling the whole story are two different things. Though when you're really ready, I'm happy to do both," I reply. He leans back again, considering me thoughtfully.

"Are you, now?" he murmurs. The question and its tone remind me of things he used to whisper in my ear and my insides clench in response, but not in the good way. "How about most of the story?"

I spread my hands in invitation. While in some ways talking to him is difficult, in other ways it still feels like the most natural thing in the world, as it's always been between us. Except that I can't sit with him, wrap myself around him, taste his lips on mine. I shake myself, refocusing.

"How long were we dating?" he asks.

"A little more than a month," I reply.

"And I was living with you?" he asks archly.

The shock in his tone should hurt, but it doesn't. Even I always thought it was fast. But then, I fought against my feelings for him for so long it's not like we didn't know each other, not like if we'd just met and decided to shack up after days.

I shrug. "It made sense. You were protecting me," I explain. And so, so much more.

He eyes me skeptically. "I don't usually move that fast," he replies pensively.

"Me neither," I admit with a small, sad smile.

"Then why?" he asks curiously.

I can't think of a way to answer his question that doesn't require me laying my heart on the floor for him to stomp on with his lack of memory, his inability to reciprocate. And the longer I try, the less comfortable this becomes, the more like a poignant reminder of our current situation.

I shake my head, throwing off the pain. "That's not something I can explain," I respond. "If you remember someday, you'll understand. And if you don't, then it's moot anyway."

But meeting his gaze, I can tell he knows why. That we must have loved each other.

"Is any of this helping?"

"If you mean, is it making me remember, I'm sorry to disappoint you, but no," he admits. "But it's helping me to understand what happened and why. So thank you."

"You're welcome," I reply simply. "Do you have any other questions for me?"

"Not right now, no," he responds. "I think I just need some time to process all of this."

I rise from the couch. "I understand. You'll be fine," I assure him. "You always know what to do, Bryce. Just trust yourself, and you won't go wrong."

He looks at me curiously. "I can see why …" he murmurs, then shakes his head. "I'm sorry. I'll walk you out." He rises and takes a step toward me.

But looking up at him, into his gorgeous face, his body as close to mine as it has been since that night, it's all too much. I put up a hand, afraid of him coming closer. He's exactly my Bryce, still. Observant, logical, considerate, kind, and heart-breakingly handsome. It's too much to bear.

"I know the way. Take care, Bryce." And without another word I turn and leave.

FIFTEEN

I stumble through the rest of the weekend, a prisoner to my own malaise. Before it's over, I decide to preemptively make plans for the following weekend to stave off further wallowing. I haven't seen or even really talked much to my mother in a while, so I make plans to visit. And, as an afterthought I ask Hunter if he wants to get together. That set, I dive back into protection mode, deeply burying myself in work.

And it's a good thing too, as after being in and out of the office so much these days, there's plenty to do. I find myself getting in early and staying late every day. Charles is happy for the relief and progress, and I don't have to think about anything but zoning permits, building materials, and the like.

On Thursday afternoon Heather calls and asks me to meet her for drinks the following day. Since I wasn't planning on heading up to my mom's place until Saturday morning, I agree. Besides which, my interest is piqued as she won't say anything about the trial, and I haven't dared talk to Charles about it since he's made it obvious he'd rather pretend like it isn't happening. I try not to think about the fact that Bryce doesn't remember any of it.

When I stride into the bar on Friday evening, I find myself anxious to hear whatever it is she has to share. I spot her waving at me from a small table on the far side of the room, her long black braids twisted prettily into a bun atop her head. And based on the barely suppressed grin on her face, I know she has good news.

I rush over to her, throwing my arms around her. She embraces me back fiercely, laughing and crying.

I pull away, keeping a firm hold on her shoulders. "Good news, then?" I ask brightly.

She squeezes my arms and nods. "The best," she responds. "Guilty. On all counts. Unanimously. They recommended the maximum sentencing, and he was given a sentence of seven years at a hearing this morning."

I sink onto the barstool, relieved that at least

something is going right. "Oh Heather, I'm so glad," I admit. "You must be so relieved."

"Beyond," she acknowledges. "I was afraid, at first, that since neither you or Bryce …" a deep blush appears on her dark skin. "I'm sorry, Sera, I didn't mean to …"

I hold up a hand. "It's okay," I assure her. "I know it must have been disheartening that neither of us were there. But I'm glad it worked out, and you've come out on the other side all the same."

"Me too," she confesses. "And I'm sorry, again. I know he probably doesn't remember how much he helped me, but I wish I could thank him anyway."

I swallow against the lump forming in my throat. "Me too," I reply softly. "Someday, perhaps."

Heather considers me carefully for a moment. "Shall we talk about something else?" she asks quietly.

"Yes, please," I respond, smiling. "And alcohol. Lots of alcohol."

We both laugh, and I go to the bar for our drinks. And we spend the evening drinking and talking about what a bastard Daniel was at the trial, Heather's job, my job, and everything in between. It's a welcome reprieve from, well, everything else.

❧

It was so nice, in fact, I don't even regret waking up slightly hungover on Saturday morning. And the pain in my head is easily put aside with a good breakfast, coffee, and a handful of ibuprofen. By the time I'm halfway to Bellingham, I find I'm actually even able to enjoy the ride.

Despite the early November chill in the air, the clouds have parted, and the sun plays spectacularly on my pastoral surroundings as I make my way between towns. I always forget how calming this drive can be, and all the little sights on the way that remind me of going home — the expansive garden store Mom and I always liked to trek to on the odd weekend, the apple cider barn where we spent fun fall days, and the vast, marshy fields filled with huge, white geese at certain times of the year.

By the time I arrive at my mom's house, I'm feeling more relaxed than I have in weeks. A twitch of the curtains tells me I've been spotted, so I'm not surprised when my mother comes rushing out the front door.

And I do something I don't think I've ever done. I leap out of the car and race into her arms. She holds me tightly, only letting go at my signal.

"Welcome home, darling," she says.

The love in her voice wraps around me, warming my aching heart. As I'm still holding her closely by the arms, I notice for the first time her hair, once a few shades darker brown than my own light brown, is now streaked more gray than not. And her hazel eyes, which are just like mine, are couched with creases. I realize she must have looked something like this for a while. But there had always been distance between us, even as we've grown closer lately. I'm ashamed it's taken such tragedy for me to be this close to her, to really see her.

"I love you, Mom," I declare spontaneously.

"Oh," she replies in surprise. "Well, I love you too."

Her smile causes me to pull her in for another tight hug.

"What brought that on?"

I pull away and go to retrieve my bag from the car. "Life is too short," I reply. "Too precious not to say it." I close the trunk and approach her. "I'm sorry it took me so long to realize that."

My mom shrugs and holds the front door open for me. "I can't say I blame you," she admits, following me into the living room. "Our relationship has never been easy."

I huff a dry laugh. "That's an understatement," I agree, smiling. I drop onto the old, flower-patterned couch with a sigh.

My mom takes a seat in the armchair next to me,

eyeing my warily.

"But I'm glad I'm here now."

"Me too," she replies. "You've been pretty tight-lipped about everything that's been happening. I've been more worried than I cared to admit. But I didn't want to press."

I nod. I know I've been withholding all but the necessary information from her for some time. And though I'm learning to trust her again, it's all been a lot. And I've barely spoken in depth about it to anyone. Even Allie, with everything she'd been going through, I'd kept at a certain distance. My main confidant of late had been Bryce, or occasionally Emily, but obviously the former is no longer an option and the source of most of my sorrow, and the latter, well, now it's so very complicated. So really, it's a good time to let my mother in a little more. Because I need it. And I think she might too.

"I appreciate that," I respond. "But I'm ready to let it all out. I think I need to, so I can move forward."

My mother raises an eyebrow. "You've given up hope," she guesses. "That he'll remember."

I blink back tears. "I'm starting to," I admit. "And I know it hasn't even been a few weeks yet, but there's *nothing*. No indication that he remembers me at all."

"Maybe you should give him a chance to get to

know you again," she suggests.

"I just don't think he's there," I reply. "He's got so much to absorb. And honestly, I don't know if I have the strength to love him like I do, to want him, when he barely even knows who I am." I shake my head and laugh through the tears that have started falling. "I don't know how he did it for so long. Hell, he had it worse — he had to watch me be with someone else first."

My mother's hand slips over mine. "This is different," she says. "He was in love with you, and that's a very theoretical thing. He didn't know what it was really like to be with you. For you, well, you two were in love and together, completely. And now you know, really know, what it is that you're missing."

Her words break my heart on a level I can barely handle. Tears fall unreservedly down my face at their truth. And I know I'm not strong enough to go from what we were, to what we'd have to be. I shake my head, trying to throw off the tears, the sorrow, but they just keep coming.

I feel my mother slide onto the couch next to me and wrap her arms around me.

"Let it all out, baby," she encourages me.

So I bury my face in her chest, and I do.

∾

AFTER A COMFORTING DAY AND NIGHT WITH MY mother, Sunday dawns and I prepare to meet Hunter at a local diner for breakfast. Still plagued by nightmares, I'm exhausted and defeated, but somehow looking forward to spending time with my half-brother anyway.

I pick him up from our father's house, purposely avoiding going in. Thankfully, Hunter bounds out and hops in the car before either of his parents catch on.

"Hey, Hunter," I greet him, pulling quickly away.

"Hey, Sera," he replies. "Figured you wouldn't want to deal with the old people."

I laugh drily. "Thanks," I reply. "What's new? Got a job yet?"

"Nah, there's really not much here," he replies.

"Oh," I say, unsure of how to respond.

"Where's Bryce?" Hunter asks curiously.

Thankfully, I was prepared for that question. I'd purposely arranged our meeting via text, so I had time to figure out what I wanted to say.

"Bryce and I aren't together anymore," I reply evenly. And I leave it there. I know he won't question it.

"That sucks," Hunter remarks. "I liked him."

"Me too," I reply softly.

Over breakfast, Hunter tells me about how he's moving to "confined" art — aka actual canvas or space that's *meant* to be painted. He thinks he might want to be an art teacher or something along those lines, so it's his attempt at going "mainstream."

I'm so not an artist, but the conversation is entertaining in a way I can't even quite explain. But in any case, it's clear that Hunter is tired of his dead-end life and he wants out. And as we finish eating, something occurs to me.

"You know, there are bound to be a lot of opportunities in Seattle," I bait him.

Hunter pushes his empty plate away and nods. "There is a really great artist's community. I've thought about moving there, but I don't really want to have to work at a fast food place just to be able to afford to share a place with twenty other dudes," he replies.

I smile mischievously. "Then I have the perfect solution," I respond lightly.

He looks up, brushing his hair out of his eyes.

"You should come live with me."

His eyes widen. "In your condo? Seriously?" he asks disbelievingly. "I don't think I could afford the rent."

I laugh. "You don't have to pay me anything," I clarify. "Just pull your weight. I could use the company. Really." I hope I'm not inviting something painful and awkward, but it seems like a pretty great solution for both of us right now. "And if it doesn't work out, no harm done."

He considers me pensively for a bit. "You do seem like you could use an assistant," he allows.

I chuckle at the idea. "How so?" I ask curiously.

"Well, you work a lot, right?" he asks.

I nod in agreement.

"So you could probably use someone to like, do your grocery shopping, pick up your dry cleaning, that sort of thing, right?"

"Yeah, I guess I could," I admit. "Think you're up for the job?"

Hunter, uncharacteristically breaking his carefully cool façade, grins eagerly. "Hell, yes!" he exclaims. "When can I move in?"

"Whoa there," I caution him. "Don't you want to talk to your parents first?"

"Sera, please," he scoffs. "I'm twenty-three. I don't need their permission."

I suppress a smile. "All righty then," I allow. "I'm going back later this evening. You can join me. Or I can come pick you up next weekend." But I already know which he'll choose.

Hunter has regained his carefully indifferent pretense. "Might as well go with you when you're already here," he replies with a shrug.

I bite back a laugh. "It's a plan, then."

∽

WHEN I TELL MY MOTHER THAT AFTERNOON SHE IS, understandably, skeptical of the arrangement, but true to her word that she wants to support me on my terms, she doesn't say much. Neither does my father, to whom I say very little as he helps Hunter load his few possessions into my car. Thankfully, I somehow manage to avoid meeting Barb, Hunter's mother. I've been through enough lately, and that's not really something I'm ready to do yet.

Hunter and I banter about the various things to do in the area, though he's clearly already got his own agenda.

When we get home, I get him settled in the guest bedroom, give him a key, and show him how to work the security system.

As I go to sleep that night, I'm hopeful for the first time in a while that the future holds something besides the painful recovery I know I still have before me. But it's not enough to stave off the nightmares.

I wake in the dark, panting, a garbled cry dying on my lips. I hold my breath for a moment, hoping I didn't wake Hunter. But his room is far enough away that, after a few moments, I decide he likely didn't hear me. As my dreams, and my reality, catch up with me, I roll over and cry myself back to sleep.

SIXTEEN

As the week dawns once more, I hunker down into work but try to keep more reasonable hours. Hunter seems to be just fine on his own, but I don't want him to feel like I've forgotten him. He's surprisingly easy to live with, and just as he promised, has done all manner of chores and errands from go. So I'm thankful when, early in the week, I have an idea that takes practically no effort to implement, that I'm hoping will make him feel like it's really his home.

There are four bedrooms in the condo — my own, my office, the guest bedroom now occupied by Hunter, and the nearly empty fourth bedroom. I clear the few boxes and forgotten pieces of exercise equipment out of the last room, leaving it bare. And the next day at lunch I go to an art supply store and pick up a range of canvases, brushes, and paints.

It takes some stealth to get it all into the room without Hunter noticing. I have to wait until he disappears on Wednesday evening to grab a few things from the convenience store down the block to set it all up. Once he's back, I giddily lead him upstairs.

"Dude, you're like totally freaking out," Hunter laughs as I pull him toward the room.

"You will be too," I singsong at him as I open the door.

He walks in, his mouth dropping open instantly at the spread of supplies. "This is for me?" he asks, clearly astounded.

"You deserve a place to work," I say, shrugging. "This is your studio now. Do whatever you want with it."

He looks at me skeptically over his shoulder. "Can I paint the walls?" he asks slyly.

I laugh. "Go for it," I reply. "This place could use some color."

Hunter smiles deviously. "Be careful what you wish for, Sera," he singsongs back at me.

It might be the first time he's joked with me, and I can't help but burst out laughing. And it feels damn good to really laugh again.

∽

BUT AS IT ALWAYS SEEMS, I'M ABRUPTLY BROUGHT back down to Earth on Thursday when Bryce calls. Reflexively, I answer, kicking myself almost immediately.

"Hello?" I say tentatively, hoping maybe it was an accidental butt-dial.

"Hi Sera, it's Bryce Hoyt," he responds.

As if I could ever forget his deep, calm, and sexy voice.

"I know. Hi, Bryce, how are you?" I ask warily.

"Good," he replies. "I'm cleared to resume normal life, mostly. So I've moved back to my own place."

My heart sinks. His apartment is barely ten minutes from mine. Knowing he'll be that close again has my pulse racing, and not necessarily in a good way.

"Oh?" I ask as calmly as I'm able. "Does that mean you're going back to work?"

"Yes, though only part time at first," he responds. "On a trial basis."

"That's good?" I hazard. Something inside me snaps at the superficiality of the conversation. "I'm sorry, why are you calling, Bryce?"

He doesn't respond immediately, and my throat

starts to constrict in a way that's becoming all too familiar.

"I was hoping we could talk this weekend. Face to face," he explains.

I note that he doesn't say why, and it makes me wonder just enough.

"Okay," I agree. "When and where?"

"My place okay? Saturday morning? Does nine a.m. work for you?" he offers.

"Yes. I'll see you then," I agree. "Bye, Bryce."

"Bye, Sera."

∾

NEEDLESS TO SAY, THE REST OF THURSDAY AND Friday are torture. I barely sleep on Friday night. Dressing on Saturday morning, I feel like a shell of myself. I pull on a dark, woolen sweater dress over black tights. Dark clothes for a dark mood. I don't bother dolling up, but as I come across the diamond earrings Bryce gave me, I can't help putting them on. It's a small bit of what we were that I can cling to through whatever happens.

By the time I get to Bryce's door, my feet are practically leaden, every step requiring immense effort, as if my whole body is protesting against the emotional torture of seeing him again.

I knock dully, and he answers, wearing jeans and a white T-shirt, looking wholly like himself again. Even the muscle definition in his arms has returned, his short hair lengthened ever so slightly.

"Thanks for coming," he greets me, stepping aside to let me in.

I stop awkwardly just inside the door, afraid it's presumptuous to do anything else.

He walks around me, but stops and turns back, as if he were about to extend an invitation to sit down. But something halts him, and he pauses, too close, looking down at me.

His right hand reaches up and, before I can even register, fingers the diamond stud in my left ear. He stares at it intensely for a moment. Frozen in place, all I can do is watch him, his beautiful face so close, his blue eyes dark and penetrating. I wonder suddenly if he recognizes them, if he's remembered, and my breath catches in my throat.

But too soon, he shakes himself, stepping back. "Those are beautiful earrings," he remarks nervously. "They suit you."

And I can only think of the last time he noticed them, when he told me he wanted to see me wearing nothing but these earrings.

But when he looks at me again there is no hint of

recognition, none of the fire that was there that last time. And I'm still too frozen to respond.

He gestures to the living room. "Please, sit down."

He seats himself in the leather armchair, so I take the couch next to him. But far enough away for comfort.

"You look well," I offer. "How is your rehab going?"

He runs a hand over his hair, and I have to look away. Some gestures are just so *him* it hurts. Not just because of the reminder of what he was, but that damn undying hope that, if he still acts like himself, that his memories are still in there somewhere.

"Cognitive skills are all back," he responds. "But zero on the memory front." And there it is. A month later. Confirmation that my Bryce hasn't come back and may never.

"What's the prognosis?" I can't help asking.

Bryce shrugs. "It's a coin toss. But they're concerned that *nothing* has come back yet," he admits. "Usually *something* does. And then piece by piece, more will."

"What does that mean? Is it all just … gone?" I press.

Bryce leans forward. "They won't say that," he replies carefully. "But Mom, Char, Em, you … I see the disappointment on all your faces. And for that reason alone I won't give up."

"What about Madison? Does she seem disappointed?" I ask pointedly.

Bryce's eyebrows shoot up. "Ah. So you know about Madison."

I roll my eyes. "Of course I do," I reply tersely. "And if you don't remember anything before sixteen months ago, then your brain still thinks you've been dating her for the last three years."

Bryce runs a hand over his mouth. "Yes, it does. And not just my brain. There are still feelings there," he admits.

I huff a joyless laugh. "Good ones?" I ask sarcastically.

"Mixed ones," Bryce allows. "And if I'm being honest, Sera, while I can't remember you, when I look at you …" He trails off, but he has my full attention now.

I press my lips together, not trusting myself to speak.

"There are feelings there too. But without the memories, it makes no sense. It's like trying to grab smoke."

And I know what he's saying. "But you do have memories of Madison," I respond with a snort.

"Except the ones that caused you to break up with her in the first place."

Bryce spreads his hands out in front of him. "I can't help that," he replies. "And I don't know what will happen with my memories. All I can do is react based on what I know."

I nod, understanding. He's going back to Madison. And I don't even need to ask if she'll take him back. She will. The conniving, superficial, gold-digging bitch.

"You're a good man," I respond, looking down into my hands, avoiding my eyes. "Better than she deserves." Tears well in my eyes and I feel so sick it's all I can do to sit here, still and quiet.

"I'm sorry," Bryce says softly. "I don't want to hurt you. But I'd rather regret doing something than doing nothing."

My eyes snap to his, unable to believe that I just heard those words come out of his mouth. The very words I spoke to him when I went after Alessandro.

Insane laughter bubbles out of me. I shake my head, a few tears spilling out. "I'm sorry," I gasp, reining myself in. When I've managed to collect myself, I look back up at him. "The universe has a very sick sense of humor. Why did you ask me to come here, Bryce? Because I know it wasn't to tell me that you're getting back together with Madison. I mean, obviously you are, but I'm sure that's not why you wanted to talk to me."

"No," he agrees. "And after telling you that, I feel like a complete asshole for even asking, but I was hoping we could be friends."

I twist my fingers together, choosing my words carefully.

"You're not an asshole," I respond. "But I'm not capable of being your friend right now, Bryce. Please understand that, while the thought of losing you is unbearable, to me it feels like I already have. And to be reminded of that over and over, well, I'm just not that strong. I've been through too much."

Bryce nods understandingly. "I went through your file," he admits. "And I know that what I'm asking isn't fair." But he looks at me pleadingly nonetheless, and I nearly crack.

"I think it would be better for both of us," I reply. "If I weren't around, pining for what was. Because I can't look at you without thinking about it. Not after everything that we've gone through. Everything that we were to each other."

"I'm sorry, Sera," he says again, and I know he means it. "I wish I remembered."

I laugh, wiping at the tears that have slipped over my cheeks. "Me too," I agree. "But you don't. And that's not your fault. But I'm at my limit, and I need to safeguard my heart again. I'm sorry I'm not stronger."

He looks like he wants to reach for me, but he stills himself. "I may not remember anything," he murmurs, "but I do know you're incredibly strong. What you've been through most people wouldn't survive. So I understand that you're doing what you need to do to."

"Thank you," I respond, rising from the couch. "Take care of yourself, Bryce, and be happy."

He follows me to the door. I pause at the threshold, looking back up at him. And I just can't help myself.

I slip against him, and before my arms are even around him, he's already wrapped his around me. While we hold each other tightly, I take one last, deep breath of his evergreen summer scent, listening to the steady and familiar beat of his heart under my cheek. And for one small moment, I'm home in his arms. But it's not long before I remember that he's not my home anymore. And the reminder that this man doesn't remember me, is just humoring me, causes me to extract myself, finally.

I drink in one last look at his face. "Goodbye, Bryce," I whisper.

"Bye, Sera," he murmurs.

And before I can do anything stupid, I go.

❧

Unfortunately, Hunter is in the living room when I get home, and there's no hiding my agony.

"Hey, Sera," he greets me.

"Hi," I reply tersely.

He studies my face for longer than I'm comfortable with. "Come on," he says, gesturing for me to follow him.

I contemplate protesting but decide I just don't have the energy. So I follow him up the stairs and into his studio.

Nothing could have prepared me for what I find. He must have bought more paint. Every canvas, every inch of wall is covered. And it's unbelievably gorgeous. It's a dark mass of blacks, blues, and purples with the occasional spots of bright color here and there. There are some recognizable motifs — a woman and a child, holding each other crying; an old man playing chess — all connected by abstract whorls, matrices, and lines.

It's a story of human emotion in three-hundred-sixty degrees, I realize as he shuts the door. I turn on Hunter, who is gazing at a portion of the painted wall as if it's nothing at all.

"This is unbelievable," I whisper. "You did all this in two days?"

Hunter shrugs and smiles. "I haven't really painted in a long time. I forgot how much fun it is," he replies nonchalantly.

I approach one of the canvases. Its colors are brighter than most of the surrounding areas. It speaks of warmth, love. And it breaks my heart.

"We're going to need more paint," I mutter.

Hunter nods. "We can paint it all over tomorrow and I can start again," he suggests.

I turn to him and shake my head. "No," I reply. "We're going to paint the rest of the house."

Hunter raises an eyebrow. "We?"

"If you'll teach me how to paint," I reply. "Yes. We."

He looks at me thoughtfully. "Painting, art, is literally pouring your soul out onto something," he says slowly. "Are you ready for that?"

I infer from the question that he understands how I'm feeling much more than I gave him credit for.

I close my eyes, roiling in the swell of emotion flowing through me. "I think it's exactly what I need."

ON SUNDAY AFTERNOON, WHILE HUNTER AND I PAINT the living room walls, my phone rings. Since I'm completely covered in paint spatter, it takes me a moment to find something to wipe my hands clean with before answering.

I don't actually make it in time but notice it was Allie, so I call her back.

"Hey, Allie, sorry I haven't called in a while," I greet her once she answers. I realize it's been a couple of weeks since we've spoken, which isn't usual for us.

"Oh, Sera, it's all good," she squeals.

"Whoa, you sound happy," I reply with a laugh. "What's up?"

"I'm pregnant, Sera," she shouts happily.

"Omigod!" I screech. "Congratulations, Allie!"

"Eeeee!" she squeals back. We both dissolve into giggles.

"This calls for a celebration. I'm taking everyone out to dinner tonight!" I exclaim.

"Yes!" Allie agrees.

"Great, I just need to get all this paint off of me," I reply, coming down off of the high of the news.

"Paint?" Allie asks, confused.

"I'll explain later. Um, Hunter will be coming with me too, which I'll also explain later," I reply.

"Okay, well, let me know when you're ready," she replies.

"Will do," I agree. "Bye."

"Bye, babe!"

I hang up, staring at my phone. The initial shock worn off, I realize it's going to be an evening of watching a happy, married couple celebrating their joyous news. And while I'm thrilled for them, it's like the final death of whatever hope had remained. Like embers bloomed back into fire, my heart burns with love lost. But I have to lock it up, cut off the oxygen. And safeguard my heart from the flames.

PART 2

"Ever has it been that love knows not its own depth
until the hour of separation."
— Khalil Gibran

NINE MONTHS LATER

The small, pink fingers wrap around my thumb. I marvel at his tiny strength, my heart overflowing with love.

"Look how hard he's squeezing!" I squeal, trying to balance my phone in the other hand and get Allie's attention.

"God, Sera, I think you have more videos of our kid than we do," Allie replies drily, coming over to observe baby Brian's tiny fist gripping me tightly. "He's only four weeks old. Too much radiation isn't good for him."

I scoff at her, even though I know she's just teasing. "Oh, please, it's a *cellphone*," I reply. "I'm not taking him on a walk through Chernobyl."

Brian squeals, drawing my attention back to him,

and I can't help but make silly faces until I think he's smiling. At this age it's so hard to tell. But I soak up every moment of it.

"So this is pretty much how I spend my week," Allie laughs. "How was yours?"

I glance up at her. "I saw Alessandro," I admit. "We had lunch."

Allie's eyebrows shoot up. "Well, that's something. It's been a few months, hasn't it? How's he doing?" she asks curiously.

I shrug. "Better," I respond. "Since he's taken Buone Case back over, he's got them on track again. He's back in his own place now too."

"He didn't ask you out again, did he?" she asks.

I huff a small laugh. "No. I think he's gotten the message," I reply.

"Who's gotten what message?" David asks, entering the room. He immediately starts cooing over Brian, though, and I doubt he'd hear a response even if I gave it.

I slide back onto the couch behind me and let him pick up the baby and take him to be changed. Being an aunt comes with the privilege of non-mandatory diaper changing services. And, you know, getting to sleep through the night.

"I swear, he's got the attention span of a gnat these days," Allie jokes as David leaves the room.

"Can you blame him? I dare anyone not to be distracted by that kid's cuteness," I reply.

Allie rolls her eyes. "So you and Alessandro, you're really just going to be friends?" Allie presses.

"Yes, Allie, I'm really not looking for anything right now, and our differences were way too fundamental," I reiterate for the thousandth time.

"If you say so," she replies, shrugging. "But I think it's about time you got back in the dating pool, one way or another."

I press my lips together impatiently. "Well, I'm going out with Em tonight, so maybe someone will manage to woo me before I get stinking drunk," I reply wryly.

Allie shoots me a dirty look. "Maybe ease off the booze and someone will *want* to woo you," she shoots back.

"Ah, see, there's the crux," I reply. "Maybe I don't want to be wooed. I'm doing fine on my own, thank you very much."

"You're not on your own. Your twenty-four-year-old brother lives with you," she reminds me. "Which, by the way, is also a huge deterrent for any would-be-wooers."

"Is 'wooers' a word?" I ask contemplatively. "It doesn't sound like a word."

"Deflecting," Allie says accusingly.

"Oh, look, a shiny object," I say, rising from the couch and grabbing my keys. "Gotta go, Allie!"

"Cute, real cute, Sera," she calls after me.

I wave dismissively over my shoulder. "See you for dinner tomorrow," I reply, then call down the hall. "Bye, David!"

"Bye, Sera!" he calls back.

And I leave before Allie can continue telling me how to run my love life. Or lack thereof.

∽

I'M TWO DRINKS IN, HAPPILY BUZZED, AND WELL ON my way to stinking drunk when Emily finally finds me at the bar on Capitol Hill.

"Hey, stranger," she greets me, wrapping me in a hug. "What's it been, like a month?" She slides onto the stool next to me.

"I've had a cute baby to fawn over, so sue me," I reply with a smile. "Wanna see pictures?"

Emily laughs. "Maybe later," she replies. "How are you?"

I shrug. "Okay. Work's great. Hunter is really coming along. The other designers say he's got real talent," I reply.

"Hmm," she replies noncommittally. By the look

on her face I know she's in Allie's boat, wishing my summary included a man.

"How about you? How are things going with John?" I hazard, trying to remember the name of the guy she was dating last time we met up.

"*Jack* and I are actually still seeing each other," she corrects. "Still pretty casually. It's only been a couple months."

"Sometimes that's all it takes," I respond, memories unwillingly pushing their way through my defenses. I shove them back, and we continue to make idle conversation for a while.

After another hour and a few more drinks, though, I can't stem the tide any longer.

"So how is your brother doing?" I ask, doing my best impression of barely interested. But Emily isn't fooled.

"He remembered a few more things," she admits. "But nothing major." I shrug, unsurprised. The few updates Emily has shared have all been the same. He remembered some paperwork or other that he'd stashed during the missing memory months. Or a movie he'd seen. Or the name of a client he'd spoken to back then but not since. But never anything about me. About us.

"Well, sounds like he's doing pretty all right then," I grouse. I hate talking about this, which is why

I usually avoid it. I must be in a more masochistic mood than usual.

"While we're on the subject, there's something else I've been meaning to tell you," Emily admits nervously. Something about her tone makes me down the rest of my margarita in one go.

"Go ahead," I reply warily.

Emily gives me a brief disapproving look. I suppress my annoyance, knowing deep down all the concerns about my drinking are not wrong, but too ruined to care.

"Bryce and Madison are getting married," she says quickly, flinching as the words tumble out.

My throat goes dry and my stomach churns. I fight a short battle with the urge but realize quickly that I'm going to lose.

"I think I'm going to be sick," I admit, bolting for the bathroom. I barely make it into the tiny two-stall bathroom, tumbling into the closest stall as the contents of my stomach reappear. I hear Emily come in behind me, and I feel the cool touch of her fingers against my neck as she gathers my hair in her hands, holding it back as I retch into the toilet.

When I'm finally spent, I sink onto the dirty, disgusting floor next to the toilet, a testament to the painful oblivion her revelation has caused. Emily crouches next to me, stroking my hair gently as I sob.

"I'm so sorry, Sera," she says soothingly. "I knew it would be hard, but I thought you'd moved past it. You barely ever ask about him anymore."

I shake my head violently. "I don't want to talk about it," I reply.

"Please, Sera," Emily begs. "I had to tell you. I need your help. He won't listen to me and you *know* Madison. She doesn't care for him, at least not more than share cares about his money, his reputation. She's manipulated him into this. We can't let …"

"*Stop*!" I screech, throwing my hands over my ears. "I'm sorry I asked. Because I don't really want to know. Any of it." I rise from the floor, swaying dangerously.

"Okay," she relents. "I'm sorry. Let's just get you to my place so you can sleep it off, okay?"

And I want to protest, but my world is still spinning, in so many ways. So I grunt my assent and let her lead me out of the bar, into a cab, and ultimately onto her couch. Where I promptly surrender to blissful nothingness.

～

I WAKE THE NEXT MORNING TO THE SMELL OF COFFEE. Cotton-mouthed and heavy-headed, I rise gingerly, wincing against the pain.

Emily drops into the armchair next to me, handing me a large cup of dark coffee. I guzzle it gratefully.

"I'm sorry about last night," she apologizes softly. I look up at her. Her hair is wet, and she's wearing a matched pink sweat suit. And she looks as contrite as I've ever seen her.

"No, I'm sorry," I admit. "I reacted poorly."

Emily laughs. "That's putting it mildly," she replies.

"When?" I ask softly.

Emily is silent for a moment, and I know she's debating whether or not to answer.

"October twelfth," she finally replies.

My head snaps up in disbelief. That's barely more than two months away. But it's the exact date that horrifies me.

"They're getting married on the anniversary of the fucking attack that did this to him?" I ask incredulously. "On my *birthday*, for fuck's sake?!"

Emily cringes and nods. "I pointed both of those things out in front of Madison. They picked it because of the attack. Supposedly to celebrate that he survived it, to turn it to something good," Emily spits. "But when she learned it was also your birthday ..." Emily's hands curl into fists. "The bitch looked *smug*, Sera. I wanted to punch her."

I have no words, I simply shake my head, looking

grimly into the dregs of my coffee cup. Eventually, I say the only thing I can. "He's his own man, Em. If he wants to marry her, what could I possibly say to change his mind?" I look down at my crumpled, smelly dress. "I need a shower."

Emily gestures to the bathroom. "Have at," she replies morosely. "I'll dig out some clothes for you."

"Just as long as it's not a matching purple sweat suit," I tease her.

She sticks her tongue out at me as I head to the bathroom.

The heat of the shower goes a long way to unraveling my tightly coiled nerves. And as I dry off, I spot the powder blue sweat suit, matching panties and all, that Emily left on the counter. I burst out laughing.

"Emily, you're a nutcase!" I call out. I hear her laughter floating under the door from the kitchen. I dress quickly, throwing my dirty clothes into a plastic bag, and emerge back into the living room.

But Emily's not alone. Bryce sits on the couch next to her. The sight of him is like a fist to the gut. He looks beyond handsome, bulkier than when I last saw him, his chestnut hair longer and curling around his collar just as it did when we first met. When his eyes meet mine, it roots me to the spot. My eyes flick to Emily, trying to convey my terror. But Emily looks so guilty that I know she planned this. And that she's not about to rescue me. She disappears back into the kitchen, leaving us alone.

"Hey, Sera," Bryce greets me softly.

"Hello," I reply quietly. I drop the plastic bag next to the couch and slink into the kitchen. I get right up next to Emily and poke her, hard.

"Sorry," she whispers. "I told you, I'm desperate."

I shake my head violently. "You can't do this to me, Em," I whisper back.

"Please," she begs. "Just try?" She looks so miserable, despite the angry pit in my stomach I shrug noncommittally, giving the tiniest of nods. She wraps her arms around me briefly before turning back to the food she's preparing.

I return to the living room, taking a seat on the small couch with Bryce, but as far into the corner as I can, so there's at least some distance between us.

"I made waffles," Emily announces, hopping up from her chair and waltzing into the kitchen.

Bryce gives me a side glance. "You didn't know I'd be here, did you?" he asks shrewdly.

I shake my head mutely, a thousand emotions swirling inside me. I'm not sure I could hold a waffle down right now if I wanted to, so when Emily returns with a plate, I surreptitiously slide it onto the coffee table, untouched.

"I'm going to get more coffee," I announce,

already unable to keep still in his presence. "Anybody want?"

Emily shakes her head, but Bryce puts down his plate and beats me to it. "I've got it," he replies, plucking my mug from my hands and striding easily into the kitchen. He returns shortly, handing me back a full mug. "Cream, no sugar."

I stare up at him, open mouthed. Emily looks at me questioningly.

"You … you remember how I take my coffee," I stutter.

Emily's mouth drops open.

Bryce looks unnerved. "I guess I do," he replies. "I didn't even think about it, I just did it." He shrugs and returns to his waffle, but the atmosphere in the room has changed to tense silence.

My eyes drift to the balcony, remembering the last time the three of us where here together and things were tense. I put my nearly full coffee mug down, unable to handle it any longer. "I should go," I say quickly, rising.

"Oh no, please, don't," Emily begs.

"Really, I have a lot to do today," I lie. "But thanks for breakfast."

"I hope you're not going on my account," Bryce pipes up. "I didn't mean to —"

"No, really, it's okay," I interrupt. "But hey,

congratulations. Um. On your engagement."

Bryce blushes and I pause awkwardly.

"Yeah, so, see ya."

I grab my purse and the plastic bag and bolt out the door as fast as I can walk. Running seems too obvious. But before I can make it to the stairs outside her door, I sense someone behind me even before the hand grabs my wrist. Large and warm, I know who it is without turning around.

"Hey," Bryce calls, pulling me to a stop. "I'm sorry. I didn't know Emily hadn't told you I was coming over."

I pull my arm out of his grasp, wrapping my arms around myself self-consciously. "It's okay," I assure him. "I just really need to go."

"Sera, if you knew me as well as you once said you did, you know I can tell when people are lying," he teases.

I smile vaguely, not taking the bait. "Was it your idea or hers?" I ask curiously. "Breakfast, I mean."

"Em's," he admits. "She said you wanted to talk to me."

And before I can stop it, a sarcastic laugh slips through my lips.

"Guess not, then."

"She wanted me to talk to you," I clarify. "To talk you out of marrying Madison, more specifically."

Realization dawns on Bryce's face. "Ah," he says. "Yeah. She's, uh, not too happy about that." He scratches the back of his head self-consciously.

I shrug. "Well, you're a big boy," I reply. "I'm sure you can handle her. And I should really get home."

"Yeah, of course, sorry. Good seeing you, Sera," he replies. His eyes search mine for a moment, and I'm almost distracted out of leaving. He too, looks lost in thought.

"Bye, Bryce," I say before I totally lose my nerve. I turn toward the stairs.

"Bye, gorgeous," he calls after me.

I stop short, whirling around to face him.

He looks as shocked as I am. "I'm sorry, I don't know why I … that was totally …" He presses a hand to his head.

"Are you okay?" I ask, taking a tentative step toward him.

He rubs at his temple for a moment. "I'm fine," he replies. "I just don't know why I said that."

"You used to call me that," I reply simply.

He looks down at me, clearly still struggling. "Then it was probably just a reflex," he replies, clearly embarrassed. I blush and look away, reading between the lines — he doesn't want me to think it meant anything and get my hopes up.

"Yeah, probably," I agree. "No worries. I'll, um … bye." I wave nervously and disappear down the stairs as fast as I can, my heart hammering in my chest.

∽

When I tell Allie the story at dinner, she's understandably shocked.

"Holy *shit*, Sera," she gasps. "His memories are coming back."

I shake my head vehemently. "After all this time? No. Nuh-uh. It's exactly as he said. A reflex. It's been ten months, Al, he's not going to start remembering now," I insist.

Allie looks at me skeptically. "Who are you trying to convince, sister, me or you?" she asks, smirking.

I glare at her. "I'm not putting myself through this," I insist. "I'm steering clear of all things Hoyt until after Bryce is married. I can't do this, Allie."

"Geez, okay, okay," Allie mutters. She gives me a sad look. "I guess I get it."

"Thank you," I reply.

But she's not completely wrong. I repeat the story to myself over and over again. Because eventually I will believe it.

EIGHTEEN

On Monday night, Hunter and I sit quietly at the table eating dinner. I'm so lost in my own thoughts, unable to stop replaying the conversation with Bryce in my head, that I don't notice Hunter openly staring at me.

"You okay?" he finally presses gently.

My eyes flick up to his. "No," I admit, dropping my fork. "I saw Bryce yesterday." I'd long since confessed the full situation to Hunter. It'd be impossible not to, having lived with him the last nine months, as well as working at the same company for most of that time.

"Shit," he replies.

I chuckle. "Yeah, that about sums it up," I agree.

"What happened?" he asks simply.

I shift uncomfortably in my chair but decide to just go with it. So I tell him what happened.

"Hmm," is his only response.

"You've got to give me more than that," I reply drily.

Hunter finishes his pasta and pushes his plate away. As he's wont to do, he sits silently for a while.

"We're more alike than you know," he finally replies, leaning back in his chair and meeting my curious gaze. "I have to protect myself too."

My brows scrunch together. "I don't understand," I admit.

Hunter sighs. "At this point it's hard to believe Bryce is actually getting better," Hunter clarifies. "So it's safest to protect yourself. Because even if he is, he's still getting married. So I get it. I get why you're holding back."

"What do you hold back?" I press curiously. I suddenly realize in the months Hunter has lived with me, he's never said a word about dating anyone. Perhaps he's as closed off as I once was. Or, am now, as it were.

An anxious, determined look spreads over Hunter's face. "You can't tell Dad."

I laugh. "Oh, Hunter. You know I can barely stand the man. I've only seen him twice since you moved here, and only because he insisted," I reply. "I hope you know you can trust me."

It kind of stings, thinking he might not, after all this time. And while we haven't exactly stayed up late talking about life and love and braiding each other's hair, the quiet bond we've shared painting and repainting the condo ad nauseum has been special to me. And so necessary for me to deal with everything. But maybe we're not as close as I thought we were.

"I know," he replies quietly. "There are just things I don't tell anyone. Well, one thing."

My finely honed intuition on when to stay quiet tingles. So I do. And as usual, after a stretch, it pays dividends.

"I'm gay, Sera." He studiously avoids my gaze.

And I find myself unsurprised. I'd thought perhaps he was asexual, but it never really mattered to me one way or the other. I'm certainly the last person to criticize anyone's love life, or lack thereof.

"Are you seeing anyone?" I ask nonchalantly.

Hunter looks at me. And I almost laugh. His expressions are all so similar, but I've come to know the subtle changes in his features well. The ever-so-slight arch of his left eyebrow betrays his shock.

"Oh, come on. It's 2019. So you're gay, who cares?"

"Dad would," he insists. "And there's already enough crap between us."

But his protests are a diversion. I don't miss that he didn't answer my first question.

"Who is he?" I push.

The corners of Hunter's mouth twitch as he rises and collects our dishes, taking them into the kitchen and loading them into the dishwasher. When he's done, he starts heading upstairs.

"Good night, Sera," he calls without turning around.

"I'm gonna find out!" I call after him.

I can hear him chuckling as he disappears into his studio. And I can't help laughing a little myself. And it snaps me out of my funk, if only a bit.

∾

I watch Hunter closely over the week that follows, but he's either the stealthiest motherfucker on the planet, or he's really not seeing anyone. I decide to follow him out of the house the following Saturday in one last-ditch effort to catch him at it. Even though I know I shouldn't. But I just can't help myself.

As I follow him into a busy coffee shop, I'm

distracted out of my pursuit as I run smack into Alessandro.

"Serafina!" he exclaims in surprise, pulling back the lidded cup in his hand to keep it from sloshing. "*Ciao*. I didn't expect to see you again so soon." He gives me his most charming crooked smile, and I have to laugh.

"*Ciao*," I reply. "*Come stai?*"

"*Bene*," he replies. "May I join you for a coffee?"

"Oh, but I don't want to keep you. It looked like you were leaving," I offer.

In truth, I'm not sure seeing him so often is a great idea. While he didn't press last time, I know he still holds out hope that he can win me back. It's admirable, if not a little annoying. And a good reminder why I don't go out very often. It's too easy to run into people you aren't expecting to see.

"Not at all," he assures me. "I have no plans today, just enjoying the beautiful weather. We must soak it up while we can."

I laugh. That is the Seattle way. We are hermits nine months of the year, sunflowers the other three.

"Okay," I relent. "Let me get a cappuccino and I'll meet you outside." As I approach the counter I also realize I'm starving, so I add a breakfast sandwich onto my order. Once I have my food and coffee, I wander onto the patio, looking for Alessandro. I spot him on the street side, people-watching.

I take him in for a moment as he's distracted. He really is every bit as handsome as he ever was, his dark brown hair now once again perfectly coifed in that messily styled manner, his beard tamed into a perfectly groomed accent to his sharp jaw and straight nose. Truly, he's the epitome of the gorgeous Italian man. Stubbornness and borderline narcissism included. Shaking my head, I proceed to the table to join him.

As I sit eating my breakfast, talking shop with him in the warm, sunny morning, I'm reminded though that sometimes it *is* nice to just enjoy someone's company on a beautiful day. It's been a long time since I've done something so normal. And, thankfully, he seems settled into the notion that a relationship of any kind is off the table, for now at least.

He's telling me a story about his new assistant when he stops cold, his eyes narrowing at something in the distance.

"Serafina," he says with a caution in his voice. "Are you speaking to the giant?"

I'm so taken aback by his question that I can't help but turn and follow his gaze. And I freeze when I see that Bryce is, in fact, approaching, walking hand in hand with Madison, his perfect five-foot-six, slim, blond beauty queen of a fiancée. My breakfast churns uncomfortably in my stomach.

"Fuck, fuck, fuck," I whisper, whipping my head back around.

"I'll take that as a no," Alessandro replies drily. "Maybe if we just …"

"Sera?" Bryce's voice cuts across Alessandro's attempted avoidance.

I sigh one last silent *fuck* in my head before plastering a smile on my face and turning around.

"Bryce!" I exclaim with false enthusiasm. "And Madison." I nod curtly at her. I don't miss that she wraps her arm possessively around his waist.

Bryce's eyes shift to Alessandro and his whole countenance changes. He narrows his eyes, his jaw clenched, his hand curling into a fist at his side. Alessandro looks at me confused, and the question in his eyes is clear, as I'm thinking it too. *He can't remember me, can he?*

"Bryce, this is my friend Alessandro Giordano," I say. "Alessandro, this is Bryce Hoyt, and his fiancée Madison Connolly."

Madison looks smug and well pleased that I know of their betrothal. She extends a hand to Alessandro, batting her eyelashes.

"*Piacere,*" she says sweetly.

"*Piacere,*" he replies genially, but uncharacteristically doesn't offer anything further. He looks to Bryce.

"I'm pretty sure we've met before," Bryce says thinly.

Neither man offers a handshake after Bryce's icy acknowledgement. Madison gives him a stern look, but he ignores her, keeping his eyes fixed angrily on Alessandro.

"Well, it was so nice running into you, but we have to be going," Madison declares, awkwardly pushing Bryce onward. "Ta!"

I flutter my fingers at their receding backs. "Bye now," I murmur.

"What the hell was that?" Alessandro asks, voicing my exact thoughts.

I look back at him, bemused. "I have no clue," I admit. "That was bizarre. He can't possibly remember you. He doesn't even remember *me*."

Alessandro looks at me appraisingly. "Are you sure about that?" he finally asks. "Hate is a very strong emotion. Sometimes stronger than love. It can be very hard to forget."

"Oh, please, Bryce never hated you," I respond reflexively. But suddenly I'm not so sure. "Did he?"

Alessandro laughs mirthlessly. "Yes, undoubtedly," he replies. "He made that quite clear."

I raise my eyebrows, but I don't ask. "I don't want

to know," I respond. "And it doesn't matter anyway. It's all water under the bridge."

Alessandro shrugs. "If you say so, *bella*," he murmurs. He looks at his watch. "In any case, it was lovely seeing you, but I must get going."

We clean up our table and head out. And with a friendly embrace, we go our separate ways. Though I'm still bewildered and disturbed. But moreover, I'm concerned that we may have upset Bryce, so, against my previous decision, I decide to call Emily and see if she can shed any light on it.

"He what?" she asks incredulously after I've explained what happened. "That's very weird. And very un-Bryce. He's never rude. To anyone. Even if they deserve it. *Especially* if they deserve it."

"Exactly!" I exclaim, satisfied that she's put to words what I for some reason couldn't. "I mean, maybe Alessandro is right? Maybe it's easier to remember someone you hate?"

"That makes no sense," Emily replies. "But I'll see if I can find out what it was all about without making it worse."

"Yes, please," I respond. "I may not be up for being bosom buddies with Bryce, but I certainly don't want to upset him, either."

"I'll let you know," she responds.

I thank her and hang up, still unable to shake my unease as I return home.

When I get back in the condo, Hunter is waiting for me with a grin.

"Boy, you must have gotten really lost after I ditched you at the coffee shop," he remarks airily.

Snapped out of my reverie, I laugh heartily. "You're a sneaky bastard, I'll give you that," I reply.

"What were you hoping to find?" he asks.

I shrug. "I'm curious, I guess. I just wanted to know if you're seeing someone or not. And obviously I'm not as stealthy as I thought I was," I allow. And I'm silently thankful that Hunter doesn't seem upset.

"In all fairness, I did dodge a direct question. I was practically begging to be followed," he responds.

"I take it then that there is a special someone?" I ask.

Hunter blushes, confirming my suspicions.

"You should bring him around sometime, then. I'd love to meet him."

"Okay, maybe I will," he replies cryptically before heading upstairs.

My curiosity about Hunter's beau fades quickly, the bewilderment at today's encounter slipping back to the forefront of my mind, despite my best efforts.

∾

I don't get respite from my concerns until the next day when Emily calls back after lunch.

"Soooo, I talked to Bryce," she opens.

"And?" I press.

"He doesn't know why he reacted that way," she replies, clearly frustrated. "He didn't really want to talk about it much. All he said was, and I quote, 'There was just something about the guy that rubbed me the wrong way.' As if that explains everything."

"And it doesn't," I agree. "Alessandro was just sitting there. He hadn't even spoken a word before Bryce got his panties in a twist."

"The doctor talked to us about lingering reflexes," Emily offers. "Sometimes, they're just there. And they don't necessarily mean you'll remember why you speak or react a certain way."

If any of Bryce's behavior had stirred hope in me, it's crushed completely at her words. It's been my own mental justification, but to hear that the doctors agree it doesn't mean anything is a finality I wasn't prepared for. And it tells me that despite my determination to keep my heart locked away once more, I haven't been all that successful, because I'm disappointed.

"That's good to know," I answer edgily. "Thanks, Em."

"Sorry, Sera," she replies softly.

Closing my eyes, I focus on staying calm and logical. "There's nothing to be sorry for, Emily. I just wanted to make sure Bryce is okay," I say. It's not untrue. "Take care, okay? I'll talk to you later."

"You too," she responds, sounding wholly unconvinced. "Bye, Sera."

After I hang up, I realize quickly that it's going to be nearly impossible for me to turn my brain off. And I don't feel like painting. So I go to my other standby, and pull a bottle of whiskey out, settling into my favorite chair by the window wall to drown the memories. It takes a lot of alcohol, but eventually I get there. Not the best choice for a Sunday night, but I reason that the alternative is worse.

Later, as I stumble drunkenly to bed, I say a silent prayer that I figure out how to move past this. Before it kills me.

NINETEEN

On Monday night the universe flips the bird to my silent plea when, three glasses of wine into my new nightly drinking ritual, my doorbell rings.

Hunter is out doing god only knows who or what, so I'm left to stumble out of my chair and answer it. And I'm not pleased at what I find waiting on the other side of the door.

Madison stands on my doorstep in teetering heels and a tight, red dress that leaves little to the imagination, her blond hair piled carefully atop her annoyingly perfect head.

"I'm sorry, I don't think we placed an order for a conniving bitch," I say by way of greeting and dismissal, starting to swing the door closed.

Madison levels a glare at me and sticks her foot in the door, preventing me from slamming it in her face.

"If you care about Bryce at all, you'll want to listen to what I have to say," she snaps.

I pull the door open angrily. "And if you cared about Bryce, you'd leave him alone and go crawl back into whatever hole you crawled out of," I retort hotly.

Madison folds her arms across her chest smugly, still leaving her foot in the door. "I'm his *fiancée*," she reminds me. "You, on the other hand, are confusing him. He's a mess, no thanks to you and your boyfriend."

And despite myself, guilt weighs on me. "What do you mean, he's a mess?" I ask tensely, not even bothering to correct her about Alessandro.

"Seeing you two the other day, reacting the way he did, it bothered him so much he can't stop talking about it, thinking about it. He convinced something didn't heal properly, that he's having some sort of aftereffect that's going to give him an aneurysm or something," she spits angrily.

I narrow my eyes at her appraisingly. "You're not worried about Bryce," I reply accusingly. "This is about the wedding, isn't it?"

She throws her hands in the air. "Of course it's about the wedding," she says sharply. "He wants to *postpone* it, for fuck's sake! Until he's sure nothing is wrong. At least, that's what he says. But I think he's just waiting to remember something. And I am not going to —"

"What, let him out of your trap?" I cut her off with a laugh. "Of course not. Couldn't have him coming around and realizing you're only marrying him for his money."

"I'm not *only* marrying him for his money," she replies with deadly calm, leaning forward and lowering her voice. "You've fucked him, Sera. So you know how good he is. Why would I give that combination up?"

My palm itches with a desire to smack the smug smile off of the bitch's face. She's a special kind of fucked up to care more about her wedding than the health of the man she's marrying, not to say anything about his happiness. But tipsy as I am, I still rein myself in, knowing it will only hurt Bryce if we fight.

"Yes, I know how *good* Bryce is. In a way you never will. And I don't know how you found out where I live," I seethe through clenched teeth. "But get the fuck out of here and don't ever come back."

Madison straightens up, laying one last icy glare on me. "I'll go," she accedes. "But if you come near Bryce again it will be the last thing you ever do. You are not going to stop me from marrying him. Even if I have to force him down to the courthouse tomorrow."

I'm so disgusted I can barely look her in the eye without losing it. "Do you even love him?" I can't help asking.

And she laughs. The bitch *laughs*. "Who needs love when he's as rich and good looking as he is? And he's *so* eager to please. So don't even think about trying anything. I've got that man wrapped around my little finger, among other things," she says with an evil glint in her eye. "Just stay. The. Fuck. Away." She turns on her heel and marches down the hall.

I slam the door as hard as I can, rattling the frames on the walls. I walk back to the dining table where I'd placed my wine glass, gripping it nearly to the point of breaking as the anger boils over inside me. And before I know what I've done, I fling the glass into the kitchen, shattering it on the fridge, where the dark, red liquid drips ominously down the stainless steel.

I pace in front of the window wall angrily. A glance at the clock tells me it's too late to call Allie. And I decide immediately to stick to my first instinct and stop talking to Emily until this is all over. Because despite not wanting to give Madison the satisfaction of knowing it, I just want to hide from all of them and wait for it all to pass me by.

But what I really want more than anything right now is to punch something. Even though it's after nine o'clock at night. There's only one place I can think of to do that. And maybe it'll be exactly what I need to exorcise my demons. Or exercise them. Either way is fine with me.

I don't bother cleaning up my mess. I simply grab my keys, wallet, and phone, calling for a cab on my way downstairs.

It's not until I'm dropped off in front of the gym where Bryce taught me self-defense that I realize this may have been a stupid, drunken idea. But somewhere deep inside I can't shake the feeling that this is where it started. Where he drew the line, asked that I choose him with all of me. And this might be where I can take that part of me back, so I can just get on with my life. It's worth a shot, anyway. And if it doesn't work, maybe I'll at least get out some frustration.

I take a deep breath and go in, striding confidently toward the guy behind the front desk. He's big and bulky and covered in tattoos, much the same as the few guys scattered around the gym.

"Hey," he greets me. "What can I do for you?"

I chew on my lip self-consciously. "I have to ask you for something. And it's going to be weird."

∾

Turns out it wasn't so weird, and front desk guy has me set up in the room with the mats, a free-standing punching bag, and a pair of boxing gloves in no time. He leaves me to it with a grin and a shake of his head, and I wonder what kind of shit goes down here that he didn't even bat an eyelash at my request.

I throw my things into a corner and use a hair tie to pull back my long, wavy hair. I'm suddenly thankful I'd already changed for bed into capri yoga pants and a loose T-shirt.

I slip the gloves on, tightening the laces like he showed me, and square off in front of the massive black bag. I close my eyes and breathe deeply, picturing Madison's face. And I punch. And again. And again. Until I'm sweating and breathing heavily.

I step back to take a break. And once I've caught my wind, I let all the sorrow, all the angst, all the fear I've felt these last months pour out of me in an attack of such intensity that, were I in my right mind, would scare even me.

"Remind me never to piss you off."

I practically jump out of my skin, whirling around

to the voice that came from the door. My jaw practically hits the floor when I see Bryce, leaning against the frame, the casual tone of his greeting betrayed by the tense set of his jaw, the downturn of his gorgeous mouth.

And I'm too tired, too emotional for this. "What the fuck are you doing here?" I sputter, still winded, ripping off the gloves.

Bryce pushes himself up, striding slowly toward me. "I could ask you the same thing. How do you even know about this place?" he asks. "You're not exactly their usual clientele."

I look at him, bewildered on so many levels. I shake my head, unable or unwilling to answer.

Thankfully, he doesn't press, but he looks at me silently for a full minute. "Madison came home angry tonight. And I got out of her that she went to see you for a little chat."

I snort derisively. "That's one way to put it," I scoff. "I'd call it delusional ranting threats from a scheming bitch."

He looks thoroughly confused and it makes me laugh.

"Did she tell you she just dropped by for tea and scones and to make sure my invitation to the wedding hadn't gotten lost in the mail?"

He stops in front of me, looking down at me

disapprovingly. The proximity is more than I can handle, and my head swims.

"I don't know what happened between you two, and I don't really need to. I told her she had no right to disturb you. That you'd been through enough," he replies coolly.

"Damn fucking straight," I say emphatically, my anger clearing my senses. "But I didn't need you to track me down to make sure she didn't hurt my feelings. I'm a big girl. I'll get over it."

I make to step back, but he grabs my wrist, holding me in place. His tight grip betrays the emotion stirring under his cool exterior.

"Why here?" he demands. The intensity radiates from every pore of him, the heat from his fingers sizzling up my arm.

I want to ask him to stop touching me, but the masochist in me never wants it to end. I feel like I'm coming apart at the seams, and I can't stop it. Unable to rein it in, my composure finally slips.

"Because I'm torn in pieces again," I sob. "And this time I choose me. It's the only choice I have left."

His eyes go wide, staring into the distance, and his hand springs open. I pull my wrist to my chest, rubbing it with my other hand as if it could remove the effect he's had on me.

"Torn in pieces ..." he mutters, his eyes glassy.

He looks over at me, his eyes focusing rapidly. "I won't settle for anything less."

My heart stops in my chest and all the breath goes out of me. "Yes," I breathe. "That's what you said to me here. That if I chose you it had to be with all of me. That you wouldn't settle for anything less."

"Yes," he agrees, his stare going glassy again, his eyes unfocused. "I was teaching you to defend yourself." His eyes snap back again, and he steps forward, closing the distance between us. "Sera …"

Before I can even take a breath, his mouth is on mine, the familiar feel of his warm lips, the taste of his breath clouding my senses. I react instinctively, leaning into him. His hands find my hair, tugging the hair band out so he can run his fingers through the tangled waves.

It takes all of my strength to push him away. "No."

And my quiet protest causes a shift in him. "I'm sorry, I don't know why I …" he stutters and stops, clearly at a loss. Clearly horribly confused.

"It's just a reflex," I respond wryly. "It will pass."

He shakes his head. "No," he objects. "That was an actual memory." His eyes meet mine. "A complete one. But it's like … looking at a small piece of a big puzzle that isn't there." The sorrow in his voice practically incapacitates me.

And despite my own pain I find myself wanting to comfort him. But I remind myself he's not mine to comfort anymore. And despite coming into his first real memory of me in the ten months since his attack, it's one of the worst ones he could remember. Because it's a reminder of the day he thought I was still trying to dick him around, not realizing how much I was already in love with him. Not that I'm sure I realized it then, either.

"Go home," I respond dully. "Fuck your fiancée. It'll make you feel better. And forget about puzzles and memories. They'll just drive you mad." I grab my things from the corner and make for the door. Under my breath I mutter, "Trust me, I should know."

He huffs a sad laugh and I know he's heard me. But he doesn't try to stop me as I leave.

THE NEXT NIGHT I GO TO ALLIE'S AFTER WORK, unable to bear the thought of another miserable night of drinking. Plus, I figure Hunter will be happy to have the place to himself for a change.

And bouncing baby Brian on my lap is just about the only thing that's made me feel halfway normal in a while. I've finished catching Allie up on all the latest between tummy tickles and cooed adoration of Brian's cherubic cheeks.

"So what now?" Allie asks. I look up at her. She looks exhausted.

"Well, you could go take a nap while I hang out with this handsome little guy," I reply, tapping the baby on his adorable little nose.

Allie smiles. "Thanks, but I don't think I could sleep right now if I tried. I can only sleep when it's least convenient," she responds drily. "It's a whole thing."

"If you say so," I shrug.

"Seriously," Allie presses. "Are you going to be okay?"

I sigh heavily and set Brian down in his bouncy chair, rocking it lightly with my foot to soothe him. "Of course," I mutter. "I'll be fine."

"Fucked up, insecure …" Allie starts.

"Neurotic and emotional," I finish. "Yeah, yeah, yeah." I wave a hand at her dismissively. "Their wedding is in two months, Al. It's practically a done deal. And I'm so over it all. Hopefully, now that Madison has had her say they'll leave me alone."

"But what if they don't? You should really …"

"Hey, so, Hunter's gay," I interrupt, desperate to change the subject.

Allie's mouth pops open. "When did you find *that* out?" she demands.

I internalize a smug high five with myself for successfully changing the subject with zero tact. "Just a few days ago," I assure her. "He's bringing his boyfriend home for dinner this Friday."

"Wow," she mouths. "That's big." I nod.

"I was pretty thrilled he trusted me enough to tell me," I admit. "It kind of explains a lot, actually. He's worried about telling our dad, though. He said he didn't want him to know at first, but he finally admitted he doesn't want to have to keep it a secret forever, either. So, you know, I'm going to try to help him with that."

"Does his mom know?" Allie asks.

"No, but he's not worried about that part," I respond. "I mean, I understand why he's nervous. It's his dad. I wish I could lend him my ability to not give a shit what my parents think." Allie laughs.

"That would sure help," she agrees. "But he's lucky to have you in his corner."

"It's been good for me too, having him around," I admit. "With my luck his boyfriend will be fabulous, and they'll be getting married and I'll be all by myself again."

Allie reaches over and squeezes my hand. "You've always got us, babe," she assures me.

I squeeze back, smiling. "I know. Thanks," I reply.

But I suppress the urge to tell her it's just not the same. And I wonder if I'll ever have what Allie has. I look down and Brian is happily sleeping in his chair, sucking on the back of his sweet, pudgy little fist. I decide in that moment that, if nothing else, I'm going to be the best auntie there ever was.

TWENTY

unter's boyfriend, as it happens, is *not* fabulous and obviously *not* ready to follow my brother down the aisle into wedded bliss. Which actually is a good thing, since Hunter is only twenty-four.

It turns out his boyfriend, who is ten years his senior, is also the annoying IT guy at Sutton Developments, Graham Forrester. Will, the head of IT at the company I once owned, is now peers with Graham and complains about him to me all. The. Time. So it's unfortunately with preconceived notions that I welcome him into the house as my brother's boyfriend. And I'm a little ticked at Hunter for not warning me. I pull him aside as Graham gazes in awe at the window wall.

"What?" Hunter hisses as I pull him into the kitchen. "It's not against the rules to date a coworker, right?"

"No," I respond, exasperated. "But did you have date *that* coworker?"

Hunter smiles and shrugs. "Yeah, okay, so he's a little obnoxiously nerdy," Hunter allows. "But he's a cool guy when you get to know him. Just try, okay?"

I sigh and fold my arms over my chest. "Oh, I have," I reply. "But I'll play nice because you're my brother and I love you."

Hunter looks startled at the declaration. "Thanks," he mutters, blushing.

And for the first time, I feel like giving him a sisterly noogie. But I resist. I mean, I am thirty years old, after all.

Unfortunately, the evening goes about as well as I expect. That is to say, not well at all. Our conversations are forced and awkward, and Graham and I don't have much in common besides Hunter. And Will, of course, who Graham doesn't seem to like as much as Will doesn't like him. And Hunter isn't exactly a rife topic for conversation as he's always so taciturn, and it's hard to tease him.

But somehow, we make it through, and by the end of the night I find I don't dislike Graham quite as much as I thought I did. Hunter obviously cares about him, so that helps his case considerably. And when I wish them goodnight, going up to my room earlier than I ever would to give them some privacy, I don't miss the sweet smiles they share. And I'm happy, at least, that Hunter is happy. At least one of us is.

❧

FOR SOME REASON I FIND MYSELF AGREEING TO HAVE dinner with Alessandro the following weekend. Normally, I restrict our meetings to lunch only, to keep it friendly and casual. But he's tempted me with a feast at Marco's parent's restaurant, and I'd be an idiot to say no. Having taken me there once before, back when we were together, I remember it being like nothing I'd ever experienced, or have experienced since.

So I dress with care, selecting a silky black dress with red heels. I let my hair flow freely around me, perfectly shining and curled. I need to feel pretty again, but I carefully stay just this side of the line, so it doesn't scream, "You're getting lucky later." Hopefully, Alessandro has truly given up that pursuit.

Though when I answer the door that evening, he looks awfully tempting in a black suit, his white shirt open at the collar, his trademark sideways smile hanging on his full lips.

"*Buona sera*," he greets me roguishly.

"*Buona sera*," I respond, chuckling. "If you're trying to charm the pants off of me, you're wasting your time. I'm not wearing any." And with a wink I take his arm and let him lead me to the elevator.

"So I see," he remarks. "It's a good look for you."

Our flirtation continues all the way to the restaurant. I can sense it's completely harmless, as he seems happy just to see me smiling for once. And I realize it has been a while since I enjoyed myself so thoroughly. I decide to surrender to it.

We end up seated on our own, the restaurant arranged in its normal configuration.

"There's no event tonight?" I ask as he sees me into my chair.

"No, I just wanted to do something special. You deserve it. And I remembered how much you enjoyed being here the last time," he replies while taking his own seat. He starts examining his menu, and I can't help but stare at him for a moment, in slight awe of the sweetness of the gesture.

"*Grazie mille*," I say to him. "Really, Alessandro. I forget how thoughtful you can be."

He looks up and shoots me a wink. "Then perhaps I need to remind you more often," he teases.

"Perhaps," I muse. "Or perhaps I'm just suffering

from cabin fever. I can't remember the last time I went out in public."

The waiter arrives, and Alessandro orders for both of us. Anywhere else, with anyone else, I would never allow it. But it only makes sense here, in his extended family's restaurant, that he does so.

"So I trust the giant is over whatever it was about me that troubled him so," Alessandro offers after the waiter leaves.

"I imagine so," I respond. "They supposed it was a reflexive reaction. He doesn't really remember you."

"Nor you, it would seem," Alessandro replies.

"For the most part," I agree. Alessandro raises an eyebrow.

"And the least part?" he asks curiously.

"He had one memory surface. But that was a couple of weeks ago. I've made it a point to avoid the lot of them since," I admit.

"I see," Alessandro replies, folding his hands in front of him contemplatively. "Is that why you've holed yourself up lately?"

I weigh his question for a moment before answering. "Yes, I suppose it is," I allow.

"*Bella*," he starts, and the concerned tone in his voice already has me on my guard. "I hate to see you so affected. Listen. It may be presumptuous, but I'm going back to Italy in a few weeks. You should come with me. Take some real time off, have a vacation."

I can't help pulling a skeptical face. "I don't think going on a holiday with you is a good idea," I respond dismissively. He holds up a hand.

"Hear me out," he urges. "I'm meeting friends at the Amalfi Coast. Lots of beaches, sun, sand. Very relaxing. You can stay in your own room, come and go as you please. No expectations."

I have to admit, it sounds pretty good. And I can't even remember the last time I took a real vacation. "I'll think about it," I concede.

A wide grin breaks across his face. "*Bene*," he says happily, clapping his hands together.

The food arrives, and we move on to less serious topics as we enjoy our meal.

It might be the food, or the wine, or the enjoyable company, but at the end of the night, when Alessandro drops me off at my door, I do something I rarely do and throw caution to the wind.

"Alessandro?" I ask, turning back to him with my keys in my hand.

"Hm?" he murmurs.

"I'll do it. I'll go to Italy with you," I declare.

He smirks, and though he's not trying to be sexy, well, he is. "I thought you might," he replies. "I'll send you the details tomorrow, so you can make reservations." He slips his hand in mine, lifting it to his lips to place a tender kiss on my palm. *"Ciao."*

"Ciao," I whisper in reply.

And I don't want my heart to race at his touch, but it does. And he knows it. Smiling, he walks away. And I let myself into the condo wondering what the hell I just agreed to.

∾

BUT THE NEXT MORNING, HE'S SENT ME THE DETAILS and I find myself booking a flight to Naples just short of three weeks away. When it's done, I feel a sense of freedom and anticipation I haven't felt in a long time. Possibly ever.

For about fifteen minutes, that is. Until my phone rings. And I notice it's Bryce. I curse loudly.

"Are you fucking joking?" I answer. "Bryce Hoyt, are you *tracking* me?"

"Don't go," he responds. "To Italy. With him. Please. I know I have no right to ask."

"None," I reply emphatically. "And best not to let the future Mrs. Hoyt know you're speaking to me. As I recall she threatened that coming near you again would be the last thing I ever did. And I don't know if talking on the phone counts, but I'd really rather not find out."

"She seriously said that to you?" he asks.

"I thought you said you didn't need to know what happened between her and I," I remind him. "Look, I can't do this. I can't get pulled back into your web of confusion. I find it fascinating that you even care, considering you only have one memory of me from before."

"I may not remember us," he admits. "But I can't shake my feelings about that guy. And that tells me he's bad news, and you shouldn't be with him. Please, Sera. I know how this must seem to you, but I can't help how my brain is piecing all of this together."

"Just stop," I beg. "I get that you're still healing, and that this all must be very difficult for you. But you've made your choices. And I've made mine. If it makes you feel any better, I'm not involved with Alessandro. Not that way. I just need some space. I need to get away. That's all." Every word I utter frustrates me more. I don't owe him any explanations. "Seriously, I should go. I don't want to get you in trouble."

"You won't," he replies simply. "I ended things with Madison."

"Seriously?" I ask incredulously.

"Seriously," he confirms.

"Why?" I ask suspiciously. "Did you remember something?"

He snorts. "I wish. No. I finally listened to Em. And I asked Madison point blank why she wanted to marry me. I guess I'd never questioned it before, when she had the opportunity to say things in her own way to make me believe what she wanted me to. But head on, she's not a good liar," he replies.

"So you know she was just after your money," I reply bluntly, not really believing he knows the full truth.

"Yes," he responds plainly. "I'm sure she cared for me in some way, but not the way I cared for her once." He sighs in frustration. "Honestly, I think I knew it all along, because I knew it then. She's not a giver."

His words pull at that stupid thread of hope in my heart, but I won't be sucked back in so easily.

"Well, I'm really glad you figured that out before it was too late," I say dully.

"I didn't just call about the trip. I had to try one more time. Please, Sera, is there any chance we can try to get to know each other again?" he asks hopefully.

My heart twinges painfully in my chest. Hope dies last, but I can't let it override my survival instincts. Not again.

"I'm afraid not," I say, my voice low and tired. "See, I already know you, Bryce. So in this case I would be the one who cared far more. And that's just not something I can handle. I can't suffer the thousand tiny rejections that doing that would mean, especially not when it could very well end with you never remembering any more about our past, and never developing those feelings again in the future. It's a bigger risk than I'm willing to take. I'm sorry."

"No, I'm sorry," he says softly. "But you can't blame a guy for trying."

"I understand. Take care, Bryce."

"Take care, Sera."

⌇

BACK AT WORK THE NEXT DAY, I CLEAR THE VACATION time through HR. Once that's done I let Hunter know I'll be out of town those weeks. He practically does a happy dance knowing he'll have the place to himself for a while. I stop myself from requesting that he not have sex in my bed. Hopefully, it goes without saying.

Graham, fortunately, seems just fine pretending he's not dating my brother whenever I see him around the office. But he starts hanging around the condo more, and I often see him disappearing out the front door as I come down for breakfast in the morning.

My slight annoyance at his constant presence is

outweighed by Hunter's clear happiness. I mean, I've never seen him so giddy. He practically speaks in full sentences these days.

On Wednesday I get a call from Emily, which I promptly ignore, sending it to voicemail. She leaves a lengthy message pleading with me not to go to Italy, and I'm thankful I don't have to suppress my eye rolls and sarcastic responses. Those two are exactly the same as ever with sharing behind my back and meddling. I'm thankful I don't have to deal with it anymore. And that I'm spared the trouble of explaining to Emily how sick I am of hurting and hoping. Because through it all, Bryce's memories really never came back. And I know that's just as hard for him as it is for the rest of us, though in a different way. But I want to spare him that, nonetheless. So instead of explaining that we should all just move on, I focus on just doing it.

TWENTY-ONE

The end of the workweek arrives, but it hardly feels that way as, when I get home, Graham and Hunter are on the couch making out. Not that they make out at work, but I'm still getting used to Graham's presence, and it's hard not to think about work when I see him. Even if it's while his tongue is shoved down my little brother's throat. Shaking it off, I grab a bottle of water and some food from the fridge and go hide in my room.

I make a few phone calls to let my mother and Allie know about my vacation plans and to catch up. And then I do something I haven't done in ages — I read. I find a trashy romance novel to download and sink deeply into my soft bed, losing myself in the kind of action I haven't had in a long time.

It seems to be the theme of the night, though, as around eleven I hear Hunter and Graham *giggling* as they make their way upstairs. And I thank the stars I won't be able to hear them from my room. Nonetheless, I take the opportunity to go downstairs and get a drink. After a short consideration, I opt for a glass of wine, hoping it will knock me out long enough to chase away the bulk of the nightmares.

Taking my glass, I turn off the lights and settle into my favorite chair in the dark, gazing contemplatively out the window wall. The dark sky is a solid mass of grey, the lights of the city reflecting off the low, late summer cloud cover. The humidity has been high lately, and I wouldn't be surprised if a thunderstorm rolled through soon.

I sip the wine slowly, enjoying the warmth that spreads through my face and chest as it does its work. By the time I'm done, it's definitely taken the edge off and I'm more than ready for bed. Alone. I heave a sigh and push myself out of the chair, arming the security system before I head back to bed. If I'm really lucky, I might even manage to sleep in.

∿

I'M WOKEN BY AN ALL-TOO-FAMILIAR CACOPHONY OF sound. The alarm blares obnoxiously through the condo. I sit bolt upright in bed, realizing the sky is already lightening, so it must be close to sunrise. I grab the bat under my bed and approach the alarm panel at the top of the stairs. It tells me the front door has been breached. I stand on the landing at the top of the stairs, peering around the wall down into the foyer.

Graham and Hunter are at the alarm panel nearest the front door, with the door itself cracked open behind them while they desperately punch codes into the system. Realizing there's no danger, I fly down the stairs as the alarm continues to blare obnoxiously.

"What happened?!" I yell over the noise.

"Graham was leaving and set it off. He panicked and tried to turn it off, but we're locked out now!" Hunter yells back.

He points at me and then at the alarm panel. I shake my head. If we're locked out, only building security can fix it.

The alarm continues to blare overhead, likely waking everyone within a few floors. I prop the bat against the wall and grab my cellphone, heading into the hallway so I can hear.

But I find a security guard already rushing toward me.

"Everything okay, ma'am?" he asks.

"Yes," I assure him. "My brother's boyfriend accidentally set it off. He tried to turn it off, but it locked him out. Can you stop it?"

The guard's eyes go wide. "I'm afraid I don't have those codes. I'm not usually on this post. I'll have to call in for another guard. It might take a few minutes."

I throw up my hands in frustration. But he continues to stare at me.

"Well, do it!" I snap at him.

He jumps, pulling a cellphone from his pocket and heading to the other end of the floor where it will be easier to hear. I feel slightly bad for snapping at him.

And unfortunately, he wasn't kidding. It takes nearly ten minutes for someone to come turn off the alarm. I make the mistake of waiting in the hall, nervously willing someone competent to come save me from the murderous looks my neighbors are now throwing me as they peep out of their doors. I can't say I blame them. If one of them had woken me up before six a.m. on a Saturday, I'd be pretty pissed off too.

Finally, a guard with the proper access comes and has the alarm off in moments. Graham and Hunter have the good grace to look horribly ashamed. The guard slips out and Graham makes to follow him.

"Oh, no, you don't," I caution.

Graham leaves the door where it is, sulking back

in to stand by Hunter. "Sorry, Sera," he says glumly. "I was just trying to head out, like I always do."

I glare at Hunter. "Have you been leaving the alarm off?" I accuse him.

Hunter shrugs guiltily. "Maybe," he admits. "It's just easier."

I squeeze the bridge of my nose. "Hunter, you know what I've been through. We can adjust the settings if you need, but …" I trail off as Hunter's stares past me, his eyes widening to the point where it's almost comical. I turn around and follow his gaze to the half-open door.

"I got a call." Bryce steps into the room.

And I realize I'd never taken him off as my emergency contact, so he must have automatically been notified when the alarm went off.

Graham takes the opportunity to slip by Bryce and out the door, pulling it closed behind him. Hunter conveniently disappears upstairs. I'm left standing there, in leggings and an oversized T-shirt, staring dumbly at Bryce.

"I'm sorry you were disturbed, but everything is fine," I reply, finally finding my voice again. "I forgot to take you off as emergency contact. I'll fix that as soon as I can." I'm suddenly extremely conscious of the fact that I'm not wearing a bra, and my hair is probably a tangled mess. I tug my fingers through it, trying to tame the worst of it.

"Since I'm here, do you mind if we talk?" he asks, taking a step forward.

I subconsciously take a step back. "I don't think that's a good idea," I reply, folding my arms over my chest protectively.

He runs a hand through his hair, and I note it looks damp — he's probably fresh from his post-workout shower. Same old Bryce. Except not. My insides twinge.

"Fine, I'll talk, you listen," he replies. "I can't stop thinking about you. I know you said you can't be friends, but I don't know if I can stay away, Sera. It's like you're a magnet, and I'm being pulled toward you whether I want to or not."

A derisive laugh escapes me. "It's too early for this," I mumble, shaking my head and heading for the kitchen. I'm going to need coffee if I'm going to deal with this shit.

Bryce stands awkwardly between the front door and the dining room, unsure of where to go as I knock around in the kitchen, getting a pot of coffee on. After a few silent and uncomfortable minutes, I emerge with a tray carrying two mugs and set it on the dining room table. He takes the hint and sits down across from me.

"Thanks," he says softly, grabbing the cup I made for him. He takes a sip. "Looks like you remember how I take my coffee too."

I close my eyes briefly and drink deeply, letting the beverage's warmth imbue me with strength. "So this magnet thing," I say. "Let's demagnetize it."

Bryce arches an eyebrow. "And how exactly do we do that?" he asks.

I can't help cracking a small smile. "Well, the traditional ways are heat, electric current, or banging on it real hard …" I trail off, my eyes going wide when I consider what I've suggested.

Bryce laughs. "Sounds kinky."

There's a sparkle in his beautiful blue eyes that I haven't seen in a long time. But then, I've purposed not to see him, despite how he manages to keep popping up.

I blush furiously. "It was supposed to be a metaphor, but I didn't think it through. Gimme a break. It's early," I reply.

"Look, I know I should take no for an answer …"

"It's okay," I interrupt him. "I wouldn't either if I were in your shoes."

"I'm just asking that we be friends, Sera," he replies softly. "Spend some time together. See if it shakes anything loose."

I set my mug down in front of me. "It's not that I

don't want to on some level," I allow. "But you don't remember, Bryce, so you don't know how hard it was for me. To get where we were. It was a long and winding path. And it *was* worth it. But it's not something I can do again, not knowing whether it will be worth it in the end this time."

He stares at me intently. "You're scared," he observes.

A small sound of agreement escapes my lips. "Yes," I admit. "I'm scared." I pause. "You once accused me of avoiding a relationship with you because I was terrified of having to really trust someone enough to be close to them." I meet his eyes. "I keep talking about you like I know you out of habit, I think. But I really don't. You're not the person I was in love with. Yet you are. Sort of. You're a new version of you. And I'd have to learn to trust you all over again. I don't know if that's something I can do."

Bryce knocks his knuckles against the side of his head. "That guy is in here somewhere," he assures me. "I think that's where this is coming from."

"Maybe," I allow. "But then again, maybe not. I'm not a risk-taker. It took me a long time and a lot of pain to admit that I loved you, Bryce. You don't know what you're asking of me. I'm not like you."

"Oh? And what am I like?" His question is sincere.

"Just like this," I supply. "Always wanting to keep trying."

"So I must have convinced you to do the same before," he challenges.

It makes me laugh, because he's not wrong. "Yes, but then we were in a place where we were both in love with each other," I reply.

"And are you still in love with me?" he asks.

It's a question I wasn't prepared for. And it requires a level of honesty I'm not sure I possess at the moment.

"I'm going to need more coffee before I can even think about unpacking that question," I admit, grabbing my mug and rising from the table. "Need a refill?" I slip back into the kitchen and top off my mug.

"Sure," Bryce replies, following me in.

But he freezes by the fridge, his eyes fixed on something next to it. I take a step back, so I can see what he's looking at and spot the frilly, white apron, still hanging from its hook on the wall. Bryce sets his mug on the counter behind him and reaches a hand out, letting the silky fabric of the apron run through his fingers before gripping the bottom, fingering the flowing edge of the fabric. I watch, frozen and fascinated, as he lifts it to his face, breathing in deeply.

"I remember this," he says.

My throat constricts. I don't want to ask. I don't want to hope. But I can't help myself. Ever the masochist, I reply. "Tell me what you remember."

He turns in place to face the dining room. "I came home from work and you were there," he points at the table. "Red heels. Sexy as sin."

I shudder as he describes the scene, remembering it all too well.

"But I had you there," he points at the couch. "And then there," he points at the floor. "And then …" He stares intently at the window wall.

"Not there," I say softly.

He turns to look at me. "I wanted to."

But looking into his eyes, I don't see recognition and love. I see pain and confusion.

"Yes, you did," I agree.

He takes a tentative step toward me, his torment written all over his face. I instinctively pull back.

"Don't," he pleads. "Just hold still." Something in his voice freezes me in place.

But I can't look, so I close my eyes. I feel him stop in front of me, and he must be very close because I can feel the heat radiating off of him.

"Look at me, Sera," he commands.

And I'm powerless to resist his husky tone. I open my eyes and look up into his beautiful face. I let my mind go numb, surrendering to whatever it is he needs to get out of his system, hoping it doesn't crush me too badly.

He raises his hand and runs it down the side of my face, along my chin. He tips my head up, lowering his face to my neck, inhaling deeply. His nose lightly grazes my ear, and a shudder ripples through me.

He pulls back abruptly, feeling the shaking of my body. "I'm sorry," he murmurs. He steps back, and then out of the kitchen into the living room. He strides to the window wall, looking out over the city.

I follow, stopping a few paces behind him next to my chair. He turns, leaning against the glass and facing me, surveying the room.

"You like to sit there," he nods at the chair.

I huff a dry laugh. "That's obvious. The cushion is shaped exactly like my ass," I joke.

"And you drink too much when you're upset," he continues. "Wine, mostly, whiskey when things are really bad."

I swallow hard and nod, wondering if it's really coming back to him, or if it's just a reaction to familiar objects. Still not quite daring to hope.

His eyes rove the paintings that now cover the walls. "Those are new."

"My brother taught me to paint," I explain. "When we ran out of canvas we just … kept going."

He walks to the wall and slides his long finger

over a dark swirl. "The guerilla artist, confined," he mutters.

"Yes," I gasp. "Hunter. He was a guerilla artist. Though he's gone traditional now. And he works for me."

Bryce looks back at me curiously. "Doing what?" he asks.

"Trim work. Interior design. That sort of thing," I admit. "He's got quite an eye."

Bryce pales and grabs back the back of the couch. "I feel a little lightheaded," he admits.

I rush to his side and let him lean on me. "Lay down on the couch," I insist.

He allows me to help him onto the overstuffed cushions, sinking gratefully onto them, lying on his side.

I grab a throw pillow and use it to prop up his head, then I fold myself onto the floor next to him. "Better?"

"Yes, thanks," he replies quietly.

"You're worrying me," I admit. "Are you okay? Should I call someone?"

Bryce takes a deep breath through is nose. "No, I think I'll be okay. My head just feels backwards," he replies.

I chuckle. "It looks like it's on straight to me," I

tease him. "I'm going to make some breakfast. You hungry?"

He nods, so I head into the kitchen. As I throw together a quick meal, I keep one eye on Bryce. After a few minutes he sits back up, looking considerably less pale and in shock. But I bring the plates out to him anyway, handing him a dish stacked with eggs, bacon, and toast.

"You used to feed me a lot," he remarks. It's not a question.

"You're a hungry guy," I reply with a shrug. "So are you really remembering, or are these all just reflexes?"

Bryce stares at me as he polishes off his toast. "Em told you about that, huh?" he asks.

"Yep," I reply, avoiding his gaze.

He doesn't speak again until his plate is clean. Setting it down on the coffee table in front of him, he dusts his hands on his jeans.

"They're not reflexes," he finally replies.

I set my plate aside, even though I'm not finished. "How can you be sure?" I press.

Bryce smiles. "The reflexes are just that — I see something, I react. I don't really understand why or feel much of anything. Well, except with the Italian," he allows. "It was hard to tell the difference between those and the real memories until recently."

"Why's that?" I ask curiously.

He levels a look at me. "Because my first real, full memory didn't come back until I saw you at the gym," he admits. "And I haven't had any more until today. Just small bits here and there."

Suddenly I'm questioning if I should've skipped eating as my stomach roils. "Is that normal?" I probe.

"There's not really a 'normal' when it comes to this kind of thing," he hedges. "Some people get everything back quickly, some never get anything back." He leans into the couch, crossing his legs, something in his manner changed. "And I don't want to scare you, Sera, but I remember now. Well, enough anyway. More than I did."

And I can't handle it. I grab our plates and return them to the kitchen, eager to turn away from him so he can't see the heat and panic rising on my face. "How much is enough?" I toss over my shoulder as nonchalantly as I can manage.

He laughs and follows me to the kitchen, leaning over the bar as I scrape off the plates. I look up into his eyes, noting they're back to their clear, sparkling blue. And he looks coolly confident, and smug.

"I don't think you're going to believe anything I say," he replies cryptically.

"You're probably right," I admit with a meager

smile, wiping my hands on a towel. At least he's finally catching on.

"So how about I prove it to you?" he challenges. I look at him, confused.

"Well, I guess you already proved you remember some things," I allow. "I'm not sure what else you mean."

"I mean, how about I prove that I remember the way I feel about you," he clarifies.

Suddenly, I'm having trouble breathing. "You remember how you feel about me?" I ask incredulously. "After all this time? I find that hard to believe."

Bryce smiles and shrugs. "Maybe I just needed the right environment. The right frame of mind," he replies. "But I do remember. The important stuff anyway. I'll admit I'm still a little fuzzy on the details, though."

I don't ask what the important stuff is. Because I know what he thinks it is, and I can't bring myself to trust that it's true.

"It sounds like you've made some good progress," I reply, dodging the bait. "Maybe we should call it a day before you hurt yourself."

He snorts, shaking his head. "You mean before I hurt you," he replies. "Not gonna happen, Evans." He suddenly seems very sure of himself, so I decide to call his bluff.

"Okay, prove it," I reply.

Smiling, he holds up a finger, then turns and bounds up the stairs. He's not gone long, returning with something clutched in his fist. He sets it on the counter in front of me. It's a small, black velvet box that I recognize all too well. It's the engagement ring I found in his nightstand on my birthday.

TWENTY-TWO

"I was going to give this to you that night," he explains.

I eye the box like it's full of poisonous spiders. "I can't take that," I reply, stepping back.

He raises an eyebrow. "You know what's in it," he accuses me with an incredulous smirk. He clucks his tongue in admonishment. "I never took you for a snooper."

"I'm not," I protest indignantly. "I was looking for a place to put something for you."

"Ah," he responds. "Did you read the inscription too, then?"

I shake my head. He opens the box, and the ring sparkles brilliantly, shooting rainbow reflections across the room. He holds it between his thumb and forefinger, angling it so I can read the elegant script written on the inside of the band.

"What have I always told you?" His voice is soft, filled with love and longing.

I look up into his eyes. I don't need to read it. The words are etched onto my broken heart. "Never forget how much I love you," I whisper.

He's right. He remembers the important stuff. A tear finds its way down my cheek, remembering all the nights I fell asleep remembering those words, wishing he would too. And now he has.

Bryce sets the ring back in the box and rounds the kitchen counter, coming to stand beside me. And despite him standing before me, it all feels unreal. "That's right," he replies. "Did you forget, Sera?"

I close my eyes and shake my head. "This all would have been much easier if I had," I reply honestly. I feel his finger slip beneath my chin, tugging it up in a familiar motion. I open my eyes and look at him.

"I know," he says softly. "And I can't undo that pain. But I remember you, finally, if not every detail of our life. But I remember this."

He drops his lips to mine, and it's more than familiar. The fire in his kiss is the fire in me that I thought had long since died. The fire that burned between us all those months ago. I burn with it, letting the feeling spread through me as his lips claim mine, truly, once again.

He pulls back, stroking a finger along my face, nuzzling his nose against mine as he used to do. "Do you believe me, that I remember you? Really remember you?" His eyes search mine deeply, begging me to accept him, to trust him.

The dam inside me breaks, emotions flooding my entire being. I nod, tears in my eyes. "Yes." It's all I can manage before needing to feel his lips on me again. I let the force of his mouth on mine drive away all the doubts, all the fear, all the pain I've felt. I can feel his own struggles melting in the purifying fire that burns between us. I can feel in his touch, in the response of my own body, how lost we've both been without this connection.

When our mouths part finally, I'm breathless and dizzy, and hopeful.

"So I guess that means you *are* still in love with me?" Bryce asks teasingly.

I press my knuckles into his strong chest and push myself backward a step. "Wouldn't you like to know," I tease back.

Bryce leans back against the counter, as in control as he ever was, now refusing to rise to my bait. His eyes flick to the clock on the microwave. "What I'd really like to know is if you'll let me take you to dinner tonight," he replies seriously.

I chew on my lip. My brain is still catching up, and I fight off the instincts I've been using to protect myself these past months. "Okay," I reply. "As long as there are no elevators."

Bryce snorts. "Deal," he agrees. "And I can't believe I'm saying this, but I need to leave. I have to go into work today. I'll pick you up at seven?"

"Deal," I echo.

He heads out of the kitchen, and I don't miss that he grabs the little black box, sliding it into his pocket on his way to the door.

I make to reach for the knob, but he shakes his head, stepping forward and using his bulk to pin me against the back of the door. He slides his hands over my hips, gripping me tightly and pressing himself into me. I breathe deeply of his scent before I look up at him.

As soon as I do, his lips capture mine, gently, sweetly, his tongue slipping between my lips, searching. It caresses mine lightly for a moment before he pulls away. And with another nuzzle of his nose, he's done, stepping back so I can open the door.

"I missed you so much," he says intently. "But I'll see you soon."

I nod. "Bye, Bryce."

"Bye, Sera."

Once he's gone I spend the rest of the day convincing myself it wasn't a dream. Well, except when I go back upstairs to yell at Hunter some more as I'd planned to do before Bryce showed up.

JUST BEFORE SEVEN I'M WAITING NERVOUSLY ON THE couch, constantly running my hands over my blue wrap dress, anxiously tapping my high heels against the wooden base of the couch.

By five after I'm sure it was a dream, or that it was temporary, and his mind has slipped back to where it was, when he didn't know he'd loved me.

And by the time the doorbell rings at ten after, I'm practically in hysterics, having already fully convinced myself that he wasn't going to show up. Feeling ridiculous, I try to breathe deeply as I go to pull the door open. But it pops open in front of me, Bryce having unlocked it himself.

"Sorry I'm late," he announces, pocketing his keys. "But hey, I just remembered I still have a key."

An ugly sob rips out of me. He looks up and notices the anguish on my face. And he's there, holding me in an instant. "I'm sorry," I blubber, the tears pouring out. "It just seemed too good to be true. And then you were late, and I …"

"Shhhh," he says, stroking my hair. "It's okay, I'm here." I sniff loudly, trying my hardest to rein in the crazy. When I feel like the panic has subsided, I pull away, wiping at his ruined shirt.

"I'm sorry I got you all messy," I grumble.

Bryce forces my chin up with a finger, looking down with sparkling eyes. "You know you can get me messy anytime," he murmurs suggestively.

I smile feebly, not really in the mood to flirt. "I'm not sure if I can do this," I admit.

Bryce shrugs. "We can stay here and eat then," he replies.

I press out of his arms and stride back to the living room, sinking defeatedly onto the couch. "No," I respond with a sigh. I gesture between us. "This."

Bryce is so still for a moment that it makes me even more nervous than I already am. Then, he quietly takes his black suit jacket off and lays it over the back of one of the dining room chairs. He calmly rolls up the sleeves of his white dress shirt, still stained with my wet tears and a little bit of my makeup.

He saunters coolly up to me, sinking down to his knees on the floor in front of me. He unfolds my arms from around my midsection, gathering my hands in his.

"You've spent the better part of a year living in a world where I didn't remember you. I get that," he admits. "So if this is all too fast, too much, I get that too. I'm just so fucking glad you hadn't moved on, Sera, you have no idea. But if you need time, or space, then we can do this slow. I told you once that I wanted us to move at your pace. And I stick to that."

"God, Bryce, *I* didn't even remember your saying that until you just reminded me," I reply incredulously. "This is for real, isn't it? Your memories are really coming back."

He pushes up and slides onto the couch next to me, running a hand through his hair. "It's been a slow trickle, all day," he confesses. "Like the memories were just waiting for a crack of light to know where they could get out. You're that light, Sera. From the moment I met you, something inside me *knew* you. Knew that we belonged together. And even after I lost my memories of you, even though I was trying to do the right thing, the safe thing, something in me still knew it was wrong. I don't think it's a coincidence that I didn't start to get full memories back until I was with you again. Really with you, and not distracted by …"

"Please for the love of all that's good don't say

her name," I interrupt. "In this house she shall forever be known as 'she who shall not be named,' got it?"

Bryce smirks. "My point is," he says, "I'm still solidly on the side of the line where I'll take as much of you as I can get."

And that one I remember. It's one of the things he said to me the first night we both confessed our love for each other. I scowl jokingly at him. "Well now you're just showing off," I scoff.

He grins, his true sunshine smile. "Is it working?" he asks eagerly.

And I laugh. "It's working," I assure him. "And while I can't promise there won't be times this all still scares the shit out of me, I'm in."

Slowly, a smile creeps across Bryce's face until he's grinning again. "All in?" he asks, running a hand down my arm.

"All in," I confirm, allowing the tingling sensation his fingers leave behind to stir me.

"Mmm," he murmurs. "Prove it."

I chuckle and raise an eyebrow. "And how exactly would you like me to do that?" I ask. Though I have a suspicion.

His eyes flick down my body. "Take off your dress," he replies.

And despite the thrill that runs through me at his

words, I have to give him the "not a chance in hell" look.

"You do realize that my younger brother lives here now and will probably walk through that door with his boyfriend — one of my coworkers — at any moment now, right?" I remind him.

"Shit," Bryce curses. "No, you hadn't mentioned he actually lives here. Or the other bit."

"So you thought he was just hanging out here at six o'clock in the morning?" I tease.

He shrugs. "I was distracted. You weren't wearing a bra," he defends himself.

I roll my eyes. "Men. I swear."

"Okay, fine. Get your gorgeous ass upstairs, then take off your dress," he amends, rising and offering a hand. I take it, pulling myself up.

"Aren't you hungry?" I ask.

He drops his mouth to my ear. "Not for food," he murmurs, his deep voice tickling my ear, causing heat to instantly pool between my legs.

"I thought we were going to go slow," I reply, slightly breathlessly.

He laughs. "I said we'd go at your pace," he corrects me. "So if you don't want to go there, we won't." He takes a step back, but it doesn't stop what he's already put in motion.

"You fight dirty, Bryce Hoyt," I reply shaking my head.

But even looking at him is too much. I feel silly that a few light touches and suggestive words have me this worked up. Though I have to allow that it's been a very long time.

"You know you like it," he replies with a wink.

I do, but I pull a page out of his book and put on my best poker face, shrugging noncommittally. I stroll casually past him, to the bottom of the stairs, knowing the wall that's now between me and the front door will shield me if needs be.

And as if I'm simply getting ready to take a shower, I untie the front panel of my dress, opening it like a robe and letting it fall to the ground behind me. Leaving me standing there in lacy, black lingerie that leaves nothing to the imagination. A small moan escapes through his parted lips.

"I guess we will be eating out after all," I say lightly, turning and heading up the stairs, biting my lip to keep a shit-eating grin from breaking across my face. And giving him a full view of my backside.

But as my foot hits the third step I hear the front door open. Bryce's head whips toward it, open mouthed. And then he makes a break for the stairs as I start to flee up them. He reaches down to grab my dress on the way.

"Leave it," I hiss.

He gives me a funny look but chases me quickly up the stairs. I burst into my bedroom, giggling, Bryce toppling in after me. And I quickly slam the door behind him.

"Why'd you want me to leave the dress?" he asks.

I grab his hand, pulling him to the bed. The thrill of almost being caught has my adrenaline pumping.

"So I didn't have to leave a sock on the doorknob," I tease. When I feel my legs bump against the edge of the bed, I pull him to me, having to rise on my toes even in heels to kiss him.

And he takes no time returning the kiss and then some, lifting me up and laying me gently at the head of the bed. It's the last gentle thing he does.

I can feel the impatience in his kiss, the hunger. His mouth and tongue work with mine furiously, his hands kneading and working down my body roughly until he slips one hand between my legs, shoving my panties to the side and using his whole hand to stroke me. He lets out a low moan into my mouth when he feels how ready I am. His hand continues its work as his mouth cuts a path down my body to meet it, leaving a scorching trail wherever he kisses, licks, and nips.

And before his tongue even finds its final mark, I'm panting and moaning and gripping the bedspread, my hips rearing off the bed like they have a mind of their own. He sets a furious pace, as if he plans to consume me bodily, his tongue and fingers working forcefully to unleash the pent-up energy now roiling between my legs. And I don't know where the feverish sting of anticipation ends, and his hot, deft mouth begins. But in what feels like seconds I'm coming so hard I think I might pass out from the sheer effort it takes to keep from screaming at the top of my lungs. As I descend, he yields, and I stop holding it all in, letting my breath out in a great sigh.

But he moves up to cover my mouth with his once more, his taste now mixed with mine. Combined with the ferocity of his need, I'm plunged back into a dizzy frenzy. I barely register his hand as it works quickly between us to free his manhood before he nudges into me, sinking deeply. As he's still fully clothed, the sudden and unexpected move causes me to gasp in surprise. But he doesn't relent. He wraps an arm around me, bracing himself with the other, and pounds into me fiercely. It's only slightly painful for a moment before it's something so much more.

I throw my head back, not bothering or perhaps unable to stem the moans pouring from my throat as he rides me. As mine did, his climax comes quickly, the groans emanating from him rising rapidly to a crescendo. He shudders over me finally, then sinks into my embrace, still fully buried inside of me. His mouth finds mine once more, his desire still obvious, but the demanding edge now gone. Like a raging inferno dying to a low, slow flame.

When we break apart, he lets out a laugh. "I haven't fucked that fast since high school." He glances down at his watch. "We could probably still even make our reservation."

"Seriously?" I ask.

He throws me a mock sharp look, then laughs. "No," he admits.

I run a hand over his chest, wishing I'd gotten to see him naked. It's something I've dreamt of frequently. "It was quite different," I remark, looking at him from under my eyelashes. "But in a good way. Obviously, I was just as turned on as you were."

"It was more that that," he replies huskily, looking deeply into my eyes. "While I was going down on you, I remembered things. Doing that to you before. Doing other things to you before. You doing things to me. It took all of my strength to let you finish. So it's a damn good thing it didn't take you long either, or I may have exploded in my pants. Also something I haven't done since high school." His lips settle into a wry smile.

"Well, while I hope you eventually remember more than just our sex life," I reply, "right now, all I can remember is that I'm starving." My stomach rumbles loudly as if to prove my point and Bryce laughs.

"Then I guess you'd best clean up and find something else to wear," he suggests, reaching down to put his clothing back to rights. "Because as much as I'd love to watch you walk around in that sexy lingerie all night, I don't think your brother and his boyfriend would care much for it."

The reminder that they were likely here for our escapades makes me blush furiously. "Oh, god, they probably heard us," I whisper.

Bryce laughs. "I'm sure you've heard them," he replies with a shrug. "I wouldn't worry too much about it."

But as I dress, I sill can't shake the embarrassment. I pick a pair of dark leggings and an emerald green sweater with a high neckline. At least fully covered I feel slightly less, well, exposed. We exit the bedroom, Bryce following behind me, and I say a little prayer that they didn't hear, or have already left again, as we descend the stairs.

As soon as I see Hunter and Graham, though, I know I'm out of luck. On both counts. The looks on their faces clearly say they heard it all. As we hit the bottom stair, I quickly retrieve the discarded wrap dress, tossing it self-consciously into the coat closet next to the stairs.

"Hey, guys," I say, attempting nonchalance. "You remember Bryce."

Bryce gives a little wave and goes into the kitchen and starts rifling through the fridge. They wave back, mystified.

"Whatcha doin?" I ask him as I wander in after him.

"Making dinner. Go sit down," he replies calmly with his head still in the fridge.

"Are you sure?" I ask tentatively.

He straightens up and fixes me with a look. "Yes. I used to live here, remember?" he teases.

"Yes, as I matter of fact, I do remember that. But the better question is, do you?" I tease back.

He narrows his eyes at me. "As a matter of fact, I think I do," he replies saucily.

I laugh. "All right, then," I reply. "I'll be in the living room."

He gives me a quick peck on the cheek, then swats me on the behind. I join Hunter and Graham in the living room, folding myself self-consciously into my favorite chair.

"Thank god," Hunter immediately says to me. "We saw the clothes and heard, well, you know. And I thought you might have gotten back with …" he drops his voice to a whisper, "the Italian guy."

I look at Hunter, confused. "Except you saw Bryce here this morning," I reply.

Hunter shrugs. "I thought maybe it upset you, so you went looking for comfort. I gotta say I'm glad it's not. That dude is bad news," Hunter grumbles.

"I remember liking you, Hunter," Bryce's voice floats over from the kitchen. He points a spatula at Hunter. "Good instincts."

"So you remember, huh?" Hunter asks. I can't help smiling.

"Starting to," Bryce admits. He looks at me and smiles back. "But I'm getting more back with every passing hour. Still don't know who this guy is though." His eyes flick to Graham.

"Oh, sorry, this is Graham Forrester," Hunter replies. "My boyfriend." Hunter shifts uncomfortably.

"Nice to meet you, Graham," Bryce replies, looking down at whatever it is he's chopping. "I'm Bryce. I'd shake your hand but …" He lifts his hands to demonstrate the knife in one and a pile of zucchini in the other. I hear a sizzle as he tosses the zucchini into a pan before going back to chopping.

"Nice to meet you," Graham replies uncertainly, still clearly wondering what the hell is going on.

Hunter also looks like he'd like an explanation. "So …" he prompts in a low voice.

I shake my head. "Later," I whisper.

"Okay. You guys need some privacy?" Hunter whispers back.

"Maybe later," Bryce calls. "Stick around. I'm making stir fry."

"God, that guy has got the ears of a bat," Graham mutters.

And I can't help but smile. "Some things never change."

TWENTY-THREE

Unsurprisingly, after dinner Hunter and Graham decide to go to Graham's place for the night. Bryce seems pretty happy with that. And as I sit in Bryce's arms on the couch, I'm feeling pretty good about it myself.

"So what else did you remember today?" I ask softly, lying back against his chest and trailing my fingers down the arm he has wrapped around me.

"Heather," he replies. "And Daniel. What happened there?"

"Ah." I sit up, turning around to face him. "He was convicted and sentenced to seven years. Heather is doing great. She's seeing someone now, and she seems really happy. She told me to thank you for your help, once you remembered."

"And Charles? How did he take it all?" Bryce asks.

I can't help but smile sadly that he's remembering, but the things he's remembering are so heart-rending.

"It was tough. But he's okay. He finally made an official succession plan. That's when I knew he'd really accepted it. And things have been better," I reply.

"So you'll be in charge of Sutton Developments one day?" Bryce asks.

"Yes," I agree. "How about you? Will you run Hoyt Corporate Services again?"

"I'd planned on it," he admits. "But I'm not so sure anymore." He pulls me close to him, running his hands down my arms. I press my palms against his chest, relishing the feel of his heartbeat under his warm, firm muscles.

"Why not?" I ask curiously.

He pushes my hair behind my shoulders and looks deeply into my eyes. "Well," he replies, "if we're both running companies, who is going to raise the kids?"

I laugh. "You mean Hunter and Graham?" I tease.

Bryce smirks. "I think you know full well I don't," he chastises me.

I press my lips together to suppress my smile. "Getting a little ahead of yourself, aren't you?" I ask.

"Technically, you haven't even proposed. I mean, you flashed a ring and all, but that seems to have disappeared."

Bryce grins mischievously. "Do you really want me to propose to you on the same day my memories came back? You seemed pretty dead set on not letting me back in unless there wasn't any chance you'd be left hanging."

"Well, I let you back in, didn't I?" I reply.

"Hmmm," he says in mock thought. "So you really must believe me. Which means …"

"I might consider marrying you if you weren't such a jackass," I reply, smacking him on the chest and attempting to wriggle backward.

But he locks his arms behind me, making escape impossible. "You know you like it," he teases me, burying his face in my neck. His lips work my flesh, and all the fight drains right out of me.

"I do believe it," I respond, ignoring his teasing and wrapping myself around him. "I just needed a little time to absorb that it was really true. That you really remembered, and that it wasn't a reflex."

He gazes seriously into my eyes. "I really remember. Not everything still, though more is coming back all the time. But I know three things, Serafina Evans," he replies, kissing me lightly on the lips. "First, that I've loved you since the moment I saw you." He kisses me more deeply. "Second, that I missed you even when I didn't remember you, I just didn't realize that's what I was feeling until my memories came back." He kisses me again in a way that causes me to moan against him. "And finally, that life is too short, too precious to live another moment without asking you to be my wife." He slips out of my arms, crouching on one knee next to the couch, the ring mysteriously having appeared in his hand. "Marry me, Sera."

I'd only been teasing him about proposing. And even though I knew he had the ring, and that he'd planned to propose before he'd lost his memory, he's right — I never thought he'd propose the same day his memories returned. But this whole ordeal has also made me realize how fleeting everything is. How much I love him. And I'd be an idiot to say no.

"I know three things, Bryce Hoyt," I respond with a grin. "First, I love you more than I ever imagined I was capable of loving anyone." I kiss him lightly and he grins. "Second, yes, I will absolutely marry you." He lets out a small, choked happy noise as I kiss him again. "And third, I think we should buy a house together and fill it with little Hoyts."

A look of sheer joy settles over him, and this time he kisses me, nearly knocking me over on the sofa. I laugh as he pulls away and slides the ring onto my finger. And it's a perfect fit, just like we are.

Bryce cups my face in his hands, radiating warmth and love, and his mouth covers mine. I press him back gently after a moment, rising from the couch. I tug on his hand, leading him to the window wall.

"Actually, I guess I know four things," I amend. I go up on my toes to whisper in his ear. "I know I want you naked and fucking me against the window. Now."

"Goddamn, baby," Bryce groans. His hands fly down his shirt buttons, and I tug my dress over my head, flinging it away from me. As he takes off his shirt, I add my bra to the pile. And when his pants and boxers go, so do my panties and leggings. And in a clash of flesh, his mouth is joined to mine, his hands roughly teasing my nipple and between my legs.

I cry out as he primes me, sinking against him and feverishly stroking him. He spins me around, grabbing my hands and placing them against the window. He runs his fingers down my back, to my hips, lifting them into position as he leans down and seats himself at my opening. I can see him reflected in the glass, lovingly caressing my backside as he teases me. I groan anxiously.

"So impatient," he murmurs approvingly. How he loves making me wait.

But I know it'll be worth it. And instead of giving in to the urge to pounce, he enters slowly, torturously. And the moan that seeps out of me is nothing short of primal. He groans appreciatively, at the sensation of our joining or my clear enjoyment of it, I'm not sure which.

But even he can't take the disciplined torment for long. Our quick encounter earlier has only left us both hungry for the full experience. So I'm not surprised when he quickly accelerates to the deep, full thrusts that send my body soaring with pleasure. The sounds of his enjoyment mingle with my own, spurring us both on as he takes me. His hands reach under me and find my breasts, allowing him leverage to drive completely into me. He hovers there, using a slight tilt of his hips to move the head over *that* spot inside me. A familiar low ache begins to build. And having learned from Bryce how to make the climax all the more intense, I slip my fingers onto the sensitive nub between my legs, pressing with our rhythm until the ache consumes me, spreading its explosive fire through my body so fiercely that my arm loses its hold, my face and chest sinking against the glass as I come apart.

As I come down from the sensation, Bryce releases me and turns me to face him. His mouth finds mine, and I get a slight respite as I sink into him, enjoying the feel of our naked bodies touching. I press him back, running my hands over the smooth muscles of his chest, then the rippling muscles of his abs. My eyes drink them in hungrily, then move down to his throbbing cock.

I drop to my knees at the sight, descending on him with my mouth. He moans loudly, his hand resting lightly on the back of my head as I work him. I pleasure him with varying stroking and sucking, enjoying every noise that he makes. It's all I can do to let him stop me before I finish him.

He lifts me up bodily, pressing me against the cold glass behind me so our hips are aligned. And then he's inside me once more, pinning me with his torso and tilting his hips into me furiously as I cling to him with my arms and legs, enduring the intense pleasure caused by the contrast of the cool window, his warm body, and the deep, intense thrusts. His head is pressed against the glass next to me, his mouth hovering over my shoulder. So when his breathing picks up as he approaches orgasm, I hear it, and use what muscles I can to spur him toward his finish. When he feels me clamp around him, he cries out and explodes inside me.

We both sink to the floor, utterly spent and gratified, leaning our warm, sweaty bodies against the chilly glass, looking up at the dark, grey sky outside.

After we've caught our breath, Bryce pulls me to him, kissing me lightly. His beautiful blue eyes find mine, his handsome face filled with love.

"I don't want to wait," he says. "To make you mine."

I smile shyly. "I'm already yours. I have been this whole time. I was just waiting for you to remember," I reply. "But now that you do, I don't want to wait, either."

"Really?" he asks, with a hopeful look.

"Really," I confirm. "I'll marry you anytime, anywhere, Bryce Hoyt. Just so long as we can do this, forever." I press my body against his.

His strong hands pull me into his lap, and I wrap my legs around him, my breasts pressed against his chest.

"God, I love you," he breathes. His words shoot through my heart, filling me with joy.

"And I love you," I sigh. "Never forget how much I love you."

He smiles. "Never again," he agrees.

TWENTY-FOUR

Two weeks later, I'm holding Bryce's hand in the kitchen at his mother's house.

"Do you remember we almost kissed here once?" I ask teasingly.

He backs me against the very counter I'd used to support myself in anticipation of that almost-kiss. "I do," he murmurs seductively. "And this time, Em isn't going to spoil it." He lowers his face to mine.

"Em isn't going to spoil what?" Emily asks, entering the kitchen.

And I can't help but burst out laughing.

"Shitty timing, as usual, sis," Bryce grouses. But he kisses me anyway, cutting off my laugh.

I sink into his embrace, not caring that Emily is watching.

"You know, this is your party," Emily grumbles. "You might want to help out a little. People will be here soon."

Bryce breaks away and shoots me a conspiratorial smile. "If you insist," he replies, helping Emily bring plates and cups out to the buffet table.

I sigh happily watching him go. There's not much he *doesn't* remember anymore, and the last two weeks have been a dream rediscovering each other, settling back into our relationship, and seeing him get back all that he lost. And then some.

Charlotte walks in with Rebecca, the former moving in to hug me first. "I'm so glad you decided to celebrate your engagement with everyone before you went on vacation," Charlotte says sweetly.

Rebecca embraces me next. "Yes," she agrees. "We couldn't be happier to be welcoming you to our family, Sera. I'm only sorry it had to be such a rough road here."

I press her away at arm's length with a smile, squeezing her shoulders gently. "I'm not," I admit. "It happened the way it happened, and in the end, it all worked out."

The older woman beams back at me, nodding in agreement. "You're right, of course," she responds with a smile.

Emily sticks her head in the kitchen. "Hey, Sera, your dad and his wife are here," she calls.

"Already?" I gasp, running out to find Bryce.

I spot him by the table setting things out.

"Baby, have you seen Hunter yet?"

He looks up at me, confused. "No, I don't think he and Graham have arrived, why?" he asks.

"Shit," I curse. "My dad and his wife are here."

Bryce's eyes widen. "I'll ask Aunt Char to run interference," he suggests.

I nod, and he runs to the kitchen to get Charlotte while I move to meet Kent and Barb. I find them hovering in the foyer.

"Kent," I call.

He looks up and his face floods with relief at the sight of me. "Sera, there you are," he breathes. He gestures to the tiny redhead next to him. "This is my wife, Barb."

I extend my hand out, which she grasps firmly in greeting. "It's so very nice to meet you, Barb," I say. I feel a hand slide on my back, and I turn to see Bryce has joined us. "This is my … Bryce." I laugh.

Bryce extends his hand to my father first, and they have a friendly shake before Bryce shakes Barb's hand too. "Please, come in," Bryce encourages, leading us all to the living room.

Behind us, I see Charlotte dart for the door to field

incoming guests, particularly Hunter. Because today, of all days, Hunter has decided to come out to our father. As if there weren't enough going on.

The next group to arrive is the Sutton Developments crowd — Charles, Suraj, and their spouses. Bryce and I position ourselves between the foyer and the living room in wait, while we watch Rebecca and Charlotte entertain Kent and Barb as Emily continues to run food from the kitchen to the buffet table. I knew the morning had been too calm — everything is in full swing now, though, so I take a deep breath as I prepare for another round of introductions.

I embrace Charles as he makes it to us, accepting his congratulations and introducing him to Bryce. It's odd seeing the two men shaking hands. They're both such a big part of my life now, and I don't miss the momentousness of the occasion. Charles introduces us to his wife, Diane, and then we repeat the whole process with Suraj and his wife, Mena. When they've all moved on to the living room, I turn back to Bryce.

"It's already weird seeing all these different people in one place," I whisper. "Was this a good idea?"

Bryce shrugs and drops a gentle kiss on my forehead. "Too late now," he murmurs in my ear. "Just focus on tomorrow. We'll be driving through the Italian countryside and eating gelato."

I let out a sigh of anticipation. "Mmmm, that was better even than dirty talk," I tease.

He smiles, but doesn't respond, gesturing to the door, where I see Heather and her boyfriend. She runs over and hugs me, introducing us to Sam, who seems like a really great guy. Though the huge smile on her face whenever she looks at him speaks volumes too. And Heather also takes the opportunity to thank Bryce personally for everything he did for her. Bryce is, as usual, gracious and humble, and every word out of his mouth makes me love him more. If that's even possible.

But it's back to it before I can spend too much time staring adoringly at him, as we welcome Tristan and his boyfriend, Max, my mother, and the Kramers all in quick succession. I spend a little extra time greeting Allie and David, fawning over Brian in his cute little sailor outfit.

But not long after, Alessandro arrives. And I watch Bryce tensely as Alessandro embraces me. Thankfully, he's on his best behavior, and he knows Alessandro and I have been through too much together not to remain friends.

Finally, Hunter and Graham arrive.

"You guys are the last ones in," I greet them. I look at Hunter. "Now or later?"

Hunter shifts nervously. "Let's just get it over with."

Graham squeezes Hunter's hand and disappears into the crowds in the living room to wait until Hunter signals him to return. Bryce approaches, bringing Kent and Barb with him.

Hunter hugs them both and they spend a few minutes catching up. I purposely keep my distance, waiting for a signal same as Graham, in case Hunter needs me. But I'm close enough to hear it when, apropos of nothing in particular, Hunter spills the beans. His declaration is met with stunned silence.

And after a time, this gem from our father: "Well, son, I'm proud of you anyway."

Barb has the good sense to smack him on the back of the head and reassure Hunter that they love him, and they just want him to be happy, whatever that means for him. Hunter catches my eye over her shoulder and smiles. I give him an encouraging thumbs-up and step away to give them privacy, pleased by their response.

A bit later I notice Hunter call Graham over. But it's then that I catch that Bryce has been watching me. Our eyes lock across the room, and a shiver of anticipation runs through me. I hope quietly that I'll always feel this way when he looks at me across a roomful of people.

As conversations ebb and flow, I slowly make my way across the room to where Bryce is. I make sure to check in with my mom, having not much more than greeted her yet. But once I make it by Bryce's side, he tucks me protectively under his arm. I wrap my arms around his torso, looking happily up into his shining blue eyes.

"Ready?" he murmurs into my ear.

I nod, and he picks up a spoon, using it to tap his glass. The room falls silent and everyone turns to us.

"Thank you, everyone, for coming," Bryce starts. "Sera and I are touched that you were all able to make it on such short notice. You all know that I proposed to this beautiful woman two weeks ago, and she accepted."

Everyone cheers and Bryce smiles, holding up a hand after a moment to call for silence.

"But you may not know I actually bought the ring a year ago." He looks down at me lovingly. "And though fate prevented me from giving it to her until now, I've loved her since the day I met her. And I'm the luckiest bastard on the planet because she loves me too."

I rise up on my toes to plant a kiss on his lips and a collective "awwww" rises from the room.

"But if we've learned anything through it all, it's not to take for granted that there will be a tomorrow.

So we promised each other that we would live each day with no regrets, without hesitation, without fear. Together. And because we didn't want to waste one more minute without joining our lives, we were married yesterday by a justice of the peace."

Gasps ring through the room.

"And so, I'd like to introduce you all to my wife — Serafina Hoyt." He raises his glass, looking down at me. "Thank you, baby, for bringing me back, and making me the happiest man alive. Never forget how much I love you." He slips his wedding ring out of his pocket, making a show of putting it on.

Grinning from ear to ear, I pull him to me once more, kissing him deeply this time, to cheers from all. "I love you too," I murmur back to him. But I wonder if he even heard me as our family and friends close on us, eager to hug and congratulate us.

I receive all of our friends and family in turn, accepting their congratulations, hugs, blessings, and everything else. My parents are both thrilled, having already come to adore Bryce. And thankfully there are few hurt feelings. Allie is really the only one who is ticked. I can see it written all over her face before she's able to corner me some minutes later after the initial wave of well-wishers has died down.

"You *didn't*," she sputters, handing baby Brian off

to David. "Please, Sera, tell me you didn't get married *without me.*"

I bite my lip, and I'm sure I look guilty as hell. "I'm sorry, Allie," I reply. "We wanted it to be just us."

"Oh, really? What about your witnesses?" she presses testily.

I shrug. "There was another couple there to get married. They witnessed for us," I reply. And instantly, I know it was the wrong thing to say.

"Strangers?!" Allie replies.

She's so loud it catches Bryce's attention. David takes the opportunity to hand him baby Brian so he can talk Allie down.

"Al, come on, it's their wedding, their choice," David reminds her soothingly.

Allie whirls on him and he shrinks back. Bryce's eyes go wide, and he smoothly carts the baby off somewhere out of the line of fire.

"No. Just no," she says to David before turning back on me. Her anger melts, leaving an expression of pure hurt on her face. "You could've called me. I would've been there in a heartbeat."

I hold my arms out to her, hoping a hug will reassure her. She accepts it but doesn't seem terribly placated.

"Allie, I love you, you know that," I assure her.

"But Bryce and I have been through so much. We just needed this to be apart from everything for a little while. Our own private moment that the world couldn't touch or spoil. Does that make any sense?"

Allie looks like a deflated balloon. "Actually, it does," she admits. She throws her arms around me and hugs me tightly again, for real this time. "I'm sorry, Sera, you're right. And really, I'm so happy for you both."

I squeeze her back tightly. "Thank you," I breathe. "You know that means the world to me."

She pulls back, nodding. "And hey, I figured out what I'm going to do with myself," she says brightly.

"Oh yeah, what's that?" I ask eagerly.

"I'm writing a book," she replies with a small smile. "About what I went through. It's really helping me work through a lot of what happened."

"That's great, Allie," I reply. "I can't wait to read it."

"Thanks," she says brightly. "Brian has been such a blessing, and he's really helped me look into my own heart to understand my *why*." She looks around. "Where'd he go?"

I laugh. "Bryce took him away when you started to go nuclear," I explain. "Let's go find him."

We mill around, ultimately finding Bryce in the kitchen holding Brian, with David nearby preparing a bottle. We hover by the door, taking it in. Bryce is looking down at Brian, cooing gently while Brian grips his finger with his tiny fist. The tenderness in Bryce's touch and the love and joy on his face split me open. It's heartbreakingly beautiful watching him fawn over the baby.

Allie rests a hand on my arm. "He's going to be a great dad," she whispers.

Bryce's eyes snap up, having clearly heard her.

I smile lovingly at him. "Yes, he is," I agree. I'm awarded with a sunshine smile in return, and it melts me that much more.

"We've got this," Bryce assures me in a gentle tone. "You guys go enjoy yourselves."

Allie gives me an impressed look and immediately pulls me back into the living room. We're headed to the buffet table to grab some food when Allie gasps and pulls me to a stop.

"Allie, what the hell?" I ask.

She shushes me and points into the foyer. I look up to see Emily leaned against the wall. Alessandro stands over her, leaned next to her, his face close to hers. He's obviously working his magic charm on her, as I know exactly what that sexy smirk means. And she's obviously enjoying it, toying playfully with the ends of her long, wavy locks and batting her eyelashes at him. I cover my mouth with my hand to hide my shocked laugh.

"Oh, Bryce is going to be *furious*," I hiss.

Allie laughs. "Then we best not tell him," she replies.

"He'll find out," I assure her. "And if he finds out I knew and didn't tell him …"

Allie stares at me in shock. "You're not really planning to tell him, are you?" she asks incredulously.

I consider Emily and Alessandro for a moment. Technically, I'm pretty sure Emily's still seeing what's-his-face. And Alessandro is probably not stupid enough to actually try dating Bryce's sister. I hope.

"They're just talking," I finally say slowly. "Right?" I give her a pointed look.

"Who is?" she asks dumbly, turning around and dragging me with her.

I laugh. "Better still," I respond.

After I've managed to sneak a few appetizers, I pop back into the kitchen to check on Bryce. Baby Brian is sleeping happily in his arms, having had his bottle, and Rebecca is gazing adoringly at him.

"I want lots of these," she says softly to Bryce. "You know, grandbabies."

Bryce chuckles softly.

"That's the plan," I interject quietly.

They both look up at me, and I catch Bryce's eye, smiling adoringly at him.

Rebecca looks between us. "Your news was timely, you know," she says to us.

Bryce's eyes move to his mother's. "Why's that?" he asks curiously.

She gestures around her. "This old place," she sighs. "I'm a widow now, Bryce. It's too much for me. I've been thinking it's time I downsize."

"No, Mom, you're not selling the house," Bryce protests.

Rebecca shakes her head. "Of course not," she scoffs. "I'm giving it to you."

Bryce's mouth drops open.

"That is, if you want it."

Bryce looks at me questioningly. I nod. I know how much he loves this house, and the timing really couldn't be more perfect. He wraps his free arm around his mother, pulling her close. His eyes shine with tears, and he seems unable to speak.

"We'd be honored by such a generous gift," I say for him. "And we would love to live here and raise our family here. Thank you, Rebecca."

Rebecca opens her free arm to me, and I join their huddle.

"Mom, can you take Brian back to Allie, please?" Bryce asks, letting his mother go.

Rebecca nods understandingly, gently transferring the sleeping baby to her arms and leaving us alone. Bryce takes my hands, pulling me to him. I slide happily into his embrace, tilting my head to look up into his eyes.

"You're really okay with living here?" he asks softly.

I smile happily. "Yes," I assure him. "And not just because I'd live anywhere with you. Or because you love this house. I love it too. It will be a constant reminder of the love in this family, for all the years they've been here. So your father will always be with us in a way. And your mother can still be here as much as she'd like."

His eyes are shining once again, bright blue and filled with happiness. "You really mean that," he whispers.

I nod.

"You are too good to be true, Sera Hoyt."

I grin at his use of my new name.

"No, I just hate house shopping," I tease him.

He laughs. "Whatever you say, Mrs. Hoyt," he mutters.

"You just really like calling me that, don't you?" I observe.

His sunshine smile breaks across his face, and it makes me sublimely happy seeing it so often. "Mhhhmmm, and I'm going to like calling you that in bed later too," he murmurs suggestively.

"Then I'd say it's about time we leave for our honeymoon," I reply. "But since there won't be any beds for a while …" I glance down the hall suggestively.

He looks around, considering for a moment before scooping me over his shoulder and bustling me down the hall to his room. He drops me on the bed, closing the door behind him.

I lay there, propped up on my arms, eyeing the tender look on his face.

"Are you going to make love to me now, Mr. Hoyt?" I ask him teasingly.

His eyes darken, and he rolls his muscled shoulders once before slowly advancing on me. When he reaches the bed, he leans over me slowly, planting his arms on either side of me so our faces are inches apart. I can feel the desire rolling off of him as he sizes me up.

"No, Mrs. Hoyt," he replies huskily. "I'm going to fuck you senseless."

"Promise?" I whisper.

He doesn't answer. At least, not with words.

⌒

Thank you so much for reading! Please take a minute to leave a review on any retailer, goodreads, and/or BookBub. Even if it's just a couple of sentences, your opinion is important to potential readers and to me. Thank you!

～

Want to know what happens with Emily and Alessandro? Get *Her Dirty Secret* (Book 4) now at https://melanieasmithauthor.com/books-her-dirty-secret.html

～

Sign up for Melanie A. Smith's newsletter to get a FREE book plus all the latest news and more https://melanieasmithauthor.com/newsletter.html

ACKNOWLEDGMENTS

My first thanks must go to my friend Nicole, who upon finishing a beta read of the second book's manuscript heavily encouraged me to write a third. Or, to quote her more exactly, "Doooo it." So thanks, Nicole, for the support and encouragement, as always. I probably would've wandered off and gotten distracted by a shiny object, but I'm so glad I didn't. And it's all thanks to you.

Next, as always, are thanks to my husband for understanding how much writing means to me, and for truly being a partner in every way.

Another as always — to the woman who spit-shines my ramblings. My darling, most wonderfulest (don't copy edit that!) BFF Jenny. If I haven't acknowledged you enough yet, well, maybe I should start sending pastries.

A huge shout out to the Instagram indie author community, as it is an immensely supportive group of talented authors who have literally shown me how it's done. I've been social media shy for a long time but have found these folks to be so welcoming and helpful. They are a constant reminder that all books have a place and purpose, and there's room for everyone at the table. Special thanks to Carol Deeley, Lindsey Powell, and Julia Blake for the support, encouragement, and commiseration. And you know, for writing fantastic books too (go read their books y'all!).

And finally, thank *you* for reading this. I write because I love it, but I publish it hoping others will enjoy it too. So I hope you did, and I hope to take you on many more adventures in the future.

ABOUT THE AUTHOR

Melanie A. Smith is a former engineer turned stay-at-home mom and award-winning, international best-selling author of steamy contemporary romance. She crafts strong book boyfriends with hearts of gold and smart, self-sufficient heroines. When she's not lost in the world of books, you'll find her spending time with family, cooking, and driving with the windows down and the stereo cranked up loud.

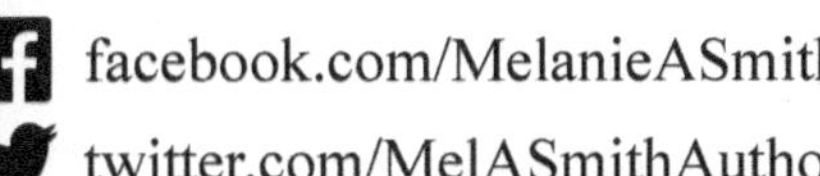

facebook.com/MelanieASmithAuthor
twitter.com/MelASmithAuthor
instagram.com/melanieasmithauthor

The Safeguarded Heart Series

The Safeguarded Heart

All of Me

Never Forget

Her Dirty Secret

Recipes from the Heart: A Companion to the Safeguarded
Heart Series

The Safeguarded Heart Complete Series: All Five Books
and Exclusive Bonus Material

Life Lessons

Never Date a Doctor

Bad Boys Don't Make Good Boyfriends

You Can't Buy Love

The Heart of Rutherford: Life Lessons Novels 1 – 3

Stand-alones

Everybody Lies

Last Kiss Under the Mistletoe

Tough Love

Finding His Redemption

Vegas Baby (Hot Vegas Nights)

Pompous Paramedic (A Hero Club Novel)

Short Stories

Cruising for Love

Hot for Santa